Ethan Reed is a pen name created by Relay Publishing for co-authored Vigilante Justice Thriller projects. Relay Publishing works with incredible teams of writers and editors to collaboratively create the very best stories for our readers.

Cover Design by Deranged Doctor

www.relaypub.com

LETHAL JUSTICE

ETHAN REED

BLURB

For Ion Frost, justice is cold as ice...

Former Special Forces Operative Ion Frost has one job left before he vanishes off the grid: deliver his dead comrade's dog tags to his nephew, Lincoln, in Clear Rock, Wyoming. It should have been a quick, easy stop.

But for Ion Frost, things have a way of getting complicated...

Upon meeting Lincoln, Ion learns that his sister, Taya, has been missing for over a week. Ion can't help but feel sorry for the kid. But time is ticking and he needs to keep moving.

His plans to disappear get put on hold, when a hidden assassin takes out Lincoln in a brutally efficient murder. With Lincoln dead and the dog tags missing, Ion is sure of one thing... Taya, the murder, and the missing tags must be connected somehow.

Now Ion is in the thick of it. He's determined to find Lincoln's killer, and deliver his own personal brand of justice. But the harder he searches, the more questions he finds. Who wanted Lincoln dead? Where is Taya?

And how long before his own brutal past catches up with him?

CONTENTS

ONE

A great shadow crept across the desert road, methodically swallowing cracked asphalt as it prowled forward. The form casting it drifted, steady and measured, approaching an abandoned vehicle parked sideways on the roadway. The car was a mid-nineties Corolla, rusted and sun-bleached, its driver-side door left open. The whistling wind chased sand across the asphalt. The shoal water of the Dori River beyond passed silently beneath the narrow one-lane bridge.

The eclipsing form approached on two armor-weighted legs. Eyes peering out behind a blast-resistant visor squinted past the harsh sunlight at the landscape before him. Scattershot poppy fields to the west provided the only color beyond the pale cloudless sky and tawny desert earth, their flowering violet blooms and green stems standing out against the lifeless terrain. The man looked closely at the poppies, surveying his environment. He noticed the pods had been scored. The opium would be collected tomorrow.

EOD Specialist Frost, United States Army ordnance disposal specialist, stalked to the rear passenger side of the car and tilted his head to get a better look. Wedged under the wheel well, set directly beside the fuel tank, crouched a magnetized copper box with a few wire leads hanging from its side.

Frost turned to look back at the rest of his team, twisting at his waist in his suit. The three men stood two hundred feet back, behind concrete Jersey barriers left behind by a previous regiment. They were dressed near-identically in Special Forces ACU gear: bulky interceptor body armor, black T-shirts, UCP camouflage trousers, and black mountain combat boots. All three held M4 carbines in gloved hands. Two wore twin turtle shell ballistic helmets, and the other enjoyed the shade of a wide-brimmed boonie.

They were just outside Zangabad, Afghanistan, a small village in the Panjwai district of Kandahar province. It was a chart-topper for IED deaths in the country, with the Taliban seeking to carve gradually away at the NATO forces until they could reclaim the region they considered their true homeland. During that time, they'd secretly rigged up numerous homes, mud compounds, and vehicles across the district with improvised bombs and killed any villagers who refused them or ratted them out.

"What is it?" Sergeant First Class Anderson, Frost's commanding officer, asked over comms. His voice snapped with humorless impatience in Frost's ear.

Frost turned back and looked again at the Corolla and the sticky bomb under the wheel well. The wires suggested the package contained a DTMF spider receiver. It could be remotely detonated from anywhere, so long as the triggerman held the paired transmitter.

Frost glanced around the flat landscape, searching for spots he might hide if he were the triggerman. Fields of poppies and grapes stretching to the west. Sprawling desert beyond the bridge to the south. The village of a dozen or so mud homes behind his team in the north. To the east, only sand and sky.

"We shouldn't be here," Frost said into his throat mic.

"You've done this a thousand times," SFC Anderson replied. "Let's get on with it and go."

"Has the village been secured? Swept for electronics?" Frost asked.

"Swept this morning, Cap says. There's nothing."

"All they'd need is a phone," Frost said.

"Heat got you shook or what, Frost?" asked Frost's squadmate, Sergeant Peña.

"Maybe they gave you that crab premature," Specialist Dean chimed, pushing up the brim of his boonie hat from his cover two hundred feet back.

The Senior Explosive Ordnance Disposal badge, or crab, was awarded to an EOD specialist after five years of in-field experience. Frost had thought the resemblance to a crab was only passing, but he took pride in his badge regardless.

"Weren't you were supposed to be the cool one?" Peña asked. "Or were you named Frost prematurely, too?"

Frost looked back at the team. It was possible they were needling him to get him past his worry. But the unusual deployment, Anderson's haste, and what he knew now about his fireteam… Frost couldn't shake the feeling that—as they stayed safe behind the Jersey barriers while he stared down a live explosive—they were reminding him of how powerless he was.

A week ago, Dean had gotten drunk and loud. He'd decided to brag to Peña about what he planned to do with the massive amount of cash they had earned by secretly providing security for the local warlord Hamid Zahir. Evidently, they'd been protecting Zahir's heroin shipments from ambush by rival Taliban forces and earned a king's ransom for their services. Dean or Peña might have later guessed that Frost had overheard—they'd acted strangely toward him ever since. Frost, in turn, had wondered how far up the chain of command he had to go to keep himself safe if he reported them.

Frost glanced again at the scored pods of the poppy field to the west. Maybe it was one of Zahir's fields, and the team was simply roping Frost into disarming a bomb on behalf of the warlord. A bomb the Taliban had left for Zahir's men and not for coalition forces.

Frost turned his attention once more to the wheel well and the dented copper box that'd been stuck to it. Maybe there wasn't even anything in it. Maybe. But he'd be surprised if he was that lucky.

"Is there a problem with the device, Specialist Frost?"

Frost stared at the IED.

"No, there's just—something's wrong here."

"Yeah, I'd say so," Peña said. "We're in the middle of Zangaboom with our pricks hanging out waiting for you to finish stalling."

"If we'd come with some support—"

"The village was cleared of T-Men two days ago, Frost," Anderson said. "Support's just a waste of manpower. Now, are there any other operational issues you'd like to discuss, or can we get on with it?"

"Yeah, come on, man," Dean said. "Let's just do this. I got a cooler of Millers waiting for me back at base."

Frost ignored Dean, addressing Anderson. "Well, *some* T-Man rigged up the bomb I'm staring at, right?"

"Can you do this, Frost?" Anderson said, terse and acidic. "Or do I have to get one of them green EOD fuck-ups to come in here and botch this?"

"Poor kid'll probably blow his damn legs off," Dean said.

"Mm-hmm. EOD fuck-ups are a dime a dozen around here, you ask me," Peña said.

"Of course I can do this," Frost said.

"Then do it," Anderson said. "Because right now, you're one excuse away from disobeying a direct order."

Frost glanced back at his fireteam. The three looked like apparitions drifting through the heat haze, ghostly shadows waiting to ferry him to the other side.

Something moved in the mud homes behind the team, where two village elders had emerged. The men were in their sixties, perhaps, but spry and animated. They hurled curses at the team as they approached, but Frost thought they might specifically be addressing him.

"Watch your six," Frost said.

The team members looked back and saw the approaching elders. Peña turned and started towards them to try to calm them down.

"Watch their hands for a cell," Frost said.

"There ain't no cell, Frost," Anderson said.

Peña spoke to the elders in Pashto, holding his free hand out in a placating gesture. But the two men weren't interested in him. They continued to angrily shout and point at Frost, brushing past Peña and continuing down the road.

"I didn't get your answer, Specialist Frost. Can you do it?" Anderson asked again.

"What're they saying, Peña?" Frost said.

"They want you to get away from their fuckin' poppy fields," Peña said. "The hell you think they're saying?"

"Frost?" Anderson growled.

Frost looked at Anderson and turned back to the IED. Something was twisting his gut, but he couldn't be sure what. The whole scene was wrong. Just what did he think would happen here? Would a Taliban triggerman leap out of the poppy fields? Or maybe Anderson would be the one to flip the switch, tying up Frost as a loose end. Pushing him to make a decision with the knowledge that he was ignoring a direct order and risking his military career if nothing really was wrong. All of it hinged on one thing: how much did his team think he knew?

Frost took a deep breath and knelt beside the car.

"I'm preparing to examine the device," he said.

A small cyclone of dust kicked up in front of Frost. His eyes stung with sweat, his clothes soaked through beneath his suit. He reached out and grabbed the copper box with both hands, gently pulling it towards him. The magnetic hold broke free from the wheel well, and Frost carefully set the box down on the dust and gravel in front of him. He felt the underlip of the lid with his fingertips. There didn't seem to be any adhesive holding it shut. There weren't any booby traps that he could make out, just a single bolt latch without a lock.

Frost exhaled, taking a moment to gauge his luck. He sucked in one quick breath, then slid the bolt open and lifted the latch in two swift moves. Nothing happened. He breathed out again.

Inside the box nestled a DTMF receiver attached to blasting caps, the caps set inside a dozen modified M112 demolition blocks. Loose nails and screws lay all around the charges in a metal nest of shrapnel.

Frost glanced back down the road and was surprised to see that the village elders were heading straight for him, a hundred feet out now, still screaming and gesticulating.

"Hey, what the fuck?" Frost said. He rose to his feet. "Peña, Dean, restrain these guys!"

The two elders marched faster. Spittle flew from their mouths as they cursed him in Pashto. They pointed at the field and at Frost.

"Where the fuck are you guys?!" Frost said.

Pop. Pop. Blood sprayed across the front of Frost's helmet, and it took him a second to realize it wasn't his. The two elders lay crumpled on the concrete.

An eerie quiet fell over the scene. Nothing but the high whistling of the wind now. Frost looked at the dead men. Blood spilled over the desert moondust that powdered the road.

He looked back at his team. Peña and Dean lowered their carbines, still standing behind the Jersey barriers. Anderson held a cell phone.

Frost tore away from the car as fast as he could, running clumsily in his bulky bomb suit. The bomb went off. A shock wave threw Frost through the air as if he'd been hit by a semitrailer. Nails and screws ripped through the protective Nomex-Kevlar of his bomb suit. Chunks of the old Corolla shot into the air—whole fragments of the chassis, the roof, and the hood. A mushroom cloud of black smoke rose into the day, trailing flame beneath it.

Frost slammed into the ground. He gasped for air and rolled onto his back to stare up into the sky. A bell rang in his ears. He glanced down at himself. His entire left side was blackened. Most of his ABS suit had been torn away. Several large chunks of shrapnel had cut into his legs, his arms, and his torso. Smaller pieces sat embedded in his exposed skin, like cancerous diamonds burning into his flesh. His blood baked in the heat of the sun and the wreckage. He groaned loudly, the tinnitus now overtaken by the white noise of radio static coming through his earpiece.

Frost looked back to the pale sky a final time. A piece of heavy metal sheeting was plummeting back to earth. Heading straight for him. He shut his eyes and resigned himself. Soon, all was lifeless again upon that desolate terrain.

TWO

A blood-red sun fell behind the Teton Range mountains and cast a wash of soft coral pink and wisteria violet over the valley of Clear Rock. Frost drove the vacant highway into town, the blued mountainscape at his back. He crossed the Hognose River and glanced over at the folded road map on the empty passenger seat. He found his exit off the highway and took it, his aviator shades reflecting the bright lights of the small town before him. The calm of the open road, that endless sky that had done him such good, now diminished in his rearview.

He parked his dark Ford Ranger in front of the roadhouse and sat there for a moment. He stared at the front door of the establishment. The old building looked like it'd been recently renovated. Sleek front signage, 54modern double-doors at the entrance. Frost glanced around the broader parking lot. The roadhouse was set at the corner of a small commercial plaza beside a lawyer's office, a small pharmacy, and a dollar store. Not a whole lot of life. Maybe forty vehicles or so.

It had been six months since Zangabad. Frost hadn't said a word to anyone about the ambush, the attempted hit, or the Special Forces working with Zahir. None of it. He couldn't be sure how high the conspiracy ran. He knew that his team had discovered he'd survived the ambush, and that Crane knew he was stateside. But maybe the captain hadn't tracked him to Wyoming just yet, Frost thought. Maybe. He ran the odds in his head and his system gave up its answer: Level Three.

Crapshoot.

He clicked open his glove box and pulled out a Glock 43. He checked the magazine, returned it, and racked the chamber. He tucked the gun into his back waistband and settled his denim jacket over it. He glanced at his reflection in the rearview mirror and pulled off his Broncos ball cap. Rough jigsaw scarring crisscrossed the top of his forehead and ran around the side to the base of his skull. Frost rubbed a hardened lump above the back of his ear, feeling the patchwork of flesh left from the inelegant stitchwork. The uneven lump where the shrapnel had lodged into his skull still took some getting used to. It was like a loose tooth that he couldn't stop poking at.

Frost set the ball cap back on his head and adjusted the brim. He grabbed a manila envelope from the passenger seat and exited the truck.

Frost adjusted his eyes as he stepped into the roadhouse. Clocked the patrons quickly. There was a handful of families and friends having dinner, most of the patriarchs obese, slow, conspicuous. Threat minimal.

A few waitresses in black pants and polo shirts milled between the tables. A group of drunk forty-somethings sat in pairs at a table in front of him. Couples date night, he guessed. Otherwise there were just a few single men alone at the bar. Sitting with their hunched backs to the room, nursing beers, thumbing their phones.

Frost counted thirty-five people in the roadhouse total that he could see. He factored another dozen or so in the kitchen and washrooms that he couldn't. He adjusted the odds in his head and lowered his threat assessment to a Level Two: Controlled.

In a booth on the righthand side of the roadhouse, a young man sat alone, facing the front door. He was a handsome kid with a short crew cut and well put together, wearing a crisp black Oxford with white buttons and an elegant silver wristwatch. He sat straight, his shirt ironed, his hairstyle functional and tidy. A Marine on leave.

The young man looked over at Frost and saw his Broncos cap. He waved him over and Frost made his way to the kid, who smiled and offered the empty seat.

"What's your name?" Frost asked, still standing.

The young man smiled at Frost's suspicion, intrigued at the prospect of engaging in the kind of *Tinker-Tailor* tradecraft he'd only seen in the movies.

"Lincoln Dane," the kid said with a furtive cock of his eyebrows. Frost tried not to smile—his life was on the line, after all—but Lincoln was like a puppy. After everything, Lincoln wasn't a bad reminder of the naivete that Frost had nearly died protecting. A grin crept across his face, despite himself.

Frost nodded and glanced around the room again before taking a seat opposite the kid, setting the manila envelope flat on the table between them.

"Why'd you wave me over?" Frost said.

Lincoln looked confused. He glanced up at the Broncos logo on Frost's ball cap and looked back at him. "You said on the phone you'd be wearing—"

"There's three other men in here wearing Broncos caps," Frost said.

The kid looked around the roadhouse to confirm, then looked sheepishly back to Frost. "Well, none of them came in here looking for nobody."

"And how do you know that?" Frost said.

Lincoln looked around the roadhouse again. "That one there came in with the woman he's sitting with. First date, looks like. And those other two are sitting by themselves with their backs to the room. Playing on their phones." To Frost's relief, he only nodded at the men he mentioned, rather than pointing.

Frost nodded to himself, satisfied that Lincoln seemed to have a decent head on his shoulders. The kid might be a little naïve, but at least Frost wasn't risking his neck for a vapid liability.

Frost looked up at the roadhouse lighting. Their booth was dim, lit by a single golden bulb hanging from a pendant fixture. Frost removed his sunglasses and set them inside his jacket pocket. He squinted and ground his teeth for a second, a dull pain rising behind his eyes. It lingered for a moment before slowly dissipating.

Lincoln noticed his discomfort. "You okay?"

Frost nodded. "Post-concussion thing. Developed a sensitivity to light. Loud noise, too. It's nothing."

"Just got back myself."

"Fallujah, you said?"

"Yessir. On leave for three months."

A young waitress came by their table, smiling brightly at both of them. "Can I start you boys off with a couple drinks?"

"I'll have a Bud," Lincoln said.

"And for you?" the waitress asked.

"I can't stay long," Frost said. He needed to get back on the road before Crane found him. Relaxing was dangerous. Even chatting with Lincoln was pushing the envelope, nice kid or no.

"You can have one beer, can't you?" Lincoln said.

Frost looked at him. Lincoln gave a warm smile, just as welcoming as the kid's dear departed uncle. The kid even looked like Brakespeare, without the years or the hardship. Frost could share at least one drink with the kid.

"Yeah, I can have one." He turned to the waitress. "Two Buds."

She smiled politely and made off to fetch their drinks. Lincoln tried his best to hide his own reaction, but Frost still caught the eager nod the kid gave when Frost gave his order.

"So... what do I call you?" Lincoln said.

"Excuse me?"

"You said you didn't want to give your name over the phone."

Frost nodded.

"So, is it Mr. X? Or..."

"Kevin Johnson, if you like," Frost said.

"That real?"

"Says so on my driver's license." Frost paused. "But no, it's not. That trouble we talked about overseas, you know? I hope you understand."

Lincoln nodded, and, just for a moment, eyes flicked from Frost's face to the manila envelope on the table—the reason they were both here. Frost slid the manila envelope across the table.

"That them?" Lincoln asked, his smile fading.

Frost nodded.

"Did you know my uncle well?"

"I did. Served three tours together. Known each other since basic at Fort Benning."

"I really appreciated your phone call. Coming out all this way, too."

"Well, he wanted you to have these," Frost said, tapping the manila envelope. He looked Lincoln over again. "You know, you look like him quite a bit."

"Yeah?" Lincoln said.

"Mm. That same... I don't know. Zeal or something. He was always full of life, ready to crack a joke, even in a war zone. You've got that same spark. It's a little eerie."

Lincoln smiled, and something in the kid's eyes told Frost that what he had said meant more than he'd guessed. He obviously wasn't the only one who missed his friend. The waitress returned with their beers and set them down and was off again. Lincoln held up his bottle in a toast.

"To Uncle Brakespeare," Lincoln said.

"To Brakespeare."

They clinked bottles and drank.

"You know, he was always good to me," Lincoln said. He stared off, his lips a tight line. "We didn't exactly see much of each other, what with him out in Boise and me here. But we bonded quick the first time he came out to visit my dad, though. Every time he drove down, he always had something new to teach me. And he called every time he heard I'd done something I was proud of. Making varsity, graduating with honors, that kinda thing. Always told me that he was giving me a long-distance high-five. He was the reason I joined the Marines in the first place, actually. I wanted to learn everything he knew. Maybe teach it to my kids someday, too."

"Well, that sounds like Brakespeare. I'm glad he had family that cared for him as much as he cared for his team," Frost said. He mulled Lincoln's words over in his mind. He had left Brakespeare behind for his promotion to Special Forces, but his new fireteam had nearly killed him and then hunted him like prey. Now, he was risking his neck for what he felt was the last man to have shown him kindness. After everything, Brakespeare's memory was stronger than Frost's fear of that risk. After the heart stops pumping, we really are just our legacy.

Lincoln looked from Frost to the manila envelope and picked it up. He opened the seal and took out the items inside. There was a letter with "Lincoln" neatly printed on the envelope in clinical typeface. Lincoln looked at the envelope for a moment and slid the letter into his jacket pocket. He reached into the manila envelope again and pulled out a set of dog tags. Lincoln examined them in his hand. His uncle's full name, social security number, blood type, and "no preference" religious affiliation stared back at him before he clenched them in his fist.

"Thank you, sir," he said. "I mean it."

Frost nodded in acknowledgement.

"Did you know he was sick?" Lincoln said.

Frost shook his head. "Not before he sent me the letter. Said he knew the cancer would take him out soon and asked me to deliver those items to you."

"You guys must have been real tight, if he asked *you* to be the one to do it."

"We were. Fought together in Jalalabad, Kabul, the Kunar Valley. Before I took up with Special Forces in Kandahar."

Lincoln leaned forward, drinking in Frost's every word, until his phone dinged and he tensed. His hand darted to his pocket and he pulled it out, but deflated after he checked the screen.

"Sorry," he said to Frost, returning the phone to his pocket. "I've been trying to get a hold of my sister for over a week now. Taya, she's... I was just hoping that was her. It wasn't."

"Everything all right?"

"I'm sure it's fine," Lincoln said, though his brow was noticeably creased. "I'm just worried. Not like her to not answer. Been keeping me up some."

"She know about her uncle passing?"

Lincoln shook his head. "Not yet." He opened his fist and stared at the dog tags again before slipping the chain over his neck, where they hung down in front of his chest.

"I think I'm going to frame these in my apartment," he said, taking another sip of his beer.

The waitress returned. "You fellas ready for another round?"

Lincoln looked across the booth at Frost and raised an eyebrow.

Frost thought about it. With Crane after him, he felt it would be wise to keep moving. He'd achieved what he'd set out to do in Clear Rock and honored Brakespeare's dying wishes. But he was having a good time with the kid, and talking about Brakespeare was almost like talking about family. Frost's life on the road was necessary to stay alive, but he hadn't realized how isolated he'd felt since he'd begun to roam. He had covered his tracks well enough, sacrificed enough, to earn some warm conversation and another cold beer, hadn't he?

Frost smiled. "Sure. Another round."

———

Frost and Lincoln exited the roadhouse an hour later into the darkened evening. A single lamplight hung high over the lot. The two men shook hands; Lincoln thanked him for making the trip, and Frost thanked him for the beers. As they walked back to their cars, Lincoln took in Frost's new Ford Ranger.

"Nice truck," he said. He looked at the cab-high truck cap set over the rear bed. "You could sleep in that thing."

"Don't I know it," Frost said. He pulled out his flip phone from his pocket and checked the time. "Say, you know where the nearest gas station is?"

"You just looking to fill up?" Lincoln said. "Because there's a Walmart a few blocks from here if you're looking for anything specific."

"Actually, I do need a new phone," Frost said. He'd had this one too long already.

Lincoln pointed down the road and gave him directions. They shook again before Frost went to his truck. He took out his keys and had just slid them into the lock when he heard the night shatter behind him. The thunderclap discharge of a pump-action shotgun echoed out over the asphalt. Frost dropped to one knee and turned, his Glock leveled at the darkness. He was still looking for his assailant when he saw the kid's body. Lincoln had been blown back against the tin-sheet siding of the roadhouse and had slumped limply to the ground.

Two shadowed figures ran up to Lincoln. One knelt and the other said something Frost couldn't hear. Then they both bolted. Frost sprinted towards them and caught a glimpse of the rear man under the dim lamplight. He could just make out sandy brown hair and a small horizontal scar on his left cheek.

Frost raised his gun, but out of nowhere a dark coupe screeched out of the blackness and swerved toward him. Frost dove sideways to the pavement and rolled to see the two figures jumping into the car.

The doors slammed shut and the tires spun against the asphalt until the rubber burned. The coupe tore off across the parking lot, lost to the night.

Frost ran to Lincoln. The kid gripped his abdomen, and a red trail of blood ran from his mouth down his shirt.

"Let me take a look," Frost said. It felt stupid; what was the kid going to do, stop him? But he was still thunderstruck from the past few moments.

Frost tucked his gun into his back waistband and knelt beside Lincoln. The kid had been shot through the chest, a giant hole of gore pouring blood out onto the surrounding pavement. Lincoln looked up at Frost, his eyes wide with horror. He gasped for air, but his breaths became more shallow. The kid wasn't going to make it. The first friendly face in Frost's life since he had left the Army, young and full of promise, was going to die. He was shocked, but he was lucid enough to feel that one bitter truth like an ice pick gouging into his gut.

Lincoln gripped Frost's jacket tight with his bloodied hands and pulled him close.

"Find Taya," he coughed out. His fingers were rigid, their grip tight as steel. His eyes were wide and desperate.

"Hold on," Frost said.

He pulled out his phone to dial 911, but the kid was gone before the first ring. His grip loosened and his head slumped forward. He watched, rather than felt, his trembling hand reach out to close the lids over Lincoln's dead, terrified eyes.

Frost stood and stared at the corpse in front of him. His breath was heavy. His head churned, trying to make sense of what he had seen, trying to decide what to do next. Who was this? It was Brakespeare's nephew, he knew that. He had known it from the spark that uncle and nephew had shared. Easily recognizable in a lineup or a crowd, an inherited trait from one's closeness with the other. But now they were both dead, the spark gone forever. The corpse was nothing anymore. Nobody. Just another body that Frost had watched die.

Frost sifted through the impulses that his combat-shattered brain was trying to process. He knew what he should feel right now, but the sensation just didn't come. His body went through the motions without him, the harsh breathing and trembling hands suggesting grief that he couldn't feel. Frost knew what this was—he'd felt off ever since he'd gotten back to the States, numb to things that made other people smile. He'd been ignoring it, trying to pretend it wasn't happening, but now he was staring at the incontrovertible proof of it. At least it didn't matter to Lincoln whether Frost grieved him or not. Emotions were useless to the kid, now.

But at that final thought, a tiny flicker broke through the fog like a lighthouse beam. Bright, blindingly so, but still narrow. *Vengeful.* What was useful to the kid? Moving. Fighting. Do what you can to set it right. It was faint, but it was something, and it demanded to be fed.

Then, outside himself, a glimmer. Frost was struck by the reflection of lamplight flashing off Lincoln's wristwatch. Frost leaned over and looked at Lincoln's rear pocket. His wallet was still inside it. He looked at his front pocket, where he saw the bulge of his phone.

This wasn't a mugging. This had been a targeted kill. But they had still been looking for something when they ran to Lincoln's body.

Frost searched Lincoln more carefully and noticed that Brakespeare's dog tags were gone. They'd been snatched by the killers.

Frost ran through the system in his head, calculating the viability of his options. Should he get the hell out of there? Call the police anonymously? Or stick around for them to arrive? He gauged the threat. If he stayed longer waiting for the cops, he would risk everything.

Frost looked back at the kid. He was in it now. It didn't matter that his instincts were screaming at him to get back on the road, to get lost. He couldn't just leave the kid in the lurch. He needed to see this through and see the killers caught. For Lincoln and for Brakespeare.

He cursed out loud and pulled out his phone. There was no way around it. He dialed 911 and waited. He would tell the police what he knew and then get the hell out of Clear Rock, making sure to disappear completely afterwards. His call connected, and he told the 911 operator what had occurred and that he would wait on the scene for the police. All the while staring down into the face of that ruined kid in front of him.

He would run. Sure. It was the smart thing to do. But beneath everything he told himself, Frost felt that urge for vengeance, small but bright, burning in his core.

THREE

F rost stayed on the line with the 911 operator, doing what he could to protect the crime scene. He pulled his truck up to a closer parking spot to block the view from the rest of the plaza and took a position by Lincoln's body. Drawing from his early tours of duty as part of an occupational force, he waved exiting bar patrons by as they wandered home. The music inside must have muffled the shotgun blast because each half-drunk man and woman seemed surprised by the blood. Eventually, the patrons seemed to peter out.

A woman emerged from the roadhouse and looked around the parking lot. She was short but tough-looking with cropped hair, toned forearms, and a hard face. She was dressed in a sleeveless blouse and dark slacks. She turned to Frost and set her fists on her hips.

"What the hell is going on here?" she asked, glaring at Frost.

Then she looked past Frost to the trail of blood on the concrete. She didn't make a sound, but simply covered her mouth with one hand and stared.

"The police are on their way. I take it you're the manager?"

The woman continued to stare at the body. "Is that Lincoln? Is he...?"

"He is. Are you the manager?"

"Yes, I... What happened?" she said.

"What's your name?"

"Sharon."

"Sharon, I'd like you to go inside, please, and do your best to keep everyone calm. Minimize the foot traffic coming out here if you can, all right?"

She kept her eyes on Lincoln's body, as though she were expecting the kid to move. "He was a good kid..." she murmured.

"Hey," Frost said, moving in front of her to break her line of sight with the body. "Can you do that for me?"

Sharon nodded. Then she glanced up at a CCTV camera angled toward the front of the bar.

"I'll need to ask Bobby if that camera's working. The ones inside, too. I know we were having some trouble before, but maybe there's some footage."

Frost nodded. "All right, get Bobby down here so we can start preparing any footage for the police. They'll need it to try to ID the men who did this."

The manager nodded firmly, exhaled, and hurried back inside the roadhouse. Frost glanced out over the dark parking lot. Thirtysomething vehicles now, likely the last of the bar rats and the roadhouse's employees. He looked at the few buildings in the plaza. They were all closed for the night. He looked at their upper façades and saw that a few had cameras mounted on them. None looked like they'd offer a view of the front of the roadhouse, but maybe they'd catch the plate of the coupe. If not, the traffic cameras in the street could give an idea of which direction the men were headed.

Frost looked at the body. On his last mission with Lincoln's uncle, Brakespeare had taken a ricocheted bullet in the back while they were pinned down in the hills outside the Kunar Valley. Frost had taped Brakespeare up himself, ignoring his friend's criticism of the patch job. Then the two had walked out of that valley, still waiting for the one bullet they wouldn't hear coming.

Neither of them would've guessed it would be cancer that wound up killing him.

Nearly an hour passed before the red and blue lights of a patrol car splashed across the night. Frost turned and let down the tailgate of his truck. He opened a hidden lockbox set inside the floor, pulled his Glock from his waistband, and set it inside the box. He'd never had issues with the cops, but after all this time on the run, he wasn't about to risk the encounter. He closed up the box and turned to meet the patrol car pulling into the lot.

The vehicle parked in front of the roadhouse. Frost could make out Clear Rock Sheriff's Department written on the side. After a moment, two officers, a man and a woman, stepped out and approached Frost. They held their flashlights up with their hands over their holstered pistols.

"Sir, I'm gonna need you to take a few steps towards me and away from the body," the male officer said.

"And keep your hands front and center," the female officer said.

Frost did as they told him. "I'm the one who called."

"What's your name?" the female officer asked.

"Kevin Johnson, ma'am," Frost said.

"All right, Kevin," she said, "I'm gonna need you to step aside with Officer Burr right here. He'll have some questions for you, all right?"

Officer Burr directed Frost towards the front of his patrol car. He asked him a few questions about what he'd seen and Frost answered. But with each question, Frost couldn't shake the feeling that his answers were being thrown out as quickly as he could give them. The officer recorded the events of the incident, of course, but he showed little interest in what Frost had to say about the events preceding or following the attack.

As they spoke, the policewoman dialed on a cell phone. She said a few words that Frost couldn't hear.

She hung up and clicked on her shoulder mic to call the homicide in over the radio. She rejoined the two men, and from a closer distance Frost could see the name on her uniform. Officer Warren.

"She on her way?" Burr said to Warren.

"She is," Officer Warren said. "Be by any minute."

"All right, Mr. Johnson, just sit tight for me," Officer Burr said.

Frost looked at the both of them. Confused.

"That's it?" Frost said.

"What's that, sir?" Officer Burr said.

"You don't want any more information from me? I told you I saw the shooters."

"There'll be time for all that," Officer Burr said.

"We might want to put out an APB on this, don't you think?" Frost said, trying to be as cordial as possible. "Before those men get out of state?"

"Don't worry, sir," Officer Burr said. "We've got everything under control."

What a fantastic way not to answer a question, Frost thought.

"Sheriff will be by soon," Burr continued, "and we'll let you tell her whatever it is you want to say, okay?"

The sheriff was supposed to be here? Frost was shocked she hadn't arrived already. The grunts had taken long enough, but was the sheriff really dragging her feet worse than they were? In a town this size with what had to be a microscopic homicide rate, the idea was ludicrous.

"Well, lookie here," Officer Warren said. A second patrol car had pulled into the lot. "Speak of the sheriff and she doth appear, Mr. Johnson."

A black Interceptor Utility truck with white-paneled doors rolled into the plaza parking lot. It parked close to the group, shut off its lights, and the Sheriff of Clear Rock stepped out. Her gold badge beamed atop her brown cavalry Stetson. She looked to be in her late forties, lean with a hardened face. Her uniform was light brown with dark pants, her tie held by a gold clip.

She walked with heavy steps towards Frost and shot a glance to the body beyond.

"You the one who called it in?" the Sheriff said.

"That's right," Frost replied.

"This here's Kevin Johnson, Sheriff," Officer Burr said.

"I'm sure the man's plenty capable of speaking for himself, now, Ted," said the Sheriff. "How about you two get started on cordoning this lot off. Make sure none of them roadhouse drunks fuss up my crime scene."

The two officers nodded and went to work, Officer Burr grabbing a roll of police tape from his patrol car. Frost tried not to think about how that should have been done an hour ago.

The Sheriff took a step towards Frost. She looked him up and down and cocked her Stetson further back on her head.

"Mr. Johnson, I'm Sheriff Carol Mendillo. But people around here call me Puck. Don't ask."

"Sheriff," Frost said.

Her face was full of contradictions. She was an attractive woman, more handsome than pretty, but she carried maleficence in her countenance. Like she'd rotted from the inside, but her outside hadn't yet caught up.

Frost cleared his throat. "Listen, I don't want to get started on the wrong foot here—"

"Yet I sense you're not about to lead with the right one," Sheriff Puck said. Frost, his patience waning, fought the urge to tell her to fuck off. She was standing less than fifteen feet from a dead man—a *good* man, far as Frost could tell—and she was throwing him sarcasm? Seriously?

She smiled at Frost, and he couldn't tell if she was being friendly or just wanted to appear to be.

He cleared his throat and smiled thinly back. "I just meant that I don't mean to sound critical, just concerned. The perpetrators are long gone, and nobody's put out an APB yet. I don't even know if Officer Burr here wrote down my descriptions of the attackers or their vehicle."

"Dispatch already relayed the pertinent information to us, sir," Puck said. "You were quite fulsome."

"Again, I didn't give dispatch any descriptions of the perpetrators," Frost said, still trying to sound more earnest than frustrated. "Same goes for the car. I really don't want these guys to get away with what they've done."

"Well, why don't you go ahead and tell me exactly what it is you saw, then," Sheriff Puck said. "I'm all ears."

She took out her field notebook and pen. It relaxed Frost to finally see an officer taking the situation seriously.

"There were two men. Three, if you count the getaway driver," Frost began. "One of them had a shotgun, which was used as the murder weapon. He had sandy brown hair and a scar on his left cheek."

"Who did? The man with the shotgun or the other one?" Sheriff Puck said.

"The gunman."

"Okay. And the make of the car?"

"It was a dark coupe. Chevy. A Chevelle, I think."

"You think?"

"A lot of their older models look alike, and it's pretty dark out."

Sheriff Puck looked around at the dimly lit parking lot. "It sure is."

"I'm pretty certain it was a Chevelle."

"A dark Chevelle," Sheriff Puck said, jotting it down. "Is that black or blue or…"

"I don't know."

"You get a plate?"

"No."

"Okay. That it?"

Frost scoffed. "Yeah."

"Okay. So, let me read this back to you. You saw two shooters flee in a coupe—you *think*—that was either black or blue. And the only physical descriptor you have for either man is that one of them had brown hair. Did I get all that right?"

"You missed the scar," Frost said, simmering at her condescension.

"The scar, right. And you want me to put out an APB on *that*, sir? You see what I mean? We'd be pulling over nearly half the state."

I'd like you to do *something*, thought Frost. "Has the coroner been called?"

"I assure you I am doing everything by the book, Mr. Johnson," Sheriff Puck said. "But these things take time. So I'm going to need you to be a little patient, okay?"

Frost nodded and hoped he looked calm.

"Look, sir, I understand you're frustrated, but take a breather. We'll get on top of this thing. Now, the deceased was a friend of yours?"

Frost nodded. "Yes."

"Okay. Now, see, I can understand your impatience a little better."

"Look, if the county coroner hasn't been called yet, would you mind doing so? That boy shouldn't have to lie there any longer than is necessary," Frost said. "It's indecent."

"No, I understand. But we've got protocols that sometimes take precedent over decency, unfortunately."

Frost nodded. "I'm just trying to understand how things are done in this town," he said. I'm honestly trying to discern if things are done at all, he thought to himself.

Sheriff Puck stared at Frost, nodding to herself, her tongue tucked in the side of her mouth.

"What are you doing in Clear Rock, anyway, if I may ask?"

"Just passing through," Frost said. "Came to see Lincoln, here. Before someone shot him."

"Yeah, well, a little tip?" Sheriff Puck said. "Folks around here don't really care for that bit of sass you been whipping up. Now, I know you're upset, but we treat one another with a little more respect around here. Goes a long way."

Frost stared at Sheriff Puck. He wasn't in the mood for a lecture. And treating one another with respect? Tell that to the dead Marine lying on the pavement with the hole in his chest.

Frost glanced away, hating how exposed he was in that moment, standing there talking to a police sheriff beneath a CCTV camera. So visible, so naked. Standing still at all wasn't something he'd cared for upon his return from overseas. Puck had turned back to her associates and was talking to them, but Frost was too preoccupied to listen in.

He looked off. He could feel himself starting to shut down. He was disappointed he'd given so much of himself away already, and for nothing, to boot. He was starting to feel that the Clear Rock Sheriff's Department wasn't up to the task. They didn't have the drive or the competence to catch up with Lincoln's killers.

The Sheriff asked a few more innocuous questions, including Frost's date of birth and phone number, and he flatly recited the information on his fake ID. He wanted to finish up with her and sort out what to make of this himself. She thanked him for his time and told him her office would be in touch in the days and weeks to come. It was further proof to Frost that the police in Clear Rock had absolutely no idea what they were doing. Here was the Sheriff, the investigating officer, letting go of a key person of interest—a potential suspect even—with nothing but a cell number connecting them to each other. Not to mention that the number was for a burner phone that Frost planned to throw away.

But there was no use arguing with her and Frost knew it. He knew now for sure that Lincoln would never see justice at the hands of the Clear Rock Sheriff's Department, barring some divine intervention.

Frost had seen men killed before. A lot. A few friends even. But that was warfare. It hurt like hell, but those were the rules of the game, and you accepted them every time you played. Lincoln's murder, though—that was something else entirely. It was something much more profane to Frost. That sweet kid, his whole future ahead of him, had his life stolen in an instant by a couple of thugs. Frost couldn't let that sit. Something shifted within him.

Maybe it was the evil he had encountered across his long tours in Afghanistan, spending years engaging the most sadistic sons of bitches that the Taliban and ISIS had to offer. The black abyss that widened with each savage crime Frost witnessed. The mass graves, the mutilations, the beheadings. The sheer carnage of unconventional warfare. Barbarism Frost hadn't even thought imaginable before he'd joined the service. Or maybe it was the attempt on his life by the Special Forces team. Betrayal at the highest level. Even after that, the mercenaries that would be set upon him the moment Crane found him. The disgusting irony of Frost now being on the run from traitorous, murderous men as if he were the criminal.

Hell, maybe it was all of it. But whatever the reason, something finally snapped inside Frost. Was he just going to sit around and let evil go unpunished? Let the killers get away with their crimes and the kid fade to dust? No, if justice was to be done for Lincoln, or for Brakespeare, Frost would have to see to it himself.

Sheriff Puck finished writing in her notebook and shut it.

"You know, we are a small town," she said, "but I'd be careful about getting your hopes up about this. Hate to say it, but people come through using that highway all the time. Them shooters are likely

29

halfway to Cheyenne by now, just passing through. Not unlike yourself, Mr. Johnson."

She held out her hand and smiled thinly. Frost shook it, but the effort felt like he was moving a mountain. He cleared his throat.

"Well, I apologize for my flippancy here," Frost said. "For any disrespect. I know these things take time. The kid there, he just—he meant a lot to me."

"I understand completely, sir," Sheriff Puck said.

"Well, would it be all right—with your permission, of course—if I just said goodbye to my friend really quick?" Frost said. "His mother would never forgive me otherwise."

It was a gamble Frost made with himself—the final test of the sheriff's competence. If she let him near the body, it was the last sign Frost needed that she wouldn't be able to solve Lincoln's murder. If she didn't, he could convince himself to rest a little easier.

Sheriff Puck thought about it for a moment. Eventually, she nodded.

"All right," she said. "But I'd get to it. The county coroner will be by any minute now."

Frost thanked her and went to Lincoln. He knelt beside the kid and looked into his face. Stared down at poor Lincoln Dane. He leaned forward and whispered into his ear.

"I'm sorry, kid. I can't grieve for you like you deserve. It's not in me. But I hope the storm I'm gonna bring those bastards is enough to lay you to rest."

And while he whispered into the kid's ear, Frost covertly reached into Lincoln's pocket and palmed his phone and keys.

FOUR

Frost sat parked in his truck on a narrow side street a few blocks from the roadhouse, scrolling through Lincoln's phone. He hoped to find a clue as to why the kid was targeted, and by some blind stroke of luck, the kid didn't keep a lock on his phone. He had to find out who had killed Lincoln and serve them up as fast as possible. Then, he could get the hell out of Clear Rock.

The last text Lincoln had received was from someone named Paul, which he had received while they were at the roadhouse together. It seemed innocuous enough, just something about Von Miller and the last Broncos game. Frost scrolled through their past messages. Not a lot there. A few more texts about catching a ball game. Comments about some superhero movie they'd recently seen. Nothing suspicious.

The next most recent text was from Lincoln's sister, Taya. The woman on Lincoln's dying breath. Frost opened up their chat and examined the messages. They were haphazard and irregular. Short conversations. Frost opened up a picture file that Taya had recently sent Lincoln of a colorful geometric pattern that had been hand-painted onto a square plywood frame, hanging on wooden planks. A barn quilt.

The painted quilts would typically be hung high on the outside of barns, over the haylofts. Each one was unique, like a coat of arms for the family that hung it. This one in particular was a mosaic of blue, white and black triangles interlocking into a pattern resembling a pinwheel, or maybe a snowflake. The photo was taken at night, the quilt awash in artificial light.

Frost had seen his share of barn quilts as a child on the rural outskirts of his small Oklahoman town. He'd come across them while ambling through the waving barley fields behind his father's house, where he'd often go to lose himself. To daydream and teach himself to shoot. He'd lost hours hunting hares in the green ash woods on the far side of the hills. He still remembered the metallic smell that would linger on his hands for days after handling that old rifle.

Lincoln had had no idea what the barn quilt picture meant. He'd messaged Taya repeatedly about it. Asked her what it was, where she was, where she'd taken it. If she was okay. Something about the picture looked like a cry for help to Frost, a plea from Taya to Lincoln. What's worse, it would turn out to be the last text he'd ever receive from her.

Frost remembered the kid's final words. *Find Taya.* He felt a heavier weight fall across his shoulders. He couldn't just find Lincoln's killers. To honor Lincoln's final request, to honor his friend Brakespeare, he'd need to find Taya as well. He needed to tell her about her brother and her uncle. Two men struck down way too early. Maybe she even knew the people who killed her brother, thought Frost. Considering how Lincoln had died, the likelihood of her disappearance being a coincidence felt slim.

Frost called Taya on Lincoln's phone, but it went straight to her voicemail. He didn't leave a message. What would he say? He hung up.

Frost stared at Lincoln's phone for a minute. He went to the home screen and checked what applications were installed. He saw Amazon Shopping, and went into the account settings, where he gleaned Lincoln's address from his default shipping information. Forty-three Bernard Street, unit 405.

The address wasn't far, and Frost found the place after fifteen minutes of driving. He found the greater trouble was working around a number of traffic cordons for some upcoming parade. The building was a modern three-story apartment, with trees growing in the parking lot and a water feature outside of the administration building. Not bad living for a Marine.

Frost was hoping to find an address for Taya in Lincoln's apartment, but he knew his chances were slim. Her address wasn't in Lincoln's phone contacts, so it wasn't likely to be stored in his laptop contacts either. And who the hell kept an address book anymore? Maybe they weren't as close as Frost thought. Maybe it was a dead end.

Frost took a long look at the building and received his system assessment. Level One: Safe. He got out of his truck and made for the front door, but paused. He turned back, went to the rear of his truck, and let down the tailgate. He reached into his hidden lockbox and retrieved his Glock, which he tucked in his back waistband. The threat level could always change.

Frost entered the building using the fob on Lincoln's keys. In the foyer, an old man in a housecoat was retrieving his mail. He turned slowly and stared up at Frost as he came in. Looked at him with a special type of unsubtle judgment that only the elderly can get away with. His eyes narrowed in suspicion.

"Don't remember seeing you here before, young man."

Frost held up Lincoln's keys. "Just staying with a friend."

The old man huffed and threw up his hand in dismissal. "Been hordes of you strangers around here lately. Like a damn bus station. But if you got the keys, ain't much I can do about it."

He shut his mailbox and grumbled under his breath as he shuffled slowly towards the elevator. Frost took the stairwell to the third floor. He didn't need to check the numbers on the door to find Lincoln's apartment. It was the one with the front door kicked in.

Frost inched up to the door, stepping from heel to toe to keep his approach quiet. It hung half open, the wood splintered around the lock and frame. A dim boot print decorated the face of it. Frost pulled out his Glock. He nudged the door open and entered.

Corners clear. The place had been turned over. Furniture was knocked sideways, drawers left open, the desk noticeably absent of a computer. It was a small apartment without many places to hide, and Frost cleared it quickly. Just one bedroom and bath beyond the open kitchen and living room. It was a typical bachelor's home. Solid dark colors against white walls. No artwork or homey adornments. Just a few pieces of mismatched furniture that Lincoln had likely gotten from friends or Craigslist.

Frost looked at the desk again, where a wireless mouse and speaker cables now lay homeless on its surface. It was clear that whoever robbed the place had taken a laptop. But, just like Lincoln's murder, nothing else obvious seemed to be missing. Lincoln had a pretty decent flat-screen TV and a nice gaming system, and both had only been moved aside to check beneath or behind them. This wasn't a robbery. There was something larger going on.

Frost felt the implications overwhelming him. If he really wanted to go through with this, he'd have to break every rule he'd made upon returning from Afghanistan: to stay off the radar, keep a low profile, be inconspicuous. He'd thrown it all out the window in the last twelve hours. And for what? What could he really do?

Frost exhaled and returned the gun to his waistband. For Brakespeare, he reminded himself. For Brakespeare. That's what for. Brakespeare deserved his best, and so did Lincoln.

Frost turned and something on the living room floor caught his eye. He picked it up. It was a framed photograph of Lincoln and a younger woman. She wore a yellow sundress. She and Lincoln shared the same round eyes, the same closed smile. The way they leaned on each other seemed playful. Familial. Love in their eyes, but not romance. It had to be Taya. At least now he had a face to match a name.

He turned the frame over, unhinged the cardboard paneling, and folded up the photo to slide it into his jacket pocket. He went to the kitchen and looked around. He opened the cabinet under the sink and found the trash bin, which he pulled out and upended onto the counter. There wasn't a whole lot. Some discarded packaging, food waste, a few loose pieces of paper.

Frost looked through the papers. A few receipts for the grocery store, a gas station, Walmart. The last was a receipt for a Black Lotus tattoo parlor. Its address and phone number were printed neatly at the top. That was about as good an idea for a lead as he could find.

Frost unfocused from the receipt and felt the kitchen's low-quality fluorescent burning into his vision. He rubbed his eyes and struggled to focus. His head was pounding with a dull headache. He dimly realized that he hadn't slept since the day before, and that in that time he had driven nine hours, drank two beers, witnessed a murder, and nearly been hit by a car. Even without his sensitivities to light and noise, which had been taxed by the roadhouse and the gunfire, he was struggling. He tried to readjust himself, to shake off his fatigue, but he knew he would be of no use until he got some sleep. He took a final glance at the apartment, pocketed the receipt, and left.

FIVE

The Ford Ranger sat shrouded in shadow in the back lot of a national state park welcome center. Hiking trails spread beyond it, snaking into the deepening woodland of aspen and whitebark. A pale moon lit the slopes of the mountains in the distance.

Frost lay in the bed of his truck beneath the cab-high cap, tucked into his sleeping bag. The cab window slid open, letting the warm night breeze in. He'd only just fallen asleep when a fan of light threw shadows across his cab before dimming once more. Another truck had pulled into the lot. The engine soon cut and the lights went out. Frost hoped it wasn't some ranger coming to tell him he couldn't park there. But that worry was quickly dispelled as he heard two men arguing in the truck.

"There," the first man said. "This inconspicuous enough for you? Christ."

"The hell you care? Acting like you got some place to be," the second said.

"Well, what's wrong with the lot behind your house all of a sudden?"

"'Cause Maggie said if she rolled up on me scoring one more time, she's leaving. Now, come on. How much for some of that new shit?"

Frost rolled over, his head still aching. It wasn't worth getting out of the truck to engage with these two junkies. He'd just suffer them until they got high and left.

"Heard about your boss's little problem," the second man said. "You really think she ran off?"

"Why not?"

"I don't know. Maybe someone finally put her down."

"Shit, who knows, man?" the first said. "I mean, she's a wild horse with a big mouth, so neither would surprise me."

Frost rolled over in his truck bed. Missing women seemed to be a trend in Clear Rock.

"You think Silver would actually do her, though?" the second man asked.

"Maybe. Why not?" the first said.

"'Cause she's one fine piece of ass, is why not."

A grunt in the affirmative. "Not a lotta that in Clear Rock. Still, she threatened Silver to walk away too many damn times. Run away with some soldier who was back in town or some shit, goin' on about some jarhead who was back in the states who could take her away from all this."

"Huh. That guy's *definitely* put down."

Frost slipped out of his sleeping bag and sat up in the darkness of his truck bed. He peered over at the truck through the opened cab window and saw it was parked a few spots over. A crew cab Sierra. The windows were rolled down, but it was too dark to see the men's faces. Frost ran the playbook in his head. He could continue to eavesdrop and see what turned up, maybe sneak around and get the plate number. Though he had no access to police databases without an encrypted computer, and that would take time to get.

No, he needed to engage them. It was the quickest way. The only way, really. It was the best lead to Taya he had. Frost needed to confront these two and find out exactly what they knew.

But how best to approach them? He decided upon deception. He didn't think it was smart to be aggressive with the men. Not right now. It would only put them on edge, and that wouldn't help him glean information from them. Frost grabbed his sidearm from beside his sleeping bag and tucked it in his back waistband. He grabbed a few tens from his wallet and exited the back of his truck.

He called out to the men as he approached and heard them scrambling to hide their drug paraphernalia. The first man, sitting in the driver's seat, looked over at Frost walking in the dim moonlight and his posture went from slack to rigid.

"The fuck you want, man?"

"I don't mean to interrupt—" Frost said, holding up his hands in a placating gesture.

"You didn't mean it, but you did it. Fuck off, man."

Frost stood by the driver's side window and got a better look at the men inside. Late twenties. The first wore a leather jacket and T-shirt. Greasy dark hair, slicked back, with a kempt goatee. The second had a tribal tattoo running up the side of his neck. He was fit, with a buzz cut. Track marks flecked the inside of one elbow, just visible in the light of the moon roof. Neither of them looked like the scarred shooter that'd killed Lincoln.

The driver pulled out a .38 Special and pointed it at Frost. He clicked the hammer back.

"I said fuck off."

Frost didn't flinch. He'd had a gun shoved in his face plenty of times before. Been shot at hundreds of times, too. Two punks getting high in some Wyoming parking lot weren't going to make him sweat.

He glanced into the cab. A baggie of brown powder sat on the dash next to a spoon and plastic lighter.

"We're cool," Frost said. "I'm just looking to score, maybe."

He held up the cash in his hand.

"Where the fuck you even come from?" the driver said, glancing around the parking lot.

The passenger reached into his jacket and pulled out a Sig Sauer pistol. He held it in his lap and looked over at Frost meaningfully. Frost saw that the man wore a black Marathon wristwatch. He took a risk. He gestured over his shoulder to his Ford Ranger.

"Been sleeping in my truck there. Fell on hard times since I got back from overseas." He looked over at the passenger. "You serve?"

The passenger adjusted himself. Uncomfortable. Embarrassed with himself. "Yeah, I served. How the hell you know that?"

Frost shrugged. "The watch, maybe. Vets know how to spot one another."

The driver glanced over at the passenger and eased up on his revolver. Frost's gamble was paying off. The driver glanced at the passenger's watch, looking confused.

The passenger held it up for him to see. "Government issued."

"Look, sorry for walking up on you like this," Frost said. "Was just maybe hoping you'd have something that could put me out for the night. I'm tweaking hard."

"Yeah? What you looking for, man?" the driver said, still guarded.

"Whatever you got, really," Frost said. "Maybe a single of that brown."

The driver looked from Frost to the passenger. The passenger shrugged. Nodded. The driver looked back at Frost.

"All right," the driver said. "That's twenty."

Frost handed him the cash. The driver opened up the center console of the truck and pulled out a small baggie of brown heroin and handed it out the window to Frost.

"You got your own gear?" the driver said.

"It's fine. I'll just snort it," Frost said.

"Suit yourself. But maybe think twice about your approach next time, man. You almost got yourself blasted."

"Appreciate it," Frost said. "My dealer split last week, and I've been crawling up the walls. You guys local? Maybe I'll give you a call next time."

"Yeah, we're local," the driver said. "You got a cell?"

"I do, yeah." Frost decided to gamble. "Did I hear you guys say you know Taya, too?"

The driver soured. "The fuck you doing, listening in on us?" He stared Frost up and down, searching for any evidence of bullshit.

The driver raised his gun again and pointed it at Frost, but Frost was already reacting. He drove his left hand into the driver's wrist, cracking it against the doorframe, and held it there. The driver's revolver discharged, sending a bullet into a distant lamppost, before the man's broken wrist released the gun and it fell to the ground. Frost ignored the roaring pain coursing through his skull all the way to the roots of his brain, feeling the sound of the gunshot like the bullet had burst in his own gray matter. He reached past the pain, pulled his Glock from his waistband, and aimed it directly at the passenger's head. It all happened in a split second.

"Toss it out the window," Frost said to the passenger.

The passenger sat in shock for a second before he threw the Sig Sauer out his window.

"Put your hands on the dash," Frost said, "and if I get even a little itchy, I'll put one in your head."

The passenger did as he was told, glowering at Frost. Frost glanced at the driver, who was moaning in agony over his broken wrist. Frost released the man's limp right hand, and the driver pulled it into the truck.

"Put your left hand on the steering wheel," Frost said to the driver.

The man did.

"Now, what happened to Taya?" Frost asked. "Go."

"Look, man," the passenger said, "we got no idea. Nobody does."

"How do you know her?"

"I don't. Not like that, I mean. I met her a party like a year ago or something," the passenger said. "You just hear shit. You know, rumors. You mess around in the dark long enough, you're bound to hear something about everything."

"Who's Silver?" Frost asked.

Both men went silent. The passenger looked over at the driver. Frost saw that he'd likely be the one with answers.

"You want to lose the other wrist?" Frost said. "Who's Silver?"

"You got no idea what you're playing at, man," the driver said.

"Look, Silver's looking for Taya, too, man," the passenger said. "I told you. Everyone is. Nobody knows where she went."

"Shut. The Fuck. Up," the driver said.

"Is she dead?" Frost asked. Nobody knows? That worried Frost, but it was also a small relief. Even if she was in trouble, at least this guy Silver hadn't found her yet.

"I honestly have no fuckin' idea, pal," the driver said, gritting his teeth from the pain in his wrist. "Like he said, it's all rumor."

Frost looked between the men, assessing their body language. He didn't think he'd get much more out of them. Not unless he was prepared to use the spare battery and jumper cables in his truck. He also couldn't be sure the stray discharge hadn't caught the ear of a passing driver, though the state road was set back a ways from the lot. But the potential reward wasn't worth the risk, if there was even a reward to be had.

Frost told them both to keep their hands on the dash, and he slowly backed away from the truck. When he'd made it to his Ranger, he fired a bullet each into the front and rear driver-side tires of the Sierra. The two men took cover for a moment before realizing Frost wasn't firing at them, and then the driver began cursing all hell at Frost.

Frost hopped into his truck and sped off into the night. He'd need to find another place to sleep.

SIX

awn fell warm over the valley. The sun sparkled brilliant on the dewed grass and the calm waters of the Hognose River. Frost stood in the middle of an upstream tributary, a klick south of the tallgrass where he'd parked his truck and slept the night prior. He stood knee-deep and barefoot in the frigid water, wearing only his Jockeys and undershirt, fishing for his morning meal.

The line of his collapsible rod went taut. Frost reeled in. The fish struggled admirably, but soon Frost had it. He gripped it tight in his calloused hands and looked at it. It was a cutthroat trout. He pinned the rod under his arm and pulled a thin, T-handled screwdriver from his waistband. He quickly plunged the end of it into the fish's hindbrain, above and behind its eyes, and withdrew it just as fast. The trout was instantly rendered braindead. Brakespeare had taught him this technique, calling it the ikejime method. The most humane way to kill a fish, and the best way to preserve its flavor.

Frost arrived back at his truck shortly after, opened the tailgate, and set the exsanguinated fish upon it. He collapsed his rod and stowed it in one of several storage bins. He retrieved a portable propane grill-stove and fired it up on the tailgate. He filled a small tin pot with water from a five-gallon jerry can, and set the pot on the stove. He set the fish on the grill, and while it was cooking, washed his hands, face, and underarms with water and soap. Then he washed and rinsed his clothes from the day previous. He dressed himself and chugged a thermos of water, used the heated water from the pot to refill the thermos, and stirred in a spoonful of instant coffee. He plated the fish and ate in silence, looking out over the Hognose River.

When he finished, Frost quickly rinsed his plastic dishes and set them back in their storage bin with the grill-stove. He picked up his thermos and went around to sit in the driver's seat with the door open. He enjoyed a second cup of coffee before pulling out his map and retrieving the tattoo parlor receipt to look up the address. He'd need to find that Walmart, too.

An hour later, Frost was parked in front of the tattoo parlor with a new burner phone in his pocket. He removed the SIM card from the old one and snapped it in half. He exited his truck and tossed the SIM card and old phone into a public trash bin.

Black Lotus was etched upon the glass picture window of the building. It was a modest shop nested in a long strip mall of chain outlets that included a shoe store, a fast-food restaurant, and a boutique coffee shop. Frost went inside.

The foyer was small. Most of the real estate was used for the parlor in the back. It was narrow, with only three steel chairs for the waiting customers. The walls were covered in colorful drawings, itemized tattoo templates, and photographs. A large viper wound around a woman's forearm. A hand holding cards inside a ball of fire emblazoned upon a man's chest. A veiled, weeping saint covering the entirety of someone's back.

"Morning," said a cheery voice.

Frost turned to see a striking woman emerge from the narrow hallway behind the glass counter. She had auburn hair with golden highlights, twisted up in a bun. She wore an attractive silver nostril ring, and a sleeve of bright detailed flowers covered the entirety of her left arm. Frost wondered if she'd done it herself.

"How can I help you?" she asked.

Frost's nose filled with her perfume. It was earthy and spiced, like incense in a palace. The scent was intoxicating. Distracting. It'd been a while since he'd chatted with a beautiful woman, but he needed to focus. He cleared his throat, trying to recapture his sense of balance.

"Morning. Are you the owner?" Frost said.

"That's right. Sarah Albany," she said.

"Kevin Johnson," Frost said.

Sarah turned her head slightly and narrowed her eyes at Frost. "Wouldn't have been my first guess."

"Oh no?" Frost said, smiling. "And what would've been?"

"Hmm. I don't know, exactly."

"Go on. Give it a shot."

"My luck, I'm likely to suggest the name of the father you don't get along with or the man who stole your wife or something," Sarah said.

"You're painting quite a grim picture of my family history."

"You see now? I'm already stepping in it. I just meant you don't look like a Kevin Johnson."

"Shame. It was my father's name," Frost said.

"Oh my God, really?"

"No. Not really."

When Sarah laughed, it rose in a pitch at the end and turned into a sort of giggle. Her laugh showed in her eyes, too. Laughing was good. Easier to get information from someone in a good mood. Frost smiled and pulled the receipt from his pocket. The smile took effort, like he was lifting something heavy. He wondered if Sarah had noticed, but she didn't give any outward indication.

"I'm trying to find some information about a friend of mine," he said. "Wanted to know if you knew anything about him. He got done up here not too long ago. Last Monday, looks like."

Sarah's posture changed at the question—nothing hostile, just a stiffening around the back and shoulders, broadcasting that he had put her on edge. Frost had either asked the wrong question, or the right question in the wrong way. She took the receipt from him and looked at the purchase and the date.

"What's your friend's name?" she said.

"Lincoln Dane."

"Oh, I know Lincoln, sure," Sarah said.

"Do you know the last time he was here?" Frost asked.

"Why do you want to know?"

"I'm—" Frost began, but Sarah held up a hand before he could finish.

"Look, 'Mister Johnson,' just because Clear Rock's a small town doesn't mean that the local tattoo parlor is some den of scum and villainy, all right? We don't need any more trouble, and I'm not selling a local kid down the river to a loan shark or what-the-fuck-ever *you're* supposed to be." She flung a vague gesture toward Frost, but he could swear he felt her pointing directly at his scars. "You seem nice enough, *Kevin*, but anyone who wants something bad enough can be polite. Buy something or leave, but please don't ask about my customers."

This had gone downhill quicker than Frost had expected. He raised his hands defensively to buy time as he thought of another approach.

Sarah had good instincts. She was already on the defensive, and any more lying would only make things worse. In this case, the truth would probably take him further than lies.

"I really am a friend of Lincoln's, but I met him for the first time last night. His uncle and I served together in the Army, but he passed away. I was in town to deliver the tags. Lincoln seemed distracted, like something was wrong. Then, at the end of the night, someone gunned him down in front of me."

"What?" Sarah asked. She looked as though she'd been slapped. "Lincoln's dead?"

Frost nodded. "The cops say they have it handled, but some things don't add up. I'm trying to find out why."

Sarah's eyes shimmered. Frost felt guilty and uncomfortable that he couldn't share in her grief, and that he had ambushed her with the news of Lincoln's death only as a means to an end. Thoughts that he was only pretending to be a person surfaced, and he pushed them under again.

"Were you two close?" Frost asked.

Sarah shook her head. "We were friends in high school. Not much after that. But everyone around Clear Rock knew one another at least a little, you know? He was a good kid. Had a good heart." She paused and shook her head. "Good hearts are wasted on this place."

"Anything you can tell me about the last time he was in here would help me."

Sarah looked up at him, her eyes wet and still narrowed with lingering distrust. Frost waited for her to make up her mind. Eventually, she sighed. Her shoulders slackened.

"I hadn't worked on Lincoln in a while, but there're two other guys who work here. One of them might've done more recent work."

She moved towards the register and reached under the counter, pulling out a large three-ring binder. She flipped through a few pages.

"It won't tell us if he just stopped in for merchandise," Sarah said, gesturing at the display case between them full of piercings and leather bracelets. "But if he made an appointment... here. Lincoln Dane. Scott was working on him last Monday. Lincoln's a talker, and he and Scott could really get going. He might know something."

She looked up at Frost. A moment passed, and Frost could clearly see regret register on her face—regret that she had trusted a stranger with information about an old, dead friend. Regret for trusting so readily. Frost could relate.

"You wouldn't know where I might possibly find his sister, would you? I've been asking around to let her know, but nobody seems to know where she's gone."

Sarah shook her head. "No, I'm sorry. I've never met her."

Frost nodded. "Thank you for your help. And I'm sorry to have upset you."

"No, of course. I hope you find her."

Frost smiled and they held each other's gaze for a moment before he made to leave. But upon reaching the door, he stopped and turned back to Sarah.

"You wouldn't happen to know a man with sandy blonde hair and a noticeable scar right about here, would you?" Frost said, running his thumb across his cheek.

Sarah sniffed. "That sounds like Andy to me."

"Andy?" Frost said.

"Andy Treece. The guy's a creep. Spends all his time over at Tick's trying to pick up girls fresh out of high school." She narrowed her eyes. "Oh my God, he's not the one who—"

"I don't know that yet," Frost said. "But I'd like to ask him a few things. I'm guessing he's local, then?"

Sarah shrugged. "Not sure. He might be. I mean, I started seeing him around in the last five years or so. He and Silver showed up around the same time."

"Silver?" Frost said. "You know Silver, too?"

"Everyone around here knows Silver, even if they wish they didn't," Sarah said. She stared off and shook her head as if she already regretted bringing his name up. "His guys won't shut up when they're getting inked, that's for sure. He made a whole lot of noise when he and Andy came to town, too. He's got that big house up on Pinewood."

"Pinewood," Frost repeated, making a mental note.

"They knew each other. Lincoln and Andy, I mean," Sarah said. She leaned on the counter, but her posture was rigid. Whether it was from discussing Silver or the news of Lincoln's murder, Sarah was becoming uncomfortable again. Maybe even ready to go on the defensive.

"How do you know that?" Frost asked, trying to connect the dots in his mind with red string.

"I saw them one morning maybe two weeks back, right out there on the sidewalk." She gestured over Frost's shoulder to the lot beyond the picture window. "Arguing. Lincoln was really letting Andy have it. He stomped in here afterwards, saying how Andy kept asking about his sister. He didn't want her anywhere near that creep."

"Andy was looking for Lincoln's sister?" Frost said.

"What I remember, yeah," Sarah said.

Lincoln's killers were looking for Taya. At least one of them was connected to this guy Silver. And the two in the Sierra had said Silver was looking for Taya himself. It seemed the girl had an enormous shadow following her, if the shadow hadn't already swallowed her whole.

It was a lot. Murder, drugs, a missing girl. Lincoln and Taya possibly caught up in some small-town underworld. Everything inside Frost told him to get out of Clear Rock. Every minute he stayed he was increasing his risk of exposure. But he thought back to Sherriff Puck. Her arrogance. Her dismissiveness. Lincoln lying there against the roadhouse wall. Frost knew that if he himself didn't get involved, there'd be no justice for the kid.

He couldn't save Lincoln, but he might be able to save Taya. It sounded like Silver hadn't caught up with her yet, but that could change at any moment. If she was still alive, he could help her and take out the men who'd murdered Lincoln. And then he'd hit the road once more before Crane found him.

Frost turned back to Sarah, who had been examining him while he was lost in thought. "One more question."

"Of course," she said.

"What's Tick's?"

SEVEN

Frost stepped inside Tick's Bar and scanned the dimly lit room. It was a small place with a few round tables throughout, each draped with a dark linen tablecloth and red glass candle holders. An empty stage loomed at the back for live music with a full PA, rack lights, a house piano. A large U-shaped bar dominated the left side of the room, with a dark walnut top and brass footrails. High leather-backed seats lined up in front of it. Red string lights hung all around, trimming the shaded windows, the doorway, the horizontal mirror behind the bar. They cast the room in a soft crimson glow. It was nicer than Frost had expected.

Frost clocked ten people in the place besides himself: a middle-aged bartender with a paunch and clean polo shirt behind the bar polishing a pint glass with a cloth, a few women shooting pool, a line of singles at the bar watching the game on a flat-screen, a table of younger guys eating nachos over pitchers of beer in the corner. The crowd posed a Level Two at best, considering the few that looked quite drunk already, being but just eleven in the morning.

Frost grabbed a stool at the bar. He noticed Kris Kristofferson playing over the speakers. He recognized the tune but couldn't place the name of the song. It'd been a while since he'd last heard it. He glanced up at the game on the flat-screen. It made him think of his father, as much as he tried to avoid it.

Every Sunday in the Frost household, the Cleveland Browns played on the beat-up cathode ray set. The games were his father's Sunday ritual. His church. He'd allowed young Frost in the living room during the games, so long as he was silent. The only sound permitted was the low volume of the TV and the outlaw country records that played on the Hi-Fi. The songs were always the same and played in very precise order.

Frost became familiar with all the Good Ole Boys this way. Willie, Merle, Waylon. He'd rise and turn the record over or replace it with the next in line and return to his Hot Wheels on the carpet. The records were the soundtrack of his youth. A soundtrack marred with the grunts and curses of his father as he shouted at the TV, pausing only to reach into the ice chest beside the sofa. His drained cans of Pabst Blue Ribbon lined the coffee table like military tombstones as the game progressed. Eventually, the Wild Turkey would emerge and shadow the afternoon sun in patriarchal darkness.

Frost had come into his father's life later than most parents are willing to tolerate children, and Frost wasn't sure his father had ever wanted him at all. Those Sundays, and the smell of Wild Turkey, were a grim reminder of that.

Maybe some old lonesome song'll take you by surprise and leave you just a little more alone.

Frost remembered now. It was "The Stranger." Track six on Kristofferson's *Who's to Bless and Who's to Blame* LP.

"What can I get you, pal?" the bartender said.

"Bottle of Bud," Frost said.

The bartender set down the pint glass he'd been polishing and tossed the cloth over his shoulder. He pulled out a frosty Bud and placed it in front of Frost on a cardboard coaster.

"You want a pilsner glass with that?" the bartender said.

"Nah," Frost said. "Thanks."

He took a sip and set the beer back down. The place smelled fresher than any bar he could remember being in. Tidier, too. The woodtop was clean of water ring stains, the floor was recently polished and free of typical barroom stickiness, the menus and straws and napkins were all set proper in their racks. Frost evaluated the bartender. He was clean-shaven with lightly moussed hair. His fingernails were clipped and clean. Frost pinned him as the owner, and the kempt bar as a broader extension of his own attentive hygiene.

"You're not Tick, are you?" said Frost said.

"Depends who's asking," the bartender said with a smile.

"Sarah over at the Black Lotus told me to head over to Tick's if I was looking for a quiet drink." He took in the bar. "Nice spot."

"Oh, Ms. Albany sent you over, did she?" The bartender began polishing another glass.

Frost nodded. "Said you take care of people."

"Sarah said that, hmm?" The bartender nodded in satisfaction. "Well, well. Maybe she's warming up to me after all."

That put Frost on edge. The man's presentation impressed Frost, but Sarah was a nice enough woman and the bartender sounded almost predatory. Either way, he made a mental note that the two had history.

Tick glanced over at Frost again, evaluating him with a more discerning eye. Frost wasn't sure what it was about Sarah's name that had prompted the double-take. He could have just been sizing Frost up as a competitor for Sarah's affection, for all he knew. But after everything he had learned about this town so far, he wasn't about to drop his guard.

"So, how do you know Ms. Albany?"

Frost shrugged. "I don't, really. Just met her this morning. I'm Kevin, by the way."

"Kevin, nice to know you," the bartender said. "I'm Tick."

Frost tilted his beer in salute. "Nice to know you, Tick."

"You over there getting a tattoo, or what?"

"Nah, not really the type," Frost said. "You got any?"

"Nah, I'm the same," Tick said. "Can't stand needles. What brought you by her shop then?"

Pushy. Definitely more than his laid-back demeanor suggested.

"Seeing about a friend. Lincoln Dane. You know him?"

Tick smiled. "Hell yeah, I know Lincoln. In here all the time. He meeting you for a drink?"

Frost looked up at Tick. Cleared his throat. He could learn from his visit with Sarah. Even if he couldn't feel the pain, he could try his best to prevent spreading it.

"You like tequila, Tick?" Frost said.

"Yeah, I like tequila. Why?"

"Why don't you pour us each a Cuervo, then. On me."

The smiled faded from Tick's face. So much for a tactful approach.

"Is the kid dead?" Tick said.

Frost nodded, suddenly wary. Could have been a lucky guess, but it came just a little too quick for Frost's comfort.

Tick set the glass down. He lowered his head and set his hands against the woodtop. Frost watched his back arch as he took in a slow breath.

"Fuck!"

A few patrons glanced over before turning back to their own business. Tick looked up at Frost again. He reached up to the underlit shelves of liquor behind the bar and pulled down a bottle of oak-aged añejo tequila from the highest shelf. He poured two shots, and the men lifted their glasses and solemnly drank.

"How'd he die?"

"Two hoods attacked him last night. Shot him dead in a parking lot."

"Jesus Christ," Tick said.

"Surprised you ain't heard yet, the size of this town."

"Nope," Tick said, shaking his head. He looked Frost over. "You police?"

Frost clocked Tick shifting his weight to the back foot. Watched him swallow and tense up. Maybe the tequila, Frost thought. Maybe grief. Maybe neither.

"No," Frost said. "I'm just a friend of the family, trying to sort things out. But I want to find out what you know."

"What I know? I didn't have anything to do with Lincoln getting killed." Tick didn't seem to be lying. His body language was rigid with indignance, back straight and chin high, irritated at Frost's intrusion.

"No, but you didn't seem too surprised he was dead. Sad, maybe, but not surprised," Frost said. "You knew something like this was coming for him, didn't you?"

"I didn't know," Tick said.

Frost waited him out. Examined and evaluated all the signals that Tick's posture could send. It wasn't much. The man was like a statue.

"I mean, I didn't know about anyone coming to kill him, but… last week, two guys came in here. Got into it with Lincoln and grabbed him by the collar. I told them to take off before I called the cops. I was ready to take matters into my own hands if they didn't listen, but they did. Lincoln told me after, those same boys had been harassing him for a while now, asking about his sister. Trying to collect a drug debt from her, he thinks. He wasn't sure. Christ. He said they told him he'd wind up paying if she didn't. If he kept covering for her." Tick shook his head. "You hear shit like that and you figure people are just talking, you know? But—Jesus, I guess those bastards were serious."

"As a heart attack," Frost said. "Do you know where his sister is?"

Tick rubbed the back of his neck. "No, I never met her."

"Know where I might find her, maybe? I think you'd agree it sounds like she's in trouble."

"Yeah, no doubt in my mind," Tick said. "But no. I've no idea where she might be. Look, if you ain't police, then who the hell are you?"

"Like I said, a friend of the family."

"A friend," Tick said. He eyed Frost suspiciously.

"That's right. Seeming to be the only one who cares that kid got lit up, too."

"I care." The bartender's eyes narrowed and his nostrils flared. That indignance again. Maybe he really had cared about Lincoln. Frost could use that.

"Then help me," Frost said. "You get a look at the two men in here threatening Lincoln?"

"Yeah, I did."

"One of them wouldn't be Andy Treece, would it?"

Tick hesitated. "Yeah. It was Andy."

"And where might I find *him*?" Frost said.

Tick sighed. "He lives in a duplex over on Boulder Lane."

He grabbed a fresh coaster and wrote something on the back, which he handed to Frost.

"You know his address?" Frost asked, reaching out to take it.

Tick shrugged. "Just the nearest cross-streets. A buddy of mine lives a few doors down. Pointed the place out to me before," he said. "What're you going to do to him if you find him?"

"That's completely up to him."

"What about Taya?"

"What about who?" Frost said. His focus leapt back to Tick's who had gone wide-eyed as he realized the slip-up.

"His sister."

"So you *do* know her?"

"I never said I didn't," Tick said. "I said I never met her. I know her name."

Sure, he did. Frost was suspicious, but an admission like that wasn't going to open up a whole new line of questioning. "Well, what about her?" Frost asked.

"You going to keep looking for her?"

"Everyone else is this town seems to be," Frost said, finishing his beer and setting the empty bottle down on the woodtop. "I might as well join in. I think I might be a little more interested in her safety than most."

Frost reached for his wallet, but Tick waved him off.

"It's on me," he said.

"Thanks," Frost said. That was a surprise.

"You know, I bet Taya just ran off or something," Tick said. "Girls her age are taking off all the time. Seems they can't wait to get out of Clear Rock."

"I can't imagine why," Frost said.

EIGHT

Frost knocked firmly on the front door of the duplex, an attached single-level townhouse on a street lined with identical models. He took a step back on the stoop and tried to peer through the front curtains of the bay window. He couldn't see anyone inside. He glanced at Andy Treece's lawn, and then over at his neighbor's. The two yards were polar opposites. Treece's was a hinterland of dandelions, haphazard patches of crabgrass, and taller ryegrass hanging awkwardly over the dismal forgotten garden. His neighbor's, in contrast, was trimmed and bespot with grass seed. Children's toys lay scattered across it; a T-ball set, a miniature soccer ball, and a small plastic trike.

Frost glanced around the quiet Boulder Lane street. Nothing moved. Nothing should've. It was midday in the middle of the week. The adults were at work, the children at school. Frost knocked again, but knew nobody was home. There was no car in the driveway.

Frost turned back to the house and glanced in through the front curtains again. The back window looked like it might be open an inch or two. He began to circle the house. The muddied stone path was overgrown with dead brush. A small garter snake slithered in the ryegrass.

"Excuse me! Can I help you?"

Frost turned to see a woman emerge from the adjoining townhouse. She stood in a blue fleece tracksuit, her hair in a tight ponytail, a steaming mug of coffee gripped in one hand. She eyed Frost suspiciously, one eyebrow raised.

"Oh, hello," Frost said. He turned and made his way back towards her. She could either be a liability, likely to call the cops on him, or an asset, as someone who knew the neighborhood. How he behaved would decide which she became.

"I was just looking for Andy," Frost said. "Do you know where he is?"

"I don't," said the neighbor. "And who are you?"

"I'm a friend of his," Frost said. "Supposed to meet him for lunch, but it looks like he forgot."

"Mm, is that right?" She blew on her coffee. "Probably at work then, I imagine."

"Probably right," Frost said. "Where does he work now, again, do you know? I'm from out of town, and I was kind of hoping to see him before I had to leave."

"That seems like something one friend might tell another. Or is that something else Mr. Treece forgot?"

Frost gave a thin grin. This soccer mom wasn't budging.

"He only told me to meet him here. But Andy *can* be a little—" Frost stared out over Treece's unkempt side of the lawn, "—absent-minded."

The woman smiled. Appreciated the joke. "Oh, I can agree with that."

Frost smiled at her. "To tell you the truth, I'm a little concerned. I've been having quite a bit of trouble getting a hold of him. He's bounced around a couple of jobs lately. Has he even been home, recently?" It was a risky lie in the event this lady knew exactly what Treece did. But the weedy lawn and the sneering mom suggested that they weren't on the best of terms.

"I haven't seen him in a while, now that you mention it," the neighbor said. "Not that we chat regularly. But I ain't seen his car in the drive for a week or so."

"Hmm," Frost said, nodding. "Well, I'll give him another try on his cell. Thanks for all your help."

The neighbor smiled and Frost threw up a wave as he walked back to his truck. She watched him leave and went back into the house. Frost turned the key in the ignition, drove around the corner, and parked again. Then he doubled back on foot to approach the house from the back.

It was a shared yard with a small patio. The two sides were similarly disharmonious to the front. Frost went to Treece's back window and saw that it had been left unlocked. He slid the window up with one swift move and ducked inside, lowering it behind him.

The house was cool and dark. It smelled faintly of bacon grease and stale garbage. Frost removed his sunglasses. He stood still for a moment in the kitchen and listened intently for signs of the occupant. Dust motes hung in the pale light that cut through the thin opening of the front shades and fell over the living room. There was a weathered leather couch, a few magazines on the coffee table, a wide-screen television. He crept down the hallway and checked two bedrooms and the bathroom.

He walked back to the living room and glanced at the front door. A small pile of mail sat on the floor beneath the slot. Bills, flyers, coupons. Treece had indeed not been home for at least a few days.

Frost looked over the few framed photographs that lined the wall. No family photos. A couple fishing trip pictures. A yellowed portrait of an older gentleman. The last photograph was a worn Polaroid of two younger men, maybe twenty years old, smiling and holding baseball mitts. One was dark-haired, the other sandy-blond. The handwritten scrawl at the bottom read: *Ron and Andy fuck up Spring Training for the Dodgers.* Cute. If this was the same Andy, the picture was taken before he'd gotten his scar. Judging by the faded ink and worn edges, the photo was about as well-travelled as the portrait of the old man. Frost took out his flip phone and snapped a picture of it.

Frost opened the front closet. He found a few jackets, a few pairs of running shoes. He wasn't even sure what he was looking for, exactly. Just something that'd help him track Treece down. He shut the closet door and rifled through the mail, but it really was all junk. Nothing to help Frost complete the portrait.

He went back into the living room and looked around. Looked back towards the back of the house. Then, he saw it: under a pile of discarded papers on the kitchen table peeked the corner of a blunt silver rectangle. He pushed the papers aside and found a laptop. Frost opened it up, but it was password protected. Frost glanced at the papers he had scattered. He rifled through them and found nothing of interest. On a shelf in the corner sat a wireless printer. Frost went to it and scrolled through the digital menu to the previous jobs. He selected the most recent one and hit reprint.

The machine whirred to life and printed three pages. Frost picked them up and sat at the kitchen table to look through them. They were a continuous email chain—encrypted, judging by the service provider— between Treece and a Ronald Fitzgerald. The Ron from the Polaroid, Frost guessed.

The emails were short and blunt, but even though they were using an encryption service and were careful to avoid language that would be damning in a court of law, the nature of the messages was clear. They were informing Treece that a large shipment of drugs—what type was unclear—was on its way to Clear Rock. That *things are going well* and *ten times the current product supply.* The words *Port of Portland* and *warehouse* and *four hundred k's* jumped out at Frost, from which he discerned that Clear Rock was serving as a distribution hub for the Pacific Northwest. And this was only one shipment. Frost tried to guess how much heroin the town was already sitting on, how many of the townspeople were already hooked. How large the devastation to come would be.

Frost felt a dull creep of foreboding. Treece wasn't some small-town alpha dealer. He was a big-time distributor, and he had helped corrupt Clear Rock into a key location for a domestic drug cartel.

Brakespeare had told Frost what a nice spot Clear Rock was. That he'd always loved returning to visit his niece and nephew when he got the chance. And Frost had seen its charm. It was a beautiful spot, surrounded in every direction by breathtaking vistas. Untouched rivers and dense woodlands and the towering majesty of the Teton Range mountains. God's country in absolute. Yet Frost now knew it was rotting from the inside out.

Frost looked over the emails again, trying to read between the lines to discern more details. The send dates on the emails were there, but most of the specifics were absent. Date of departure, date of arrival, address of the warehouse—all left out. Only confirmation that everything was on schedule and running smooth.

Frost folded the pages up and tucked them in his inner jacket pocket. He wondered why Treece would print the emails in the first place. Perhaps he wanted to show someone else, but didn't want to send them electronically? But he was using an encrypted provider, thought Frost. The risk was almost hypocritical. There were a lot of questions to be answered yet.

A key crunched into the front door lock and shattered the low threat level he'd been sitting on. Frost shot to his feet and prepared to engage. He could not climb out the window nor reach the back door in time. He drew his sidearm and stepped into the corner of the kitchen closest to the front door wall. Unless the man warmed to an intruder standing in his kitchen, Frost was likely going to have to fight his way out.

The door slid open and daylight washed over the linoleum floor of the front hallway. Frost could make out vague details of the man who stood in the doorway: a lean build, a gaunt face, a sandy splotch of hair, and a horizontal line across one cheek. Frost adjusted his grip on his handgun and turned off the safety as Andy Treece walked into his home.

NINE

Treece muttered something dismissively as he kicked at the small pile of mail that had stuck under the front door. The pile slipped free, and the door shut behind him. As he walked forward, Frost noticed that he was holding a bag of groceries. He would be coming back to the kitchen, and his hands would be full. Frost could get the jump on him.

Treece walked to the kitchen doorway, but stopped before he entered the kitchen. Frost's hasty hiding spot wasn't perfect, but the kitchen table should have obscured him enough in the back window reflection that Treece couldn't use Frost's own vantage point against him. Still, the man's head tilted sideways as he examined something Frost couldn't see.

"What the fuck..." Treece muttered. He walked forward to the kitchen table, where his laptop lay open and excavated from under the pile of discarded papers.

Now was Frost's chance. Take the bastard's knee, knock him off-balance and limit his movement. Pin him and attack his head if he needed disorientation. He would use the gun only as a club or a last resort, so the sound didn't attract attention.

Frost lunged forward just as Treece turned to check the corner. Frost still struck out with his knee, but Treece was fast enough to backpedal so that Frost's strike only caught his instep. The distributor stumbled, falling backwards and taking the groceries with him. Frost moved to pin him, but Treece flung something dug out from his grocery bag. By sheer dumb luck, the heavy glass jar struck Frost in the temple.

His skull exploded in pain and the trauma sites across his scalp ignited like fault lines filling with lava. He dropped to one knee, clutching his temple with his free hand. Behind the lights dancing over his vision, Frost just saw Treece regaining his feet. God dammit.

"Motherfucker," Treece growled, picking up the dark glass jar he had struck Frost with. Frost tried to bring his hand up to block the blow, but Treece brought the jar down on his head again. Frost heard himself bellow in pain as he fell to the floor.

Pain. Swimming in it. He was a child again, merciless at the hands of his father. A recruit, his whole body burning from the trials in Boot. A soldier, his body shredded and pummeled by his team's bomb. But he had survived pain. He carried every pound of it with him, but he had survived it. He continued to survive it every agonizing day of his life.

He drove his fist forward, putting the strength of his core behind the blow. His fist met the soft organs of an unprotected stomach, and Treece gave a shocked grunt of pain. Frost's vision still hadn't cleared, but he swung forward with his gun hand and scored a glancing blow across Treece's jaw. The jar dropped from Treece's hand and shattered, apparently having had enough blunt force trauma for one lifetime.

Frost tried to blink away the spinning room and the blinding stars to no avail. He needed to be able to see before he risked using his gun. He settled for an uppercut instead, stepping forward and using his body's momentum to drive his fist into Treece's side where he hoped a floating rib would be. He didn't need to see to take this asshole down.

Then, the dark shape ducked down to something at his feet. He came up holding something reflective and lunged at Frost with it, but Frost stepped away in time to dodge the strike. Treece had grabbed a shard of glass from the broken jar. The man was resourceful enough, but it was obvious that he was getting desperate. Frost took his chances and held his gun in a short-armed CQB stance, unsure if he was even aiming the barrel at Treece.

"Why did you kill Lincoln, Treece? And where's Taya?" he growled.

Treece gave a short, breathless laugh. "Is that what this is about? That stupid kid and his slut of a sister? Jesus, they've both caused us enough trouble."

"If you're trying to convince me not to shoot you dead, you're doing a shit job of it," Frost said.

"You won't kill me, if you want to know where dear, sweet Taya's gone. Probably so you can tell her that her brother died like a bitch with a load of my buckshot in his guts, right?" He laughed. "But I think you've run out of time."

Frost's vision started to clear, enough to see a pair of dog tags peeking from Treece's cheap button-up shirt, which had lost a few buttons in the struggle.

"How do you figure? Because it looks like I've got you dead to rights, Treece."

Then Frost heard it. His vision was coming back, but his head still felt like it was splitting, and the approaching police siren tore into him even further. He watched Treece tap smugly at a cracked smartwatch on his wrist.

Treece lunged forward again. Frost raised his arm to deflect the blow, but his disorientation got the best of him and Treece slashed into Frost's forearm. Frost brought the butt of his pistol down onto Treece's head. He connected, and hard. The man collapsed to the floor with a grunt, completely limp.

His head a nimbus of pain and his arm pouring blood, Frost assessed his situation. He was wounded and standing in a house that was not his, holding a gun over the unconscious homeowner. It didn't matter if Treece was a drug lord or whether the Clear Rock police were incompetent, this situation looked about as bad as it was going to get. He was at Threat Level 4: SNAFU.

He staggered to the back window and opened it to climb out. Behind him, Treece groaned in pain. Frost would be back for him. This wasn't over. Not by a long shot.

TEN

Frost squinted through the bright sunlight and tried to keep his focus on the road as his migraine pulsed behind his eyes. He pulled his sunglasses from his jacket pocket and shoved them onto his face. His left forearm, rush-wrapped in a clean bandage from his first aid kit, stung sharply. His forehead throbbed, and he touched it gingerly with two fingertips. They came away red with blood. Frost grabbed the Broncos cap from the passenger seat and threw it on. It hurt like hell, but he couldn't have anyone seeing his wounds. He thought about what to do. Where to go.

He drove on. It was a small town. There weren't many. If he could find a spot to stop, he could sew up his wounds with the first aid kit. He could suture them himself, too, but he didn't have the tools. He could try a pharmacy, but his current state would draw attention. And a hospital was out of the question. There was only one viable option. Familiar from his time overseas. Go to ground with what few allies you have.

He ran through his system in his head. He'd have to take his chances. Frost arrived at the Black Lotus fifteen minutes later. He parked his truck in the small lot behind the building and walked around to the front through the narrow alley. He glanced up at the corners of the buildings to see if there were any security cameras mounted on them. There weren't. He pulled the brim of his hat lower, ignoring the burst of pain as the band gripped his head like a vise, and went inside the Black Lotus.

Sarah stood at the counter writing in a ledger when Frost walked in. She looked up with a friendly customer-service smile, but it vanished when she saw the blood slick on his face. Her eyes widened further at the slash on the side of his jacket and the exposed flesh beneath it.

"Oh my God." She ran around the counter. "What the hell happened to you?"

"Bar fight at Tick's. I need your help," Frost said. She was friendly. She seemed smart. Unlike Tick, Frost's backup option, she hadn't seemed like she had anything to hide. But he couldn't tell her the truth and risk involving her more than he already had.

"Of course." She pulled off his hat and winced at the gash beneath. "I'm seeing a cut on your arm and at least one head wound. I'm gonna assume it's not just a surface cut?" He wondered where she'd learned to evaluate wounds like that. Either way, he admired her ability to keep a cool head in a crisis.

"Probably some blunt trauma," Frost admitted through gritted teeth. The fluorescents in the ceiling burned through his sunglass lenses and straight into his skull.

"Jesus Christ," Sarah said.

"Do you have a first aid kit?" Frost said.

"Yeah, but this is bad," Sarah said, taking in his wounds. "You need to see a doctor."

"It looks dramatic, but it's more appearance than function," Frost said. "I've sewn up worse myself, but I don't have the supplies right now."

He'd already decided that it would not be worth the risk of going to a hospital, of the police possibly being called. Not with Crane on his heels.

"But maybe a doctor—"

"I can't," Frost said. "Please. I need you to understand. I think I'm Lincoln's only chance for justice. If I go to a hospital, then it all falls apart."

The moment hung between them. He had put it all on the table, infused his voice with desperation. His inability to feel his plea, to actually mean that desperation with any authenticity, felt manipulative. But this was what Crane had reduced him to. This was the ghost that was left behind. Whether she saw the lie or the truth beneath, Sarah let it go.

Sarah locked the front door and flipped the Open sign to Closed. She guided Frost down the narrow hallway at the back of the parlor. Behind a door at the end of the hallway stretched a steep stairwell leading to the second floor. Thin curtains hung over its high narrow windows, the wooden steps creaking loudly beneath them as they went up. A single door loomed at the top of the stairwell. With Sarah's help, Frost climbed upward.

On the other side was an attractive studio apartment with exposed brick, hardwood floors, and a charming vintage wall radiator. Judging by the farmhouse chandelier hanging over the thick wooden dining counter with its pendant light bulbs encased in converted mason jars, the kitchen had been recently renovated. Frost saw them and couldn't help but laugh. Christ, he thought, I'm about to bleed all over the world's smallest Pottery Barn.

"What is it?" Sarah said.

"Nothing." No humor like gallows humor. Sarah might not appreciate it, though.

She sat him down at one of the wooden barstools at the counter and disappeared into her bathroom. Frost looked around. A large cabinet dominated one side of the room, its face made up to look like a large barnyard door. It looked like a Murphy bed. There was a small sofa, a few potted plants, but most notable was the artwork. A wooden easel with a half-finished canvas on it dominated the corner of the room. A table stood beside it filled with dozens of paint tubes, brushes, and charcoals. Numerous finished pieces leaned against the wall atop a gray drop cloth smattered with acrylics and oils.

Other pieces hung from the walls. They were mostly abstract, expressionist pieces. Dark and brooding and earthy in a way that implied a kind of smothering chaos. Frost felt like if he stepped into one of the paintings it would take all his pain away… right before it drowned him for the pure fun of it. He admired that her art could make him feel that way—could make him feel anything at all.

Sarah returned from the bathroom with a frozen package of meat, a large Tupperware container full of medical supplies, and a stack of towels. A black cat hopped up onto the counter beside Frost. It stared at him with suspicion, as if it hadn't made up its mind about him just yet. Frost liked cats. He knew they operated on mutual respect and he respected that. It was more than he'd gotten from his military team, that's for sure.

"Who's that?" he asked, as the cat's raised tail drifted away like a shark's fin. He'd been deemed uninteresting.

"That's Sid," Sarah said. "Short for Obsidian. Now take this off."

She helped Frost out of his jacket, dropping it to the floor. Sid returned and curled up in the discarded fabric.

"You going to take those off?" Sarah asked.

Frost looked at her and saw she was gesturing at his sunglasses. He shook his head. "I get migraines," he explained.

"Well, that gash in your head ain't helping. Here, you might as well take that off too, if I'm going to get at your arm," Sarah said, gesturing at the waffled thermal sweatshirt he'd worn under his jacket.

Frost nodded and slowly began to take it off. He appreciated Sarah's matter-of-factness. Sarah saw him wince as he did so and helped him pull the sweater over his head. He caught her stare just a little too long at his shoulders. It only took a moment, and then Sarah was back to business.

Sarah folded a towel on the kitchen counter and set Frost's wounded forearm over it. She reached into the Tupperware container and pulled out a set of latex gloves from a box. She ruffled through the container. Frost looked at the numerous supplies in it.

"That's quite a haul," he said.

"I used to date a nurse. You can never have too many medical supplies in a tattoo parlor."

"You have a needle and thread in there?" Frost said. "Suture threads?"

"I do, actually," Sarah said. She took them out of the container and laid them on the counter.

"Great. As long as we've got running water and some unscented soap to clean the wound and the needle, we're good to go."

"You've done this before, huh?" Sarah said.

"Medical training."

"You a doctor?"

"Army."

She grabbed a bar of soap, a bowl of water, and set a small pot to boil in the kitchen. She stood over Frost.

"Lean your head back," she said.

He did, and she began wiping the blood from his head wound, drying the water with a separate towel. Frost winced in instinct and Sarah apologized, but went on with a tender swiftness. His head wound cleaned and dried, she moved on and did the same for his forearm.

"Do you have a needle driver?" Frost asked.

"This *is* a piercing shop," she said.

She pulled out a needle driver from the container. Sterilized the driver and the needle with boiling water and prepared the suture thread. She handed Frost the bottle of vodka.

"Drink," she said.

"Little early in the day."

"Says the man getting in a bar fight before lunch."

Not a bad point. Frost smiled appreciatively and took a long pull of the vodka. Sarah stood up and leaned his head back again and set to work stitching up his wounds. She was gentle but precise in her care —well used to prodding vulnerable strangers with sharp objects.

Frost looked up at her. Got a waft of her perfume again. That earthy incense scent, rich and disorienting like the depths of her paintings. A thin strand of her hair fell down from behind her ear. Across her eyes. Frost glanced up at them. They were vibrant Kelly green, set behind thick dark lashes. Like emeralds seen through a coal-dusted window. Some secret garden you couldn't quite get to.

"I know that's not really what happened," she said softly.

Her breasts brushed lightly against his arm as she worked over him. She was beautiful, capable, and talented. And she was far, far too good for him.

Frost thought about lying to her further, but immediately shut it down. He was still too unfocused to lie well. Plus, one question to Tick and she'd find out. Not worth it to lie anymore. He also suspected that the truth would endear Sarah to him, securing her as an ally and a resource.

"No," he said.

She glanced down at him for a moment. Again, he caught her gaze and their eyes lingered. She turned and grabbed a pair of scissors from the container and cut the excess thread from his stitched head.

"So what, then?" she said and went to work on his arm.

"I made a judgment call, and then I made a mistake," he said. "And like the last time I did, it nearly killed me."

"Is that what happened to the side of your head here? All these scars?" Sarah asked. "Was that the 'last time'?"

"Yeah. An IED in Afghanistan."

"You've seen a lot of combat?"

"What's a lot?" Frost said.

"Enough."

"Yeah, I've seen enough."

Sarah finished up on his arm and snipped the loose thread with the scissors. Frost took another swig of vodka, then held the bottle out for Sarah. She smiled and went to the cabinet, grabbing two rocks glasses. She poured them each a tall glass. They clinked glasses and took a sip.

Frost examined the stitchwork on his arm. She'd done a fine job. Tight and tidy. She moved around to his back and removed the few bits of glass and cleaned and bandaged him up.

"Thank you," he said. "I mean it. You didn't have to do this."

"You're welcome," Sarah said. She took another sip. "Did you kill anyone today?"

Frost looked up at her. That, at least, he could be straightforward about. "No, I didn't kill anyone."

"Who did this to you?"

Frost hesitated. "Andy Treece." He watched her body language, searching for a reaction.

"Jesus Christ," Sarah said. Her shoulders went taut. She shook her head, her face tightening. "That mother—"

"It's all right," Frost said. "I went by his place, looking for information about Taya—Lincoln's sister. Treece and I had some words."

"And what was this? A knife?" Sarah said, gesturing at Frost's forearm.

"Chunk of glass. Treece might be a weasel, but he's a resourceful little weasel."

"Weasel's too kind. Some of my best friends are weasels." She glanced down at Sid, who had burrowed into the folds in Frost's jacket. "Ain't that right, my little weasel?"

The cat gave no response. Sarah turned back to Frost.

"If Treece isn't dead, where's he now?"

"I don't know. I left him face down in his apartment, but had to run. He called the cops."

Sarah grunted in frustration. "A little ironic, that." So she at least knew something about Treece's illicit activities. He could ask her later.

She threw back her vodka and filled it again. Frost wondered if he'd struck a nerve talking about Treece.

"You two got a history, or something?" Frost said.

"With Andy? Never," Sarah said. "I just know his type, that's all. Walks between the raindrops, takes whatever he likes."

"Root of all evil." Frost grunted and Sarah nodded grimly.

"He's the one who killed Lincoln, isn't he?"

Frost winced. He had already decided—lying wouldn't get him what he wanted here. "Yeah. He is."

"That *fucker!*" she shouted. She rose up and pounded the top of the counter with her fist. Her nostrils flared, and she looked like she was about to throw her glass against the wall.

Frost stared at her. Her reaction revealed a much greater affection for Lincoln than Frost anticipated. Either that, or a much deeper hatred for Treece. Frost wondered if her passion could rub off on him.

"You going to tell me what happened between you two, or not?" Frost said.

"Nothing happened between me and Andy," Sarah said, her anger turning on Frost. "I already told you that."

"Something happened. Look at you."

"What about me?"

"Fuming. Swearing. Throwing back vodka like you just took Berlin."

"You going to give me shit now, after all I just did for you?" she said. "I'll drink as much as I want. It's my house."

"All right. Then drink." He wasn't about to get in her way. Truth be told, he ached all over and digging for information wasn't improving his exhaustion. He was ready to give up and give in, for just a little while. He laid the meat gingerly against his head and gasped at the stinging cold.

Sarah took Frost's advice in stride and threw the glass back, then breathed out in a long, hissing sigh. Frost gave up the chase. He was tired. She was angry. Maybe he could stop pushing his luck and just keep being honest.

"Your paintings are beautiful," Frost said.

Sarah snorted. "You're trying that hard to get into my pants, huh?"

"I mean it," Frost said. "Ever since my last tour, it's been hard to feel anything at all. My emotions feel dull and far away, like they're still overseas, buried in the desert. Your art feels safe to me, but the kind of safety that would mean death if I surrendered to it. Like stopping and resting would mean death by indulgence. Does that make sense?"

Sarah didn't look at him. She rolled her glass between her thumb and forefinger and stared at her paintings. "Strangers from out-of-town maybe get to put some miles of road between them and their problems before the past comes to collect, but some people can only stay still and paint."

Her bravado from before was gone. Her posture hung limp, defeated. Something about what Frost said had taken the fury from her. He didn't know if it was her poisoned town, her connection with Treece, or Lincoln's death, but something had her in its grip.

Frost knew that he couldn't say anything to help, so he did the only thing he could think to do: He reached out and grasped Sarah's hand. She didn't pull away.

"This place is different, now," she whispered. "The good is bleeding out of it. People leave or die."

Then Sarah turned, and, to Frost's surprise, she kissed him. He tried to let go of her hand, but she held on. He tossed the frozen meat onto the counter with a solid clatter and reached up with his freed hand to cup her face. Her hands caressed his chest, and the warmth of her touch spread across his shoulders, stomach, and back. She pressed into him, melding into him, kissing him as though she wanted to descend into him. Frost moved his hand to the small of her back and pulled her close.

She let go of his hand to trace her fingers up his inner thigh. Her breath hitched hot in their mouths, shallow. Frost felt the blood pounding in his head, but he winced as the pain redoubled under the increased stimulation of his excitement. His head shrieked and his arm throbbed.

"Sarah," Frost breathed, tearing his lips from hers. "I don't think I can—"

"No need to exert yourself, handsome stranger," she whispered. "We can find ways to enjoy ourselves without reopening your wounds."

Frost opened his mouth to respond, but her lips closed over his again. He felt her warmth against his. He felt her need, and needed her in return. The pain became secondary. The outside world faded. His arms wrapped around her.

In the following moments, Frost tried to feel something beyond the burn of his carnality; the joy of companionship, the fear of vulnerability, Sarah's grief. It didn't work.

ELEVEN

Frost and Sarah lay naked in Sarah's bed, passing the last glass of vodka between them. She lay against Frost, one leg resting over his so that they were intertwined. He could feel the warm, smooth skin of her thigh pressed against him. He could even feel her pulse, just now beginning to slow. Every time she moved her leg to adjust herself, he felt the need to take her again tingling at the back of his brain. To take his mind off it, Frost glanced through the dark window curtains and out into the bright day.

"It's going to rain," he said.

"How can you tell?" Sarah asked, following his eyes.

"I can feel it in my head, like a change in the air pressure," Frost said. He smiled to himself and closed his eyes again. "Think the shrapnel's like a barometer or something now."

He heard Sarah chuckle. Then she sucked in a preparatory breath, as though in preparation for a difficult conversation. Frost braced himself. "So... I buy that you really did know Lincoln, but was that story about how you knew him actually true? Or just more bullshit cover story?"

"I really had only met the kid once," Frost said. "But I knew his uncle well. He was a good friend of mine. Family, really."

"Was he killed? Your friend?" Sarah asked.

"No. Cancer."

"Were you there?" Sarah said. "When Lincoln was killed?"

Frost turned to her. Slowly, he nodded.

"Oh my God," she said. "That's awful."

"I'm still looking for his sister, to find her and tell her what happened to him. What happened to her uncle."

"That poor family."

"Yeah," Frost said. He plucked the vodka from Sarah's hand and took a sip.

Sarah cocked her head, as though he'd said something she didn't like. "What?"

"Nothing."

"Come on, man."

"It's just—I'm pretty sure the girl is mixed up in something bigger. Think Lincoln was, too. That's what got him killed."

Sarah grabbed the vodka back and took a sip. "Mixed up in what? Treece's business?" Sarah said.

Frost nodded.

"You're really going to try to find him again?"

"Yes, I am," Frost said.

"I want to help you," Sarah said.

"No," Frost said. "That's really not a good idea."

"What do you mean no? Do you know anything about Clear Rock? You need someone who knows a thing or two about the people, the businesses, the roads. Plus," she said, gesturing to his head, "you haven't exactly done stellar as a lone wolf, slugger."

Frost looked over at her, but Sarah had evidently said her piece and was awaiting his response. He'd have to lay everything on the table and hope that she understood the gravity of the situation.

Frost climbed out of the bed, stumbling slightly from the vodka. He grabbed his jacket from the kitchen stool and handed the folded email printouts to Sarah. He tossed his jacket on the end of the bed as she began reading.

"This isn't a couple dime bags being sold at a party," Frost said. "This is the real deal."

Sarah's eyes went wide as she read through the messages. "Jesus. What is this—Port of Portland?"

"My guess is that's where the overseas shipments are being smuggled in. And then driven from there into Idaho, here in Wyoming, who knows where else."

"That motherfucker," she said under her breath.

"Yeah," Frost said. "So you can see why you shouldn't get tangled up in this. *I* don't want to be tangled up in it."

"But you are," Sarah said.

"I am." It was Brakespeare's town. And Lincoln's. All the justification he needed.

"And so am I."

"Sarah, I—"

"No, listen to me," she said sharply. "You asked me what happened between me and Andy. I'll tell you."

She leaned back and took a deep breath.

"I was engaged," she said. "Two years ago. Long story short, I discovered Charlie was using H shortly after he proposed to me."

Frost hadn't been expecting this. He welcomed the information, but he felt as though he had forced Sarah to give him something she hadn't been ready to explain. Again came that feeling that he wasn't a real person anymore, just a machine using the real emotions of the people around him to achieve his goals. He fought it down and climbed back in bed beside her.

"It was a tale as old as time, really," Sarah said. She chuckled, but the sound was dry and pained. "Sweet, beautiful, stupid football star messes up his knee in an injury, and it never heals right. Gets prescribed Oxy for the injury and he uses it to numb the pain, but he finds out it works pretty well to kill the memory of his dead athletic dreams, too. So he tries to score on the street, where our sweet prince finds a cheaper, stronger poison called heroin."

Frost nodded. Sarah was trying her best to sound detached, but her eyes were boring a hole in the wall in front of her.

"When he switched from snorting to needles, he couldn't hide the track marks. So, I kicked his ass. Basically locked him in this room for three days while he detoxed. It was awful. I've never seen someone so sick. He was begging me to score for him. But we made it through. And he cleaned up. The church over on Clinton had NA meetings that he started going to. Started exercising, keeping busy. And we started planning our wedding."

Sarah took another sip of vodka, holding the glass in both hands. Frost had known a few addicts before and during his time in the military, and he knew that going cold turkey on heroin was no easy feat. He must have been one tough son of a bitch. She must have been tough as hell on him, too. They would have made a good team.

"But one night, he went out with a few work buddies. Got drunk. And that was it. Police found him in his car early the next morning. The needle was still hanging out of his arm." Sarah's eyes narrowed and the corner of her lip curled into a snarl. Her eyes were still fixed on the middle distance, but the intensity there would have been enough to bring a grown man to his knees. "I talked to his buddies, asked them what happened. They told me Andy Treece finally got him to cave. Charlie never told me, but Andy was following him—calling, texting, showing up at his work. At the bar. No matter how many times Charlie told him to fuck off, Andy kept coming back. And eventually Treece sold him the dose that stopped his heart. After everything that Charlie and I went through, that piece of shit killed him. And there was nothing I could do about it."

Sarah held up the email printouts. "So Andy Treece isn't above ruining lives one by one. But he's gone big time, and he's poisoning my whole town, too. So I'm going to help you find that bastard again, and he's not getting away from you this time. If you don't stop him, I'm going to pull his fucking heart out myself."

Sarah's anger concerned Frost. He wanted to find Taya, get her safe, and tear apart the drug empire that had corrupted Brakespeare's hometown. Sarah seemed to agree, but her pain could be a liability, leading her to poor decisions. Still, they seemed to see eye to eye on what justice meant for a man like Andy Treece.

Sarah's thousand-yard glare ended and her eyes softened, her posture slackening. Then she blinked, as though surprised by something. "I just remembered something Lincoln said to me, in the shop one morning."

Frost looked over at her.

"He'd shown up late to his appointment," she said. "Apologized and said he'd run behind with his sister. He drove her to the doctor's that morning. I asked him if everything was all right, and he said it was fine. Come to think of it, he was almost happy."

"Happy?" Frost asked.

Sarah looked over at Frost. "Yeah. He said that it was an OB-GYN appointment, and then he said something about 'jinxing it.' I was frazzled at the time and didn't think anything of it, but it sounded like his sister might be pregnant."

"You sure that's what Lincoln told you?" Frost said.

"I think so, yeah," Sarah said.

Frost leaned forward and grabbed his jacket from the end of the bed. He reached into the pocket and pulled out the photograph of Lincoln and Taya that he'd taken from Lincoln's apartment. He thought that it looked recent. Lincoln looked the same as when Frost had met him at the roadhouse. The early stages of his sleeve tattoo peeked out below his T-shirt. Taya wore a flowy sundress that hung loose over her stomach. If she was showing, he couldn't tell.

"What's that?" Sarah asked.

Frost handed her the photograph.

"Lincoln and Taya," Frost said.

Sarah took the photograph from him and looked at it. She tensed suddenly. "Oh my God," she whispered.

"What is it?" Frost said. Her tone caused him to brace for what came next, despite himself.

"I know her," said Sarah, staring at the photograph. "I mean, everyone knows who this is. I just didn't know that this girl was Taya."

"What do you mean?" Frost said. "Who is she?"

Sarah looked from Frost and back to the photograph one more time.

"That girl there is Silver's mistress."

Frost sat up in the bed and tried to connect the dots. Silver's mistress? Was that really the only reason Silver was after Taya? He was simply looking for his girlfriend, the woman carrying his child? And what did killing Lincoln have to do with all of it?

"Jesus Christ," Sarah whispered. "This *is* the real deal, huh?"

"As real as it gets," Frost said. "Taya's not safe, and she's got two distributors in a drug empire looking for her. No reason to think they're not out for blood after what they did to Lincoln. If you know anything else about her, even the most unimportant detail could be crucial in keeping Taya safe."

Sarah looked over at Frost and nodded. After a moment she got up and walked across the room to retrieve a silk robe from her closet. Her demeanor was cold, but whether it was from her anger earlier or something new entirely, he couldn't tell.

"When Silver and Treece came to town a few years ago," Sarah said, "things got—I don't know, weird. Obviously. Treece was the one out on the streets pushing product. Clients started coming in here with more than just *my* needlework on their arms, you know?"

"And Silver?" Frost said. "What about him?"

Sarah shrugged. "The people around here only see him from afar, when he's not holed up in this gated mansion in the woods... it's clear he has money. I've heard he takes private planes to Denver, Salt Lake City, and Vegas nearly every weekend. God, he was at Benito's the night Charlie proposed, and sent us a $500 bottle of baco noir from his corner booth. I didn't even want to accept the bottle, but Charlie said it would be rude if we didn't. Every time I looked over at Silver, he was staring at us like a fucking gargoyle. Or a shark."

Sarah came back to the bed and sat down.

"And now with Lincoln being killed—I mean, this shit can't be a coincidence."

"What shit?" Frost said.

"*Disappearances*," Sarah said, throwing her hands up in finger quotes. "Dozens of them here in the last few years. Unsolved. People just vanish. I told you that this place has gotten worse since Silver and Treece showed up, and I didn't just mean the drugs. The police never called them murders, and they never figured out where they went."

"Yeah, I met your Sheriff," Frost said. "So I can't say a bunch of cold cases surprises me."

"Mhm. Puck. She's something else, eh? And there you go—even her. She only became Sheriff when the last one 'disappeared.'"

"What?"

"Yeah," Sarah said. "Only weeks ago now. You believe that? Sheriff Gomez. Great guy, but clearly in over his head once the town started going to shit. Lost a lot of weight toward the end. And then one day he just up and disappears, like he never even existed. And nobody seems to give a shit. Or they're too scared to talk about it."

"Goddamn," Frost said. He grabbed his flip phone from his jacket pocket and scrolled through until he found the picture he'd taken in Andy's hallway, showing a Polaroid of young Ronald and Andy together. He showed it to Sarah.

"Is that guy Silver?" Frost said, pointing to Ronald in the photo.

Sarah examined the picture closely. "Honestly, I don't know. It could be Silver. Dark hair, white, mean-looking. But I don't know." She handed the phone back to Frost. "Sorry. You think that's the same Ronald from the emails?"

"Why not?"

"And that this Ronald Fitzgerald is Silver?"

Frost shrugged. "Maybe. You never heard Silver's real name spoken before?"

Sarah shook her head. "Just *Silver*. Always Silver." She stared out the window, into the storm clouds gathering on the horizon. "That poor girl."

"I'll find her," Frost said.

"How?"

"I'm going to talk to your friend Tick again, for one thing."

"Tick?" Sarah said, cocking her head to one side. "What's he got to do with this?"

"He didn't tell me everything he knew about Taya," Frost said. "I'm gonna find out why."

"Well, I've no appointments for the rest of the day," Sarah said.

"No," Frost said. "I told you, I don't want you tangled up in this."

"And I told you I already am," Sarah said. "Besides, I can help you with Tick. Think he's got a bit of a thing for me."

"Yeah, I got that impression," Frost said. She had a point–that would be useful.

"So there you go."

"Sarah—"

"Look, I'm in this whether you like it or not," Sarah said, her hands on her hips. "The drugs, the disappearances—this shit has to stop. So either you and I work it together, or I'm going to go it on my own. It's your choice."

Frost sighed, but he couldn't argue. He fully believed Sarah when she said that she would involve herself whether or not she had his help.

Even in nothing but a bathrobe, she held herself with the poise of someone who was tired of being backed into a corner, and was getting ready to fight their way out, no matter what came next. He might as well use her help, and she might as well use his. Begrudgingly, Frost nodded.

"Good," Sarah said. "I'll just hop in the shower quick, and then we'll go."

Frost nodded and lay back in bed. He put his forearm over his eyes and thought through a plan for approaching Tick. Threatening him might work, but it would be safer to use his connection to Sarah—

"Well?" came Sarah's voice, still close.

Frost looked up and saw that she hadn't moved. Her hands were still on her hips, but her head was tilted toward Frost in a posture of mischievous interest.

"Well, what?" he asked.

"Aren't you going to join me?"

TWELVE

Tick's Bar was livelier in the afternoon, a modest crowd of shift workers downing beers and divorced women sipping their three o'clock Tom Collins. Frost saw the two regulars from the morning still hunched at the bar watching their third game of the day, looking only slightly worse for wear. Two kids in the corner played pool over a pitcher. They barely looked old enough to drive.

Tick watched Frost walk in and didn't work hard to hide his displeasure at seeing him again. His face was congenial enough, but Frost clocked the thin smile, an absence of warmth in the eyes. Yet Tick's mood changed when he saw Sarah follow Frost inside, his back straightening and his eyes flickering to life.

Frost and Sarah approached, and Tick set down two coasters in front of them. He smiled at Sarah.

"Ms. Albany, a pleasure to see you, as always." He turned to Frost. "Chris, wasn't it?"

"Kevin," Frost said. Like hell the bartender had already forgotten his name. He was trying to posture in front of Sarah as subtly as he could manage. All Frost could think was how petty it seemed.

"Kevin. Right. My mistake," Tick said. He looked over at Sarah again. "So, what can I get you two?"

"Some information, maybe," Sarah said, smiling.

"Information?" Tick said. "About what?"

"Taya Dane," she said.

Tick straightened up, the playfulness disappearing from his face. He looked over at Frost. "What is this?"

"What's what?" Frost asked. Talk about a quick change of tone. Whatever torch Tick carried for Sarah, apparently it burned out when Taya entered the picture. He wasn't sure if Tick was scared or angry, but the subject still struck a nerve. He was being defensive, but why? Despite Frost's misgivings with bringing Sarah, she knew Tick better than Frost did. He hoped she had some insight he didn't.

"Look, I told you earlier, pal," Tick said, "Got no idea where Taya is. Like I said, she probably ran off."

"And you were about as convincing as I imagine those boys' fake IDs are," Frost said, gesturing to the kids playing pool.

Tick glanced over at them and then back at Frost. His nose twitched, like he smelled something foul. "So you *are* some kind of police, then? Because if you're not, I'm about to tell you where to go." Tick looked over at Sarah. "This guy shaking you down for something, or what?"

"And like *I* told *you* earlier," Frost said, "that ain't it. I'm just a friend of the family."

"And you know I keep my nose clean, Tick," Sarah said, smoothly intervening. "He's here to help, and I'm helping him. You help us, we help Taya."

Tick softened and a thin smile came across his face.

"You got a real good-cop, bad-cop thing going on here, huh, Sarah? Real Mulder and Scully."

"Mulder and Scully? That ain't so bad," Sarah said. "What do you think, Kevin?"

"It does feel like I'm running around chasing ghosts," Frost said.

"Look, I've told you everything I know. Got nothin' more to say to you," Tick said.

"Come on, Tick," Sarah said, her voice low. She leaned forward a little on the bar, her head tilted and her smile playful. Frost was reminded of the look she had given him before inviting him into the shower. "I thought you and I got along."

Tick shook his head and laughed. He knew exactly what she was doing.

"You ought to be ashamed of yourself, Ms. Albany, but at least you're the devil I know. Not like *some* people," he said, shooting a skeptical glance at Frost. "Taya came in sometimes for a drink. Haven't seen her in a while."

"How often does she come in?" Frost asked.

Tick shrugged. "Not a lot."

"And why was that such a dirty little secret?" Frost said.

"Because I believe in maintaining discretion as it relates to my customers, is why," Tick said. "Privacy, you know? Not blabbing about their personal lives to every wannabe Dick Tracy that comes walking through my door."

Frost would have been able to smell the bullshit if he'd been standing upwind. Even if Tick was as noble as he claimed, he was far too guarded about Taya.

"Whoa. Gear down there, Tick," Sarah said. "We're just concerned about Taya, that's all. Just trying to make sure she's okay. We're all after the same thing here."

"Why wouldn't she be okay?" Tick asked.

"No one's seen her in some time," Sarah said, "and we think she might be caught up in something nasty. And even if she ain't, she needs to know about her brother, right?"

Tick took a breath and closed his eyes, as though he were deep in thought. He looked over at Frost. "Fine. Sorry about that. I shouldn't have insulted you."

Frost shrugged. "Fox Mulder and Dick Tracy? I ain't complaining."

Tick laughed to himself. Frost noted Tick's quick change of heart and wondered if the cause was Sarah's influence or her reassurance that they would keep Taya safe.

"We're really just trying to make sure Taya's okay. That's all this is," Sarah said. She leaned against the counter again, but this time she placed her palms down in a gesture of peace.

Tick watched Sarah for a moment. Frost watched the man's lip pull slightly inward as he chewed gently on it. Thinking. Then he pulled out his phone, scrolled through a few screens, and nodded. He placed a coaster on the bar counter.

"I gave her a ride home once," Tick said, writing on the coaster. "She got a little too in her cups."

"When was that?" Frost asked. Depending on how long ago it was, she might have moved. If it was recent, it might poke a hole in Sarah's pregnancy theory.

"I don't know. Three, four weeks ago?"

Well. Consider that hole poked.

"She usually tying one on when she comes in here?" Frost said.

"No," Tick said, handing the coaster to Sarah. "Not at all. One or two maybe, but that's it. That night, she was drinking with purpose. And that's the last time I saw her."

———

The address was set in a row of four-story brownstones not far from where Lincoln had lived, in a collection of houses that had been renovated to hold individual apartments. Frost and Sarah parked out front. Frost glanced at the building and then at Tick's scrawl on the coaster. He hadn't included an apartment unit, just the building address. Sarah glanced at the coaster and appeared to come to the same conclusion.

"Maybe she didn't tell him her apartment number," Sarah said. "He said he just dropped her off."

"He also said she was completely drunk," Frost said.

"Yeah, I heard that," Sarah said. "So, maybe she's not pregnant, then. Maybe I misunderstood Lincoln. Or hell, maybe she is drinking regardless."

"Or maybe Tick's misdirecting us for some reason," Frost said. He looked at the building again. What would Tick have to gain from misdirecting them? "Maybe this is just some random address."

Sarah ran her fingers through her hair. "Well, let's find out."

Frost cut the engine and the two got out of the truck. They walked up the front steps of the building, where Frost pulled on the front door handle and found it unsurprisingly locked.

"Here," Sarah said. She was scrolling through the digital directory intercom. "There we go," she said. "T. Dane. Unit 201."

Sarah buzzed the unit and they waited. No one answered. Frost couldn't say he was surprised by that, either.

Frost stepped down off the stoop and glanced up at the second-floor windows. He glanced down the block and saw that a narrow alley edged the building. Worth a look.

Frost and Sarah entered the alley and saw that a fire escape system dominated the side of the building. They went and stood beneath its the second-floor steel landing. The bottom of the ladder hung about ten feet off of the ground.

Sarah looked up at it. "I could stand on your shoulders, maybe, or—"

Frost backed up to get a running start. Sarah turned at the sound of his footsteps, and he jumped and grabbed the bottom rung of the ladder with one hand. He hung there for a moment, swinging from his momentum, before he began climbing. The still-healing gash in his arm ignited in pain, but he held fast and hauled himself up.

"Never woulda guessed you'd been stabbed," Sarah said with a chuckle. "Hey, if you need anyone to hobble you before you run a 10k, I'm a mean swing with a softball bat."

Frost released the mechanism that held the ladder in place, and it slid down its rails to Sarah. Frost knelt down in front of the apartment window. He removed an ID card from his wallet and was preparing to try to jimmy the window latch open when Sarah squatted beside him.

"Wait," she asked, her brow furrowed. "Are you sure this is 201?"

"See for yourself," Frost said.

He gestured into the apartment. Sarah leaned forward and cupped her hands against the glass to peer inside, then pulled back with a look of shock. The entire apartment had been turned over, just as Lincoln's had.

Frost set to work on the single window latch. He considered the Threat Level, but could hardly place it above a Two. There didn't seem to be any movement inside the apartment, and it was likely that whoever turned the place over was long gone. He swiped the card swiftly beneath the centimeter-wide opening under the window, and the hook latch swung open. He lifted the window and slipped inside, making sure to hold it open as Sarah slipped in behind him.

The apartment was larger than Frost had expected, with high ceilings, exposed ductwork, and hardwood floors. Incredibly modern kitchen appliances littered the floor alongside expensive-looking artwork torn from the walls. The upturned sofa and loveseat were handcrafted and upholstered in mahogany leather. If Taya wasn't the mistress of a drug boss, she was certainly living like one. To Frost, the place looked like it had been paid to be furnished by a professional—before it had been trashed, at least.

Frost held his finger to his mouth, telling Sarah to remain silent while they checked the apartment. They cleared the bathroom and the back bedroom before coming back to the living room. Sarah knelt down over the upturned coffee table, cradling a picture frame in her hands. It was a copy of the photograph that Frost had taken from Lincoln's place. Taya and Lincoln together, smiling, with Lincoln in his fatigues and Taya with her brother's arm slung over her shoulder.

Frost glanced around the unit. There were a lot of reasons to raid Taya's place. Her drug lord boyfriend might have been pissed that she mouthed off to him, or ratted on him, or ran off with his baby. Maybe he wanted to send her a message, or maybe he was looking for clues about where to find her. Maybe he was actually worried.

Then came the familiar click of a key from the outside of someone else's front door—a sound to which Frost was becoming wearily accustomed. Sarah quickly rose to her feet and looked at the front door and over at Frost, her eyes wide with panic. The doorknob turned. Frost could get to cover, but Sarah was out in the open. Too late for her to hide, and he wasn't about to leave her.

The door swung open and two burly men in black suits stepped calmly into the apartment. One had a trimmed goatee and a horseshoe of hair ringing his head, and the other was tall and lean with the hooked nose of a predator. Judging by their posture and their even demeanor, neither were surprised and both were ready for action. Frost's Threat Level escalated to Four. These two were trouble.

The men strode into the broader living room area.

"Who are you?" Baldy growled at Frost.

"I could ask you the same thing," Frost said. Keep them talking. Keep thinking of a way out.

Baldy laughed. "You hear this shit?"

"You two are trespassing," Hooknose said. He took a step towards Sarah, continuing to close the gap. Frost was running out of time, but he was still hesitant to make any sudden movements that might provoke them. Not while Hooknose was so close to Sarah.

"You guys must work for Silver, then," Frost said.

Baldy didn't answer, but the way his upper lip twitched was enough of a tell.

"Got yourselves a key to the unit and a good spot for stakeouts, don't you? If Silver owns this apartment, and I'd bet my truck he does, that would make you his errand boys," Frost said with a derisive smirk. Divert their attention to him. Draw the gun as a last resort.

Baldy cracked his knuckles. He wasn't interested in talking. Hooknose inched closer to Sarah.

"How's the weather up there, fella? I hear there's a chance of rain," she said, staring up at him.

Hooknose smiled and began to make his move, but Sarah inhaled and hawked a gob of phlegm directly into his eye. He shouted and flinched, and Sarah took the opening to drive the heel of her palm into his throat. The tall man stumbled back, holding his hands to his throat and choking for air.

"Gotta watch that weather report, fuckface," Sarah said, backing away.

Frost moved to get between the two, but Baldy was already charging at him, fist raised. The clumsy punch was easy enough to deflect, and Frost took the opening to drive his fist into the man's floating ribs. Before he could recover, Frost swung another punch into Baldy's solar plexus, driving the air from his lungs with a wet cough. He didn't give the thug time to recover and swung another punch into his right orbital. Frost felt Baldy's skull crack slightly beneath his knuckles.

Frost turned to see Hooknose struggling to pull a gun from an underarm holster, still choking on his constricted windpipe. Before he could free the firearm, a reclaimed wood side table crashed into him. Frost barely had time to acknowledge Sarah, heaving with the effort of the throw, before he closed the gap between himself and Hooknose, who was struggling to stand.

Frost stomped on Hooknose's hand, still reaching for his gun, pinning the man's wrist between his own chest and Frost's boot. Frost ducked down, pulled the gun from its holster, and slid it across the room toward Sarah. She didn't move to pick it up, but he could hardly blame her. Suddenly, her eyes darted to something he couldn't see.

"Behind–" she warned, but it was too late.

For the second time in as many days, stars exploded behind Frost's vision as something slammed into his head. Frost grunted in pain and stumbled off of Hooknose. He heard unsteady footsteps coming toward him and began to pull himself together, but froze when he heard the metallic click of a semiautomatic's hammer being pulled back.

"Back the fuck off." Sarah's voice. Through swimming, starbursting vision, Frost saw the tattooist holding Hooknose's gun in unsteady hands, aiming at Baldy, who had regained his feet despite the beating Frost had given him. Hooknose coughed and rose unsteadily to his feet.

"Fuckin' bitch," he wheezed past his pummeled windpipe.

"Don't wear it out," Sarah growled. "Now sit the hell down. We've got some questions."

Sarah's voice was convincing enough, but her hold on the gun wasn't. Frost watched the two men decide whether to call her bluff, their bludgeoned brains calculating. Instead, they just ran. Frost stepped forward to pursue, but his own battered skull sent up a lightning storm of white spots behind his vision. He lurched and fell to one knee as Baldy and Hooknose half-ran, half-staggered from the apartment. Baldy cast a nervous glance back at Sarah, but kept going. Hooknose, however, turned in the doorway.

As he ran, he pulled out a phone and snapped a picture, the camera flash creating an agonizing nimbus of light in Frost's field of view. Frost's blood went cold. He did his best to raise his hand in front of his face. He had no way of knowing it would work.

"Shit," Sarah and Frost both breathed as they watched the two go. He couldn't follow. He could barely stand. His skull felt like it was being opened with God's own hammer and sledge.

"Are you okay?" he asked Sarah.

"Yeah. Are you?" she asked.

He only shook his head, and even that hurt like hell. "Christ," he gasped. "You fight dirty, Sarah Albany."

"Rules of engagement are for assholes," she returned. She looked at her hands and seemed to finally realize she was still pointing the gun at the door. She let her arms slacken. Despite her bravado, her breath was uneven and her free hand still shook with uncontrolled adrenaline.

"I can understand that. Maybe better than most. Well, come on. Let's get out of here."

"We need to call the police," Sarah said, looking around the trashed unit.

"I really don't think it's a good idea for us to stay any longer," Frost said. "Those two might be calling for backup."

"Maybe, but the police need to know about this," she said. "The more eyes we got looking for Taya, the better, don't you think?"

Frost glanced around the unit. He loathed the thought of working further with the Clear Rock sheriff's department, but she wasn't wrong.

"Let's call it in from the truck, at least," Frost said. "I'm not about to explain to Sheriff Puck that I got assaulted breaking into a drug lord's mistress's apartment."

"In that case, it might be better if we head down to the station. I've got a deputy I'm friendly with. I might be able to convince him to keep us up-to-date on things as they progress."

"You've got just about everyone in this town wrapped around your finger, don't you?" Frost said. At this point, he was wondering if she could give Silver a run for his money as resident crime boss.

Sarah raised an eyebrow at him and smiled out of the side of her mouth as she made her way toward the fire escape.

THIRTEEN

Frost and Sarah pulled up out front of the Sheriff's Department Office, a beige brick building squatting at the center of a broad parking lot dotted with police cruisers. The sun sat low in the west and threw their shadows over the pavement as they walked across the small parking lot. Frost felt a deep unease about walking through the front doors of a police station—partly because of the massive number of laws he'd broken in the past twenty-four hours, but also because he knew he'd be captured by the lobby surveillance cameras. Yet one more image of himself recorded in binary. One more way Crane might zero in on his location.

Sarah walked up to the receptionist and asked if Deputy Kim was on duty. The receptionist told her that he was and asked her to wait a moment. Frost looked around the office. He noticed a trio of young officers in the break room, leaning back in their chairs, sipping coffee, shooting the breeze. None of them seemed to take note of him, and he looked away before they could catch him watching them. They were comfortable enough on their own home turf.

A minute later a young officer emerged from the back hallway. He was a fresh-faced kid of Korean descent, wearing the standard-issue Clear Rock police uniform: black boots, beige pants, utility belt, and short-sleeved beige button-up. He approached Sarah with a bright smile.

"Ms. Albany," Deputy Kim said. His back was straight but his shoulders were slack, on-duty but clearly pleased to see Sarah.

Sarah smiled back. "Donny, how's the force treating you?" she asked.

"Same as ever, Sarah: glorious and merciless."

"Nerd." Sarah laughed. Frost watched her. She was relaxed around Kim as well, and her smile seemed more natural than the one she'd aimed at Tick.

"That's between me and my unfinished Cowboy Bebop tattoo, madam. And who might this be?" he asked, gesturing toward Frost.

"Deputy Don Kim, meet Kevin Johnson," Sarah said.

Frost shook his hand. "Deputy."

"Please, call me Donny," Deputy Kim said, shaking firmly back. "So, what brings you two in? Everything's all right, I hope."

"I'd like to report a missing person."

"Oh, no," Deputy Kim said, his brow furrowing. "Well, please, let's chat in my office." He motioned for them to follow him down the hall.

Deputy Kim escorted Sarah and Frost down the short hallway to the back of the station. Frost tried not to make too much of a show of checking his corners or counting the exits, but old habits died hard. The fluorescent lighting was boring a hole in his skull even with his sunglasses, and something about the pitch of their air conditioner returned that feeling of a splitting skull. Kim eventually ushered them both into a cramped office, where he sat behind his desk and offered Sarah and Frost a seat in the two empty chairs before it.

"Who is it that's gone missing?" Deputy Kim said.

"Taya Dane," Sarah said.

Deputy Kim leaned back in his seat. "Jesus. That poor family. And why do you think she's gone missing, exactly? You two close?"

"No, we're not close," Sarah said. "But Tick asked me to check up on her as a favor. Mr. Johnson and I just came from her apartment. It's been broken into, completely trashed. And Taya's nowhere to be found."

"Is that right?" Deputy Kim said. He looked over at Frost.

"That's right," Frost said. "There were two men there when we arrived as well, walking down the hallway when we came upon her floor. I think they were probably the ones that did it. They were sweating, edgy, you know?"

"You say anything to each other? You and these men?" Deputy Kim said.

"No," Sarah said. "Didn't really occur to us that they were suspicious until we saw the apartment." Frost was impressed. They had discussed a game plan on the way to the station, but he still enjoyed watching Sarah talk on her feet.

"We're just really worried about Taya," Frost said.

"No, of course. Obviously. Sounds like she's in trouble. You know—" Deputy Kim stopped himself. For the first time since they had walked in, his shoulders went rigid.

"What is it, Donny?" Sarah said.

Deputy Kim looked at her. He paused. His mouth opened, as though testing the words, and then closed again. After a moment, he leaned forward onto his desk.

"You know, I shouldn't be telling you this," he said, "but some of the details about Lincoln's murder are just... bizarre."

"What do you mean, bizarre?" Frost said.

"Well, for one," Deputy Kim said, "the bullets we removed from him were made of silver."

"You see that a lot around here? Silver bullets?"

"A little more in the last few years, maybe?" Sarah said.

Deputy Kim stared across the desk at Sarah. He seemed to know what she was driving at and looked afraid to agree. He nodded.

Sarah looked over at Frost.

Deputy Kim cleared his throat and opened a desk drawer.

"Well, now, let me get the paperwork started on this missing person report," he said. Deputy Kim searched through the desk drawer, and a second cabinet, then stood. "Pardon me. Just give me a minute. I've got to go grab one of the forms."

He exited his office and walked down the short hallway. Frost and Sarah didn't say a word to one another. They didn't have to.

A moment later a raised voice caught their attention outside the office. Frost turned towards the lobby and saw Deputy Kim being dressed down by Sheriff Puck. She jabbed a finger at the missing persons paperwork in his hand, and Deputy Kim turned and pointed towards his office.

"Shit," Frost said.

"What?" Sarah said.

"Puck," he said.

"Is that a problem?"

"We're gonna find out."

Sheriff Puck walked down the hallway, the form in her hand, and entered Deputy Kim's office without him. She sat behind his desk and looked at Frost and Sarah.

"Mr. Johnson, Ms. Albany," Sheriff Puck said. "Didn't expect an out-of-towner to start rolling with the local ink."

"Didn't realize the Sheriff's Department cared about that sort of thing," Sarah said.

Sheriff Puck laughed insincerely. "Now what's this I hear about Taya Dane? You say she's gone missing?"

"Yes," Sarah said, "that's right."

"And that her apartment has been broken into."

"Yes," Frost said. What was all this about? She seemed like she was playing dumb.

"Well, that doesn't sound good," Sheriff Puck said. "I gotta say, Mr. Johnson, seems like trouble follows you wherever you go, huh?"

Frost didn't reply. He didn't like where this was going.

"Well, I'll have a few of my men head over there tomorrow morning to check things out," Sheriff Puck said.

"*Tomorrow?*" Sarah said. She looked from Puck to Frost in disbelief.

"It follows today," Sheriff Puck said, her expression flat. She almost seemed annoyed that they had reported a crime.

"Why not right now?" Sarah said. "I don't know if Donny mentioned, but her place—"

"Deputy Kim told me everything, Ms. Albany," Sheriff Puck said. "But we've got limited manpower at the moment."

Frost frowned as he considered the three officers picking their teeth in the break room. The Clear Rock Sheriff's Department might have been plenty short on brainpower, but their manpower was doing just fine. Puck must have noticed Frost's scowl because she fixed an expectant gaze on him.

"We hopping back on the wrong foot, Mr. Johnson?"

"I'm just wondering why you'd want to sit on this," Frost said. "Did Deputy Kim tell you we saw two men leaving the scene?"

"Is that so?" Sheriff Puck said. "Another two mysterious men leaving the scene of a crime, huh, Mr. Johnson?"

"There might still be evidence they were there, if you get men on the scene soon," Frost said.

"You wouldn't be telling me how to do my job again, would you?" Sheriff Puck said.

Frost held his tongue, in part because of his awe at Puck's continuing refusal to do her job. Last time they spoke, she was cavalier. This time, she was almost hostile.

"And what exactly were you two doing there?" Sheriff Puck said.

"Trying to find out what happened to Taya," Sarah said.

Sheriff Puck nodded to herself. "How'd you get in the building?"

"The door was open," Sarah said. "We told you, two men—"

"No, no," Sheriff Puck said. "Not how'd you get into her apartment— how'd you get into the building in the first place? If she wasn't home to buzz you up."

"A neighbor happened to be leaving," Frost said.

"Is that right?" Sheriff Puck said. She crossed one leg over the other and sucked nonchalantly at her teeth. "Hmm."

Frost took a breath. "You a Clear Rock native, Sheriff Puck?"

"Born and bred, Mr. Johnson."

Frost nodded. He was starting to suspect Sheriff Puck's ineptness was something more. He thought about when he'd asked Sarah, another Clear Rock native, to identify a sandy-haired man with a scar, and she'd named Treece immediately. Yet when he'd asked Sheriff Puck the same in front of the roadhouse, it didn't even register for her. But was he really supposed to believe, in a small town like this, that the sheriff didn't know the resident drug dealer? The odds were slim to nil that the Sheriff didn't actually know who he was talking about.

And if she did know who Treece was but hadn't followed up on him, despite Frost identifying him as Lincoln's killer, that only led to one conclusion.

They wouldn't get anything out of this visit. The Clear Rock Sheriff's Department was working with the enemy.

FOURTEEN

A cool dusk light fell over the valley in cobalt and heliotrope. Shadows splayed out over the road as the Ranger drove over them. Frost and Sarah sat in silence inside the truck. They hadn't said much since they'd left the station. Frost had risked a lot for that trip into the police station, and all he had done was put himself in the line of fire for a legion of corrupt cops. His detour for Lincoln and Brakespeare was becoming more and more dangerous.

Sarah's phone dinged and she pulled it from her jacket to check the message.

"It's Donny," she said.

"Apologizing?" Frost said.

"Yup," Sarah said, looking at her phone. "He says he's sorry about Puck. Not much he could do about it, though."

Frost said nothing.

"And that he'll keep his eyes and ears open for any sign of Taya," Sarah said. "Now, what's gotten up your ass?"

Frost sighed. "Sorry."

"Something eating at you, slugger?"

Frost's eyes flicked from the road to Sarah. She was staring at him. Watching him like she cared what he thought. "Every minute that passes increases the likelihood that Taya is no longer *just* missing, you know what I mean?"

"Don't say that."

Frost thought about the situation and switched tracks. "Where in Clear Rock would you store a large cache of drugs?"

Sarah tilted her head. "Well, if Silver's running things, why not his mansion?" she said. "More than enough room."

"Yeah, maybe," Frost said. If Treece and Silver were distributing, that would mean a fleet of cars—maybe even trucks—coming and going on a regular basis. "Someplace big, where you could hide a truck. Maybe more than one."

"So, a warehouse or something?" Sarah said.

Frost shrugged. "I'm just thinking that maybe if we find the drugs, we'll find Taya." Or at least find out what happened to her.

Sarah ran her fingers through her hair. She had to know what he was saying was true—the chances of her still being alive were growing slimmer by the minute.

"I don't know," she said. "There's a lot of places in Clear Rock to hide bulk goods."

"Such as?" Frost said. That was a genuine surprise for a town this size.

"Um, well, there's the lumber yard warehouse on the edge of town. There's Pete's Storage. A number of abandoned buildings in town. Pick a direction and point, really."

They came upon a red traffic light and sat idling in silence. Frost looked out over the countryside. Not another car in any direction. Nothing. No sound but the low purr of the engine. He looked at the dark mountains on the horizon in front of him. The sky had cleared and it had yet to rain. Frost wondered what else he might be wrong about. Then, he saw the hawk.

Frost wasn't sure how he hadn't seen it before. It sat on the other side of the intersection, tearing away at some shapeless furred roadkill. It looked up, and its golden eyes shone like hellfire in the reflection of the red traffic light.

Frost thought it might be a ferruginous, noting its white coat and rusted markings. He turned on his headlights and the road lit up in front of him. The hawk didn't move an inch. It just stared.

The traffic light changed to green, throwing emerald over the hawk, and Frost slowly released the brake. The truck crept forward into the intersection, drifting towards the hawk. Frost made to drive around it, but Sarah touched his arm.

"Wait a minute," she said. "Back up."

Frost looked over at her.

"I just thought of something," she said. "Turn around and head to the north side of town."

Frost stopped the truck and put it into reverse and backed up into the crossroads. He turned right and began to head north as directed. After a moment, he glanced behind him in the rear-view mirror. Looked over at his side mirror. The hawk was gone.

———

Years ago and countries away, Frost and Brakespeare descended the Afghani foothills with their fireteam. They stalked toward an occupied city, a dense settlement of two-story clay buildings that valleyed towards a river at its west end. Dark violet and steel lapis colored the dusked city walls squatting before the team and the Hindu Kush mountains looming behind.

"Any movement?" Frost whispered into his throat mic.

"Negative," growled their team leader, Master Sergeant Holt. Frost wasn't sure why, but Holt seemed to have a personal stake in this region's liberation. With each new guerrilla atrocity, their leader had grown more on edge. "Looks like they're under curfew."

"Yeah, well, heads up, Snowman," Brakespeare said. "They're all gonna wake up if they hear that Zahir's Most Wanted is skipping through their streets."

"He's just a poor sport, is all," Frost said. Zahir's operation was about as poorly put together as his bombs. Frost was aware of the warlord's hatred for him, and he was hardly concerned.

"What's he got a hard on for you for?" the fourth member said, SFC Gage. Gage wasn't aware, but the rest of the unit was starting to pay attention to how often he talked about dicks in combat. Frost had gotten off easy with a callsign like Snowman, but Gage was cruising straight for Callsign: Chub.

"Snowman keeps clipping his IEDs," the fifth member said, Sgt. Noonan. Noonan barely spoke, and Frost could only guess that it was because the small man had an unusually deep voice. That was fine enough with Frost; the rest of the unit did enough talking for ten men.

"I heard he's even put out a bounty on your head now," Brakespeare said.

"Bullshit," Frost said.

"How much we talking?" Gage asked.

"Why, you still got student loan repayments to make?" Frost said.

"Don't be silly," Gage said. "I dropped out of college first semester."

Brakespeare laughed. "Well, I'd hurry up if you were gonna collect. Snowman's off to greener pastures tomorrow."

"That how you'd describe Kandahar?" Frost said. He had barely been briefed on the region, and wasn't at all sure what to expect.

"Fuck, already?" Gage said. "Thought that wasn't for another week or so."

The men halted at the foot of the hillside, hiding among the scraggly brush and boulders. They scanned the townscape below. Nothing moved.

"We sure Zahir's even here?" Brakespeare said.

Holt pointed to a cluster of buildings on his right. "Intel says he's holed up in the compound there to the west. Three blocks up."

The men held still for a moment.

"All right," Holt whispered. "Radio silence from here on out."

The five men crept down the dusted road at the base of the foothills, their carbines drawn. Like specters separating from the dim shadows of the dying day. They descended the narrow road that led into the city, gazing up at the balconies and rooftops through the reflector sights on their carbines. Laundry hung from many, a few others held satellite dishes, the lot of them overcrowded by power lines. But no faces. No voices. The city seemed dead but for the American fireteam stalking its streets.

The team turned right and saw the compound at the top of the road, a three-story clay building surrounded by a ten-foot concrete wall. The team approached, clinging to the walls of the neighboring adobes to minimize their exposure. Frost wished they could have come later, when night had fallen completely, but time was short.

Hamid Zahir never stayed in one place for long. If they were going to catch him, they needed to do it now.

Frost looked up the dusty street. A griffon vulture landed in the road next to them, lazily flapping its wings. It bent its serpentine neck and picked at something in the road, some morsel of roadkill that had been left behind. It never once looked up at the men, not even as they passed it.

Brakespeare held his hand out and up, directing the team members to the top of one of the buildings. Mounted on a rooftop parapet was a small electronic CCTV camera. It panned with the soldiers, watching soundlessly as they approached the compound. Frost looked ahead and saw two more parapet-mounted cameras at differing distances down the street. He pumped his closed fist up and down, signaling the team to rush. They jogged towards the compound now, the barrels of their weapons sweeping the area. Noonan and Gage kept pace in reverse to cover their six.

They came upon the large wooden door of the compound wall and backed themselves flush against it. They collected themselves for a second and listened. But for them and the security cameras, nothing moved. The stillness unsettled Frost. They had been spotted. When would the shitstorm start? MSG Holt took a step out and faced the door, raising his carbine to the cheap lock set inside it. They were ready. Breach and clear.

But the abrupt hissing whisper of a bullet cut through the silence and muzzled the assuredness of the men. It ripped through Holt's calf and burst out the other side. He cried out and dropped to one knee. He backpedaled toward the fireteam, staring up at the rooftops, trying to locate the sniper as he scrambled in the dirt with his obliterated leg. The team turned their stances square against the darkness and did the same, and Frost moved forward to haul Holt back onto his feet.

"Do you see him?" Brakespeare shouted.

"No." Holt gasped. He bit down hard on his lower lip as he tried to put weight on his wounded leg, instead leaning himself up against the wall of the compound. Suddenly, the team was blown out in a brilliant whiteness as two mounted floodlights came to life on top of the compound walls.

"We gotta get the hell out of here!" Gage's voice, shrill with panic.

Another bullet hissed through the air, this time straight through MSG Holt's head. The clay wall behind him exploded with gore, and his lifeless body toppled over in the dirt. The other four men bolted for cover behind a single small car parked in front of the compound. Another shot from the sniper rang out and shattered the car window.

"Christ, where is this dickhead?" shouted SFC Gage.

He leaned out from behind the car, but he must have judged the angle wrong. A shot ripped through his neck and he collapsed dead in the dusty road. Blood bubbled from his wound and mixed into clumps in the dirt.

Frost turned to see the thick gate door behind them creak open an inch. The muzzle of a Kalashnikov emerged from the gap. Frost swung his carbine around and fired into the darkness and heard the liquescent piercing of flesh and the collapse of a body.

"He's on the roof of the building with the cart in front, on the east side of the road," Brakespeare said into his mic. "Keep him occupied!"

Frost turned and saw Brakespeare darting across the road towards the wooden door of an adobe home. Noonan had taken a position on the hood of the car and was returning fire to cover him. Frost watched a dark shape duck behind a low rooftop wall across the road to the east. Brakespeare kicked open the home's front door and dashed inside, barely breaking stride.

Frost held his gun upon the opening at the front gate. He looked up at the CCTV camera mounted on the compound wall. It panned over and focused on Frost and Noonan. Frost swore he could hear the whir of the camera focusing on him. He thought about shooting the cameras out, but didn't want to waste ammunition. He didn't know how many he'd have to take out in the house. Besides, their cover was already well blown.

"Brakes, you in position?" Frost called into his mic.

"Sure am, Snowman. Made it to the roof. He doesn't know I'm here."

"All right, give us some covering fire. Noonan and I are gonna clear the house."

"Wait," Sgt. Noonan said. The man's eyes were wide. The quiet sergeant clearly wanted to stay put, but to Frost, that meant death. They were two men down and pinned in hostile territory, with a compound full of men at their backs and a sniper pinning them down at their front. If anyone could watch their backs and stay alive, it was Brakes.

"We're sitting ducks here, Noonan!" Frost said. "If we can establish a foothold in the compound, we can at least get some cover on our backs!"

"I got your six, Sergeant. Stay close to Frost," Brakespeare said over the comms. His voice was warm, reassuring even over the airwaves and the distance.

Frost heard Brakespeare open fire from the house across the road and ran. He threw himself against the wall of the compound beside the gate and, once Noonan was positioned on the other side of the doorframe, donkey-kicked the wooden gate inward. As he'd hoped, an anxious gunman inside lit the doorway up, revealing his position. Fragments of the wooden gate splintered and sprayed out onto the street.

Frost tore an M84 flashbang from his belt, pulled the pin, and tossed it inside. A second later it burst in a nimbus of phosphorous and the firing stopped. Frost ducked into the doorway and put two rounds through the gunman's chest. Noonan followed, providing an overlapping field of fire, but the courtyard was empty.

Frost led the way into the house and cleared the first floor. It was nearly barren. A television, sparse furniture, some electronics. Not much else. Frost turned as he heard a man darting down the stone staircase and fired upon him as he hit the first floor. Frost ran up the staircase to the second floor and startled a younger man trying to fit the magazine into a beaten Kalashnikov. Frost shot him twice through the chest before the man even touched the trigger.

Frost looked around the small room while Noonan watched the door. It seemed to be the surveillance hub, cluttered with cheap monitors and ancient electronics. A single modern Toshiba laptop sat solitary among the detritus. Frost found the floodlight switch and turned it off. On the monitor, the road in front of the compound went dark again. He and Noonan swept the rest of the room, finding no one.

"No sign of Zahir. We're coming back out to regroup. What's the status on the sniper?"

"Plugged him when he popped back up to look for you, you maniac. Keeping an eye on the street now."

Frost and Noonan descended the stairs and returned to the bullet-shredded gate through which they had entered.

Then came the flat breath of a silenced pistol. Frost spun to see Noonan clutching at his underarm which was quickly becoming soaked with blood. Red spittle flecked his lips. Frost was almost stunned in disbelief. They had cleared the building, hadn't they? Who was left?

"What..." the sergeant said, his small voice almost a whimper. A towering figure emerged from the shadow of the stairwell, beneath a concealed chamber that neither of them had noticed, and buried a Ka-Bar combat knife hilt-deep in Noonan's neck. Frost felt his heart plummet.

Frost opened fire, but the newcomer kept moving, dragging Noonan's body as he ran. One of the bullets found their target, but instead only clipped the dead soldier's vest. The last man standing fired at Frost as he moved, and Frost was forced to run for cover behind the threadbare couch in the lobby. They had circled around one another now, and the assailant was closer to the gate than Frost. The newcomer turned and bolted, only dropping Noonan's corpse once he was past the threshold.

"Brakes, do you have eyes on the gate?" Frost shouted into his mic.

"Sure do, you need some cover?" Brakespeare asked.

"Shoot the motherfucker coming out!"

Frost heard distant gunfire and bolted for the gate. The last man standing was crouched in the crook of the bullet-riddled car's open door, inserting the key into the ignition without climbing into the driver's seat where Brakespeare could line up a clearer shot. Even over the gunfire, Frost could hear the man cursing furiously under his breath.

Frost had a clear shot. He took it. The man dropped dead, slumped against the driver's seat.

Frost didn't miss a beat. He tore across the street to the house where he had seen Brakespeare holed up. Frost nearly collapsed in the house's man room, quivering as the adrenaline bled from his brains alongside the thoughts of images of Holt, Gage and Noonan dead in the street. Brakespeare found him downstairs and Frost was dimly aware that he even risked setting his gun down to talk Frost through his panic.

When Frost was level again, he caught Brakespeare up on what had happened. They decided to ensure that the compound was clear and that there wasn't more information to be gleaned from the area.

The two men tore through the compound once more, searching for any clues that Zahid had been there. When they were done, they reconnoitered back at the compound's front gate. Brakespeare looked out the door at the carnage in the street as though seeing it for the first time.

"Jesus Christ," he whispered.

"Hamid was never here. There's not even a car in the driveway," Frost said. Their fireteam had died for nothing. He felt his pulse rate rise, and he took a deep breath to calm it once more. He was even. He was level. No need to dwell on it further.

"They knew," Brakespeare said.

Frost thought of the sniper across the street. "Absolutely." Judging by the disorganization from the men inside, however, they seemed to think that a sniper and a gunman at the door would have taken care of the squad. Frost and his fireteam were supposed to have died in the street, never having set foot in the compound.

"There's a fuckin' leak somewhere, man," Brakespeare said. "I mean, how many people outside of us even knew we were coming here? It's supposed to be a fuckin' black op."

Frost nodded. He gestured at the mounted CCTV cameras. "Did you see the setup upstairs? Those things are wired up for remote viewing."

"As in, Zahir might be looking at us right now?" Brakespeare said.

"Him and anyone else with a link," Frost said.

"Fuck's sake," Brakespeare breathed. Then, his eye seemed to catch something unexpected outside. Brakespeare checked the rooftops and crept back into the road, where the last man standing slumped against the battered car's driver's seat. Frost joined Brakespeare, and found his friend examining the dead man's face. "Jesus."

"What?" Frost asked. Brakespeare's expression, wide-eyed and tense, scared Frost further. What else could go wrong tonight?

"You don't recognize him?"

Frost cocked his head and looked down at the man again. He recognized him now.

"That's not—"

"Yeah, it is," Brakespeare said. "Mohammed Zahir. Hamid's firstborn son."

"Oh, Christ." He'd shot a warlord's son. And worse…

Brakespeare turned and stared up at the mounted CCTV camera pointing directly at them. He looked back at Hamid Zahir's dead son.

"Well, if there wasn't a bounty on your head before…" Brakespeare muttered.

Frost turned and stared up into the black eye of the watching camera and nodded. He looked back at the dead man in front of him.

Brakespeare nudged him and gestured towards the sky. Frost looked up. By the pale moonlight he could see the griffon vulture circling above him. The smell of the dead grew overwhelming.

———

The Ranger rolled down the road in Clear Rock's industrial northside. A few rundown textile factories, a scrap yard, and a lonely out-of-place motel trailed by as they wound through the darkening streets.

"What exactly are we looking for?" Frost said.

"There," Sarah said, gesturing out her window. "The guy on the stoop."

They pulled into the parking lot in front of the motel. Frost glanced at the shabby building. It looked like it hadn't been updated since it was first erected in the seventies. Flaking oil paint bespotted the façade, and faded orange-beige curtains hung from its small windows.

At the far end of the motel, a single man sat in a plastic chair on the portico. Drinking a bottle of malt liquor, smoking a cigarette, playing on his phone. He had a fuzzy beard and greasy hair and wore clothes that looked like they used to fit, as if he'd lost a fair bit of weight quickly.

"That guy was my fiancé's dealer," Sarah said. "His regular dealer. Besides Treece."

Frost looked at the man. Early thirties, maybe. If he was a dealer, he might be armed, but Frost doubted it. Regardless, Frost's system pegged him as a Level Three.

He glanced over at Sarah. She was opening old wounds in coming here, and by interacting with the dealers that led to her fiancé's death. It was a courageous thing to do for someone you'd never met, sure. But Frost still found himself hoping that her personal stake in what they were doing wasn't going to make her a liability.

"It's been a long time since I've seen him," Sarah said, looking out the window at the dealer. "Looks the same. Worse, if that's possible."

"I'll go have a chat with him," Frost said, still considering her past.

"No," Sarah said. "He knows me."

"That's what I'm afraid of," Frost said. He regretted saying it as soon as the words left his mouth, but Sarah simply looked back at him with an expression that told him all the different ways he could fuck off. Frost only nodded. If she thought her taking the lead would give them better chances, she could give it a shot.

Sarah stared at the man a moment longer before exiting the truck. Frost got out with her, and they crossed the parking lot to the motel portico.

"Max," Sarah said to the man.

The man turned slowly from his phone. His eyes fluttered and Frost clocked dilated pupils. The man was high as a kite, and it definitely wasn't on anything that would let him move faster than a stumble. Level Two, now.

"Sarah?" the dealer said. His face split into a wide, dreamy smile. "Hell you doing on the wrong side of tracks?"

"I wanted to ask you a few questions," she said.

The dealer looked over at Frost. "Your friend cool?"

"The coolest," Sarah said.

"He don't look cool," Max said, staring Frost up and down.

Sarah took in the motel window and the room beyond it. "You alone?"

The dealer nodded, his smile widening. "For the hour, at least. Got myself a lady friend popping by." He looked over at Frost again. "You sure he's cool? He's making me nervous."

The dealer sniffed his wetly nose and took a long pull of his malt liquor.

"Where do you get your supply from?" Sarah said.

Max laughed. "What? The fuck kind of question is that?"

"A simple one," Frost said.

"Why the fuck do you wanna know that?" the dealer said.

"Because I do," Sarah said.

"Look, there's not a lot there I can tell you, girl," the dealer said. "Now, you want me to hook you up, I can do that, but—"

"Where do you meet to re-up?" Sarah said, cutting him off. She stepped closer. Her posture wasn't threatening, and neither was her tone, but there was something about her demeanor that worried Frost. She was too calm. Max was picking up the same impression, and was clearly becoming nervous. Frost wondered exactly what history the two of them shared.

"Yeah, that's not a consistent thing," Max said, leaning away from Sarah. "I call them when I need more, and they always deliver to me. Every time. I go where they tell me."

"Deliver where?" Sarah said, her voice still unnervingly placid.

"A new spot each time. A parking lot. Behind the Walmart. Wherever. They tell me."

"Deliver in what?" Sarah asked.

"It's never the same. Different cars, different drivers."

Sarah moved one step closer and squatted so that she was eye level with Max. "Max," she said calmly. "I know that Andy Treece sold Charlie the heroin that killed him. But I also know that he scored from *someone* else many, many times before that. There might be a way for me to consider that water under the bridge. If that *someone* could give us some details we can use, for example. But if he can't, there might be a few years of pain and anger that I need someone to answer for. And that cool guy behind me? He's not gonna be so cool."

"Sarah—" Max stammered, but Sarah shook her head. Max's eyes darted to Frost, and Frost, at a loss to do anything else, simply cracked his knuckles as menacingly as he could.

The dealer shook his head and looked off. He thought for a second and looked back at them.

"Yeah, I got something for you," Max said. He hesitated and shook his head. "You two are gonna land me such a fuckin' beating. One of them guys showed up one time in a white van. Few weeks back now."

Frost sighed internally. A white van? Hardly distinct.

"But the van looked new. And I remember thinking it was weird because they didn't usually drive vans. Just cars and pickups. So after we did our thing and I paid him and loaded up my car, he drove away. And I saw, on the back of the van, the bumper plate holder. You know, like, the license frame thingy?"

"Yeah, and what'd it say?" Frost asked.

"It said: *You want discreet...*"

Sarah finished the slogan. "*...go with Pete.*"

FIFTEEN

Twenty minutes later, Frost and Sarah arrived at a privately owned storage unit facility on the edge of town. It had five rows of identical concrete buildings, each housing ten large storage units. The property itself was surrounded by a chain-link fence lined with razor wire, parted by a mechanical sliding gate at its entrance. A small office by the gate was flanked by a short parking lot that held three white vans and one large moving truck. The vans were unmarked but for their license plate holders that, along with the siding on the moving truck and the custom lightbox marquee at the front, read: Pete's Storage. If you want discreet, go with Pete.

Frost and Sarah parked the Ranger across the street and down the block from the yard. Frost scanned the surrounding area for mounted cameras and didn't see any. He didn't see much of anything or anyone, besides the loosely arranged lots of dead or dying businesses. Just a concrete graveyard of mattress warehouses, clearance furniture shops, and a boarded-up auto garage.

Frost got out of the truck and walked to the back and opened the tailgate. He reached into a compartment and pulled out a set of laser rangefinder binoculars. He came back around and hopped into the truck again. He peered out through his windshield towards the yard office. To Frost's surprise, the office was dark. Nobody seemed to be inside.

"Those are impressive," Sarah said. It took Frost a moment to realize she meant his binoculars.

"I like to birdwatch," Frost murmured.

"Birdwatch?" Sarah said, smiling. She gestured to the truck bed behind her. "What else you got back there?"

"All I need. My whole life travels with me." Frost realized that he hadn't told Sarah about his life as a drifter. He wondered what she thought of that.

"Sounds heavy," Sarah said.

Frost nodded and patted the dashboard in front of him. "Yeah, but this baby's got a lot of torque."

He glassed the yard again. Looked beyond it. In the distance, he saw a service road winding up into the wooded hillside. He set the glasses down and put the truck in drive.

A few minutes later, Frost and Sarah came to a stop on the dirt shoulder beside the service road. Set halfway up the hills, they parked the Ranger and got out. They walked back a dozen feet or so and found a sight line through the woods. The storage facility was laid out about a hundred feet in front and thirty feet below where they stood. They could see everything.

Frost passed the property over again with his binoculars. It seemed still, but his vantage point wasn't as good as he would have liked, and he couldn't be sure.

"Anything?" Sarah asked.

In a middle aisle, Frost saw three men standing in front of a closed storage unit. A car pulled up and parked beside them in the shadows, and as it did, the headlight played off a familiar face. Frost handed the binoculars to Sarah.

"Middle aisle," he said. "Halfway up."

Sarah looked. "They're waiting for something."

"You see the guy on the right?" Frost said.

"Oh, shit," Sarah said, pulling the binoculars from her face. She looked over at Frost and grinned. The guy on the right was Treece. She peered through the binoculars again. "Damn, he looks like Satan used him as dental floss. You really beat the hell out of him."

Frost held out his hand for the binoculars and Sarah handed them back. He watched as Treece pulled out his phone and checked its screen and held it to his ear.

Treece began to pace and gesticulate wildly. It appeared to Frost that he was letting whoever was on the other end really have it. Treece hung up and put his phone away and continued to pace, checking his watch.

Frost lowered the binoculars, considering if there was any way he could get close enough to hear the conversation without blowing their cover. But Sarah gestured to the road that led up to the storage facility.

"Look," she said.

Headlights pierced the night and Frost returned to his binoculars. Another moving truck had passed through the gate and drove into the middle aisle where it stopped in front of the three men. The driver cut the engine.

"Here we go," Frost said. Time to see what was waiting for Treece behind door number one.

The two men standing with Treece went to the front of a storage unit, lifted the gate, and turned on the light. The driver got out, went to the back of the truck and opened it, lowering the steel ramp onto the pavement. Treece yelled at the driver, and the man held up his hands in apology. Frost guessed this was the man Treece had just been on the phone with.

The driver disappeared into the storage unit behind the other two men and a minute later all three emerged. They each piloted semi-electric pallet jacks, each jack carrying four-foot-high pallets wrapped in plastic.

Frost handed the binoculars over to Sarah. She looked.

"Jesus," she said.

"Look at the plate on the truck," Frost said.

Sarah did. It was a California license plate.

"Whoa," she said. "This really is cross-country."

Frost nodded. "Guy's even got a Lakers freshener hanging from the mirror. This shit is coming in all the way from LA."

Sarah stared over at Frost, her eyes wide. She could hardly believe what they were watching. She handed the binoculars back to Frost and he looked again.

The men finished loading up the pallets and walked the empty jacks down the steel ramp back to the storage unit. The driver climbed back into his truck and started it up. He drove straight ahead and looped around the lot, heading towards the front gate. Treece and the other two men climbed into their car and drove to the gate as well. Soon, both vehicles were beyond the gate and fading from view.

Frost lowered the binoculars and looked over at Sarah. He thought back upon the email correspondence he'd lifted from Treece's house.

"So, we've found where they take the goods for distribution," Frost muttered.

"We have to do something," Sarah said.

"I'd say you're right," Frost said. "Unless you want Clear Rock looking like southside Chicago."

They climbed into the truck.

"We should call the FBI," Sarah said.

"Yeah? And when they pull up and ask Sheriff Puck just what's going on, whose report will they believe?" Frost asked. He believed what he said, but his certainty that Crane would find him the moment he reported to the feds also worried away at the back of his mind.

"You really think that Puck is a part of all this?" Sarah asked.

"She's going out of her way to make Taya harder to find. Not just for us, but for her fellow cops as well. I don't know how well we can count on law enforcement."

Sarah sighed. She cast a glance back at the storage units, crouching in the shadow of the setting sun. She ran her fingers through her hair and turned back to Frost, who met her gaze.

"This is a lot. I don't know how you're doing, Kevin, but I need a little time to think this over. Think we can head back to the Lotus?"

Frost thought for a moment about the time left in the day and the ground he still had to cover. He looked into Sarah's eyes and thought about how little she knew about him, despite the trust she was placing in him. Hell, she didn't even know his name. He was lying to her every moment they spent together.

Frost nodded and pulled the truck in reverse, leaving the storage units behind.

———

Frost pulled up in front of the Black Lotus and stopped, but kept the truck running.

"You're not coming in?" she asked. "You're welcome to stay the night."

"Got some business I need to take care of before I can rest."

"More birdwatching, huh?"

Frost nodded. "Something like that."

"Suit yourself, slugger. If you change your mind, my door's always open. Metaphorically, at least. After today, I'm probably gonna barricade the Lotus until you're back."

Frost winced. That had been on his mind—he and Sarah had exposed themselves to corrupt cops, had their pictures taken by Silver's thugs, and been very vocal in Tick's bar about their search for Taya. Would Silver go after Sarah here at the Black Lotus? This was the exact reason why he hadn't wanted to involve her. But, he admitted grudgingly, she had been able to get information where he hadn't. She had even saved his life in Taya's apartment. But now she was a loose end. A vulnerability.

"Are you sure you don't want to come with me?" Frost asked.

"I've had enough action for today. For the week. I'll be fine, Kevin. Just keep your phone on you, all right? And be back here as quick as you can." Sarah leaned over and gave Frost a quick peck on the cheek and stepped out of the car. Frost watched her jog back to her tattoo parlor.

He drove away once Sarah was inside. He needed to get back into Taya's apartment—and this time, without being seen. If he could go over the place without being interrupted, he might be able to find something that Silver's men hadn't discovered. He had to be thorough, and the attack that day had robbed him of that opportunity. Still, re-treading old ground made him edgy. It was only a matter of time until Crane found him.

He drove to Taya's and parked down the street from the brownstone. Outside the car, nothing moved in the evening suburban shadows. Frost tucked his sidearm into his waistband once again. In the past two altercations, he'd been hesitant about discharging it with the amount of heat that could bring, but heat didn't mean a damn thing if one of Silver's thugs shot him through the throat.

This was it. Look for cameras, disable them, and a quick sweep of the apartment. Easier now that he was alone. Frost put on his ball cap and climbed out of the truck. He ducked quickly into his trunk for a pair of pliers and a heavy flashlight. Being alone again felt right. No more mistakes, no more hasty decisions. In and out, without anyone being any the wiser. Frost pulled the bill of the cap low over his brow and disappeared into the night.

SIXTEEN

F rost indeed found a camera in the back alley where he and Sarah had entered the building the first time. He was preparing himself for an even more limited window of time to enter and leave after he cut it from the grid, but as he walked another circuit of the building, he was surprised to find the building's front door swinging open. An old woman had walked out with her dog, and Frost jogged toward her, holding his phone to his ear.

"No worries, someone's letting me in! Stay upstairs, I'll come on up to you," he said into his phone to nobody. He gave the woman a friendly wave, which she returned, and he ducked past her through the open door.

Just goes to show, Frost thought, *espionage and hospitality really do go hand in hand.*

Frost approached Taya's apartment and saw that the front door was wide open. He paused in the hallway and listened for voices or footsteps inside the unit. He heard none. He walked slowly to the threshold, pressed to the wall, and paused again just outside. He was shocked to see the state of the apartment.

The entire unit had been put back together. The furniture was set back upright—the detached leg of the sofa even hammered back in place—all sign of struggle from before had been cleared away entirely, including from the fight with Silver's thugs.

As soon as Frost set foot through the doorway, he heard a voice.

"Breaking and entering now, Mr. Johnson?"

Frost turned to see Sheriff Puck standing alone in the kitchen over a small stack of mail. She held an open bill up to the light in a blue-gloved hand.

"The door was open," Frost said. So much for no more mistakes. He had gotten sloppy since his Army days.

Sheriff Puck nodded and set the envelope down.

"I'm starting to think trouble ain't so much following you, as you're leading it by the nose," she said.

"Got worried that the state of things might change if the police really did start their investigation tomorrow," Frost said, stalling for time. What the hell was she doing here? How was the whole place cleaned in a matter of hours?

Puck sighed, though clearly from condescension rather than exasperation. "Seeing as you and Ms. Albany were so put off by my itinerary, I figured I would see to things myself."

Frost took the opportunity to examine the apartment while she spoke. Sure enough, everything had been put back into place. Even the broken furniture seemed to have been mended.

"You know, you and Ms. Albany suggested that Taya's apartment had been broken into." She made a show of prowling through the apartment, tracing the walls and furniture with her fingertips. "Looks fine to me."

"Yes, it does," Frost said.

He stared hard at Sheriff Puck and she stared right back. The two of them both knew the score, but he didn't know the play. Would Puck try to arrest him for suspicion of Taya's murder after finding him here at the scene? How much would she try to get away with?

"Still think that this peaceful, small town could really have such a nasty disappearance on its hands?"

Frost looked around the apartment again. He couldn't confront her. Not under these circumstances. "I guess Ms. Albany and I were mistaken."

"I guess so," Sheriff Puck said. "Still think you saw two men leaving here this afternoon as well?"

"Suppose I was mistaken about that, too," Frost said.

Sheriff Puck nodded and smiled, clearly happy to see Frost was starting to play ball. Then her smile vanished as her phone began to vibrate on Taya's kitchen counter. She plucked it from its place on the granite countertop and turned away from Frost to answer it.

Frost knew immediately she was speaking to some kind of superior. It wasn't her eagerness to take the call, but her posture had changed entirely. One moment she was threatening and commanding, the next her shoulders were rigid with anxious subservience.

Yet if Frost was looking to glean information about the investigation from Sheriff Puck's responses, she didn't give him much to work with. Just a few mumbled affirmatives before hanging up and turning back to face him once more.

"The Clear Rock Sheriff's Department has officially closed their investigation into the death of Lincoln Dane," Sheriff Puck said.

"Excuse me?" Frost said, despite himself.

"We're closing the case. No leads. Well, other than you, I mean," she said.

"What about Andy Treece?"

"Who?" Puck asked. Frost stared at her. She was nearly smirking. "Anyway, we've concluded that Mr. Dane's death—"

"Murder, you mean," Frost said.

"We've concluded that Mr. Dane's death was simply a mugging gone wrong."

"He wasn't robbed."

"On the contrary, his phone and keys were missing."

"And what about Taya?" Frost said.

"What about her?"

"She goes missing around the same time her brother is killed and that's just a coincidence?"

"Just because she's not here doesn't mean she's missing, Mr. Johnson," Sheriff Puck said. She glanced around the apartment again. "And like we've already established, everything seems fine. Perhaps she went on vacation."

"Andy Treece shot and killed Lincoln Dane," Frost said. "I was there. I saw him do it myself. He and a second man did it."

"I don't know who Andy Treece is," Sheriff Puck said. "Look, you've got things ass backwards here. I'm telling you it is the Sheriff Department's conclusion that Lincoln Dane was killed by a mugger or muggers and that they left town immediately afterwards. Likely even left the state. And on the basis of that conclusion, the case is now closed and no further investigation of it shall be conducted. Tell me what's so difficult to understand about that? Now, if you think that this Andy Treece fellow was somehow involved, well, that's your prerogative, but we have no evidence to support it—"

"Only my eyewitness testimony," Frost said.

"–only the eyewitness testimony of a man who also baselessly claimed that his sister's apartment had been ransacked." Sheriff Puck stepped forward and thrust her face into Frost's. She lowered her voice. "Now, you think about this and you think about it long and hard: Do you really want me going back over this murder and taking a closer look? You were there when Lincoln Dane was murdered and you're here when Taya Dane has her apartment broken into. Any sensible person might suspect you've got an axe to grind with the Danes, don't you think? Any sensible jury, at least. And murder is a capital offence here in Wyoming."

"Except that this apartment *wasn't* broken into," Frost said. "Right?"

Sheriff Puck grinned thinly, and Frost could see she'd finally grown tired of the dance.

"I don't want to see or hear that you're even remotely associated with the Danes, is that clear?" Sheriff Puck said. "Stay in Clear Rock as long as you like. Enjoy its small-town charm. But if I hear that you're still sniffing around Taya or Lincoln Dane after tomorrow morning, you might not be able to avoid this whole damn thing coming down on your head."

"That almost sounds like a threat, Sheriff," Frost said.

"I'd take as a goddamn divine edict if I were you, Mr. Johnson," she said. "Unless you really want to see yourself sent up to Rawlins on a homicide. Sitting on death row, spending your last thoughts on this earth wondering why you ever pissed off the Clear Rock Sheriff's Department. Now, how's that for a fuckin' threat?"

The games were over now. Sheriff Puck was wrapped up in this whole mess from the top down. Maybe she was being paid off by Treece. Who knew? Either way, he could see that she wasn't just spewing hot air at him. That there was weight behind her threat, and venom in her bite. He wondered how many lives she'd already destroyed, if there were prisoners in Rawlins right now who'd been put away because of her. Frost left Taya's apartment without another word.

"Enjoy your stay, Mr. Johnson!" Puck called after him.

Frost walked back to his truck and climbed in and sat there for some time. After a while, he felt a strange sensation coming over him, as if he was being watched. Not by the Sheriff, he thought, but by someone else. He'd had the same strange feeling ever since he'd first arrived in Clear Rock—since he'd returned from overseas, really, but it had started very small then. Nothing more than a shifting breeze on his shoulders. And he'd simply chalked it up to the legitimate paranoia of knowing that Crane and his men were scouring the country trying to find him. That he was being hunted. But now he thought that it was something else.

Frost looked over his shoulder, out his window, and across the street. Just as he did, a pair of car headlights turned on, blinding him momentarily. Frost took a few moments to shake the dizzying effects of his photosensitivity until he looked up to see the car pull out of its parking space, heading towards him. It passed slowly by his window and Frost made out the unmistakable shape of a black Lincoln Town Car.

The car drove past the truck and away from Frost. Soon it was gone entirely, disappearing down an adjacent side street. Frost thought about following the Lincoln, but decided against it. He was exhausted and needed to sleep. He had made one mistake and almost landed himself in jail. One more, and he might land in a grave.

He thought about returning to Sarah. He thought about her bed and her smile. The way she called him slugger. And when he thought about those things, he felt... nothing. Cold. He turned his truck around and headed for the edge of town.

SEVENTEEN

Frost drove out of town hoping to find a quiet spot by the Hognose River again. Yet his thoughts kept drifting back to Pete's Storage. To Treece, the shipment, California—something wasn't right. There were details that didn't fit, and he hadn't recognized them. He had to have more pieces to the puzzle than he thought.

He pulled the Ranger over to the side of the road and put it in park. He grabbed the folded email printouts from the overhead cab and went through them. Read the messages again. The quantity discussed was too big to fit inside one storage unit. Perhaps Treece had other units, but then why hadn't the men loaded the truck with their contents as well?

Maybe Pete's Storage was just a pickup and drop-off point, not used for long-term storage. Frost tried to imagine the possible scale of this operation, and where its heart might be. He thought back on what he'd seen so far, what Sarah had mentioned to him. Nothing spoke to him.

He folded the pages and placed them back in the glove box. He turned off the overhead light and turned his truck around, heading back to Pete's. He couldn't sleep before he'd cracked this. His wounded brain cried out for rest, but his theories needed to be put to bed first.

Frost parked his Ranger up in the hills again and walked back to where he and Sarah had knelt in the woods. He glassed the storage property again with his binoculars. And there was Andy Treece. Frost couldn't believe it. The distributor was still pacing back and forth in the shadows of the middle aisle, speaking into his phone.

After a few moments, Treece ended his call and put his phone away. He spun clumsily on his heel, apparently still tender from the morning, and climbed back into his car. Frost sprinted back to his truck. He needed to get back down the hill quick and tail Treece.

The fight that morning seemed like a lifetime ago. He could hardly believe it was the same day. The same month. He'd broken into two homes, fought off attackers at both, and uncovered a national drug operation. Not to mention meeting Sarah. Going to bed with her. It had been one of the longest days in his life. And it wasn't over yet.

Frost hopped into his Ranger, killed the headlights, and floored the accelerator. He took care to remember the twists and turns of the road, nearly driving off twice. But he made it to the bottom and took the main road towards Pete's Storage.

Up ahead he saw Treece's headlights exit the property and head down the road. The taillights of the car now stared back at Frost in the distance. Two red-hot embers glowing in the dark. Demon's eyes staring backwards, coaxing Frost onward. Leading him deeper into the shadows. Into malice.

Frost soon saw that Treece wasn't heading home. He turned north and then onto the highway that led out of town. Frost merged onto the highway at a good distance behind and turned his headlights back on. He drove on for a while, keeping breathing distance between himself and Treece, until he saw Treece's car turning onto the next exit. Frost followed.

The exit off the highway lead to a rural two-lane road and Frost took his time turning onto it, watching the dim glow of Treece's headlights in the distance. Frost followed the glow as it snaked down the winding road until it disappeared entirely. He cut his headlights again.

Frost reached the crest of the hill and saw Treece's car descending into a valley of flat prairieland, bristling with foxtail barley and needlegrass. The valley was pocketed with dense woodlands of linden, cottonwood, and apple trees. He watched Treece slow up and pull off the rural road onto a narrow drive. Frost pulled his truck over and waited.

The driveway led up to a large farm property. Barbed-wire fence posts lined its acreage and rolled hay bales marked the grass. In the distance, Frost saw a large wooden barn sheltered by surrounding greenwoods, its façade glowing bright amber as Treece drove up to it.

Frost scanned the dark night in front of him. He needed to get closer. He chose a small dirt pass flanking the farmland and took it around the east side of the property. He parked behind a small copse of dense birch trees, exited his car and knelt down with his binoculars in the shallow ditch that lined the pass. He stared unaided over the farmland for a moment. He could see now a handsome two-story farmhouse beside the barn, and the sawtooth peaks of the Teton Range beyond it like pitch-black pyramids against the starred sky.

Frost glassed the property with his binoculars. The barn was larger than most barns he'd seen growing up in Oklahoma. Large enough to house a midsize jet, Frost thought. Or, of course, a national supply of heroin.

Treece turned his car off and stepped out, where he crossed the property and disappeared into the barn side door. Frost lowered his binoculars. His instincts were telling him something that he couldn't quite articulate. He looked back at the barn. At Treece's car, at the farmhouse, and back at the barn again. And there it was.

The barn quilt. Hand-painted on a plywood frame and hanging over the barn doors. The last picture Taya had sent Lincoln was a picture of this barn quilt. Taya had been here, on this farm, and snapped a photo of the quilt before she disappeared. Frost glassed the property. She must have stood right where Treece had parked to take the picture.

So she'd known everything, Frost thought. She'd known what Treece and Silver were involved in, and she'd tried to warn Lincoln about it.

No wonder the kid had been killed.

EIGHTEEN

F rost sat watching the property for nearly an hour, but nothing else occurred. Treece might have gone out the back of the barn and into the farmhouse, but no lights came on in either building. The car didn't move. Frost decided he'd pressed his luck far enough and went back to his truck. He set the binoculars on the passenger seat and looked through Lincoln's phone again. He opened the maps application and pinned his current GPS location to make sure he'd know exactly where the farm was. Then he turned and drove back to the main road with his headlights off, leaving them dark until he'd reached the highway.

Taya could have been trying to say anything with that photo. Why hadn't she just asked for help if she'd needed it? Or sent him the address? The photo was a quick snap, so maybe she'd been in trouble when she'd taken it. Maybe she'd planned on conveying more to Lincoln, but never got the chance.

Frost picked up Lincoln's phone from the passenger seat and scrolled through older texts between Taya and Lincoln as he drove on. There was a photograph from a few weeks back that Lincoln had sent. It was a photo of Taya and Tick, their arms around one another, smiling brightly.

So they did know each other well, Frost thought. He'd suspected as much, but here it was in zeros and ones. But why would Tick lie? Not once, but twice. It wasn't just bartender-customer discretion, as he had claimed. No, Frost was certain now that Tick knew more than he was telling about Taya. Maybe he even had something to do with her going missing. He might himself be involved in this whole drug operation—the bar would be an ideal selling point, and Tick, selling alcohol to minors, didn't seem overly concerned about the law. Frost frowned as he remembered Sarah saying that her fiancé had overdosed in a bar's parking lot. She hadn't mentioned which one.

Frost set Lincoln's phone down and pulled his own from his pocket. He dialed Sarah, praying she'd answer. Thankfully, the ringback gave way to a click and a woman's sigh on the other end.

"Hey, you," Sarah said. Her voice was slow and drowsy. "Didn't think I'd be hearing from you again tonight."

"I need two things," Frost said. "You wouldn't happen to know where Tick lives, would you?"

"You're still going?" Sarah said. "Jesus, you don't quit."

"If there's questions that can be solved before I sleep, my brain won't allow me to skip 'em," he said. One more lie to Sarah. He felt like his skull was about to crack open.

She chuckled on the other end of the line. "Yeah, Tick's invited me to a few parties at his place. Got a place over on Russet Drive. Hold on." After some footsteps and rustling, she said "Sixty-five Russet."

"Beautiful," Frost said. "I owe you one."

"How about a few?"

"Well, there's reason number two," Frost said. "You mind if I come by tonight?"

"Not at all," Sarah said. Frost could hear the smile in her voice. "Got any sleuthing to share with me, slugger?"

"Let's just say I've got barn doors on the brain."

"Hope that's a euphemism for something."

Frost laughed. "No, ma'am."

"Darn," Sarah said. "I'll leave a spare key in the mailbox out front."

"See you soon."

"And, Kevin—"

The name stung Frost. She still didn't even know his name. His headache broadened, spreading across the back of his skull.

"—go easy on Tick, okay? He's a good guy."

"I will," Frost said. He hung up and tossed his phone onto the passenger seat. The jury was out on Tick, and as far as Frost was concerned, it was up to Tick just how easy tonight was going to be on him.

———

Tick's house was a gray, single-story rambler on the quiet side of Clear Rock. Frost parked on the street and looked over at the house. There didn't seem to be any lights on, but Tick's house was well-shuttered. Frost checked his watch. It was almost midnight. He'd wondered if Tick was still working at the bar or if he'd closed for the night. When Frost had stopped by the bar, Tick had been there in the morning and the afternoon—it was unlikely that he was still on his shift. But he still had no way of knowing if the man was still awake, or if he was alone.

Frost pulled his Glock from its concealed space in the cab and tucked it into his back waistband. If nothing else, Clear Rock had taught him to prepare for the worst. He walked to the front door and knocked. He heard movement inside, perhaps the sound of a television. Frost heard the gentle scrape of a peephole cover lifting aside, and then the louder click of a lock's bolt opening. Tick opened the front door, but only a few inches.

"Mr. Johnson?" Tick said, obviously surprised. "What are you doing here?"

Tick glanced behind Frost, as though expecting to see someone behind him. Frost guessed that he was looking for Sarah.

"Sorry, I know it's late," Frost said, glancing past Tick to see if he was alone as well, but unable to tell with his limited field of view.

"It's almost midnight, man. What the hell are you even doing here?"

"Look," Frost said. "You've blown me off twice today, even though I've told you I need to know as much as I can about Taya to help her. The sooner I get a straight answer out of you, the sooner you start never seeing me again."

"I don't know who you think you are, Johnson, but—"

"Or I could call the police," Frost said. "Seeing as I now know you lied about how well you knew Ms. Dane, they might want to speak to you in regards to her disappearance. You might even be the last person who saw her." Not that calling the police was a remotely viable option. Still, Frost hoped his bluff would work.

It did. After a long moment, Tick sighed and stepped aside to invite Frost in.

Frost scanned the place quickly. A living room opened into a small kitchen and dining room, and a single hallway led to two bedrooms and a bath. A wooden door sat opposite the front hall, and Frost figured it led to the basement. The entire place was neat and tidy, as

Frost had expected, but very sparse. A minimalism of scarcity, it seemed, and not of design, as though Tick poured any money he made back into the bar.

A single dark leather sofa and a black coffee table sat in the living room. Magazines were neatly stacked on the table. Porcelain coasters. A mounted flat-screen on the wall playing *The Public Enemy* on Turner Classic Movies. Every edge of the room was perpendicular to one another. It reminded Frost of a curated Zen space. Made him think of the vacant Buddhist stupa he'd visited in northern Afghanistan. The lonely echo of its empty caverns.

Tick shut the door behind Frost and stood in his foyer with his arms crossed. He did not offer him a seat.

"You've got five minutes," he said.

"I'm not looking to hurt Taya," Frost said. "I simply made a promise to find her."

"To her dead brother, and her dead uncle, right? Sure," Tick said.

"You wouldn't have let me in if you didn't think I was trying to help her, would you? You know I'm telling the truth."

"That, and you threatened to go to the cops," Tick growled.

"I still will. She was in deep with a drug lord, Tick. Very close with him. Maybe even close enough to be carrying his child," Frost said. Tick waited too long to feign his surprise, and Frost caught it. "But you already knew, didn't you?"

"I don't know what you're talking about," Tick said. His upper lip twitched in a barely restrained snarl. Frost wondered what the chances were that the bartender would get violent.

"Yes, you do. You know a startling amount about Taya Dane, Tick. And if you don't start cooperating with me to help get her to safety, I'm going to have to assume that you're hiding information about her because you want to hurt her. As Lincoln's last living will, I can't let that happen." Frost watched Tick's expression. The bartender's eyes had widened, and they darted to the front door. Tick was regretting letting Frost inside.

"What do you think you're going to do?" Tick asked.

Frost didn't answer, simply pulling the gun from his waistband and letting it hang by his hip.

"Jesus fucking Christ!" Tick shouted.

"Just tell me what you know about Taya so I can get her somewhere safe, Tick."

"You're a goddamn lunatic," Tick muttered.

"And you're a fucking dead man," a woman's voice growled behind Frost. He felt something sharp jabbing into his back—the point of a knife. Whoever this was, she had used Tick's yelling to cover her approach. It was a savvy move, and judging by Tick's wide-eyed expression, he hadn't expected it either.

"Go back to your room," Tick whispered.

"Like hell," the woman said. "Drop your gun."

Frost sighed. "Okay. I don't want any trouble." Then, he pivoted on his foot away from the point of the knife, spun himself around, and caught the attacker on her wrist, wrenching it so that she dropped the plastic box cutter she'd been holding to the floor. Frost kicked the blade into the corner and caught four long fingernails to his cheek for his trouble. At least, for the first time that day, it wasn't more blunt force trauma.

Frost made to incapacitate his attacker, but froze. Her hair was mussed with sleep and her eyes were bright with rage, but there was no mistaking it. Frost was looking into the face of Taya Dane.

NINETEEN

A few frantic explanations later and Frost was seated on the sofa with Taya while Tick stood leaning against the kitchen counter waiting for the tea kettle to boil. He'd asked Taya if she was hungry and she said she wasn't, but Tick was making her a sandwich anyway. The baby had to eat, even if she didn't. Frost found himself surprised at the genuine care that Tick was giving to Taya. The bartender seemed to honestly care for her well-being.

"And so how long did you and Uncle Brakespeare serve?" Taya asked, one hand resting on her rounded belly.

"Both did several tours," Frost said. "A few years together. He was a good man. A great friend."

Taya nodded. "He was. He bonded with Lincoln more, but he was always kind to me. And I always knew I could rely on him if I needed him. I can't believe he's gone."

"I'm sorry to be the one to tell you."

"No. Thank you," Taya said. "Lincoln and I can honor him the way he deserves, once this is all over. And it really was something for you to travel all this way to give Lincoln those tags."

An awkward silence emerged. Taya seemed to sense it, her eyes narrowing.

"So, why don't you really tell me why you're here now. What happened to my brother?"

Frost looked hard at Taya. Looked over at Tick as he brought the tray of sandwiches and chamomile tea into the living room. Frost could understand why Tick hadn't told Taya—that news was hard enough to break to a stranger. But if Taya was in hiding, then he was her only link to the outside world. And he hadn't told her about her own brother's death.

Tick avoided Frost's gaze, clearly ashamed.

"I'm here because your brother told me to find you," Frost said. He took a deep breath. "Those were his last words."

Taya clasped her hands in front of her mouth. "Oh my God, no." She gasped into her hands. "No, no, no."

Tick put his hand on her shoulder and pulled her in and hugged her.

"I'm sorry, sweetheart," he said.

She looked up into Tick's eyes. "You knew. You knew, didn't you?"

"I—I'm sorry, I just—" Tick said. "I only found out this morning, I swear."

"I asked Tick if I could be the one to tell you," Frost said. "Just in case he found you first."

Tick looked over at Frost, eyes soft with relief. Grateful for this small kindness.

Taya turned back to Frost. Tick handed her a linen napkin, and she wiped her eyes and took a breath. She stared down into her milky tea for a moment. Steam rose off the top of her mug, rising and vanishing.

She finally met Frost's eyes again. "How did he die?"

"He was murdered last night. Shot by two men in front of the roadhouse off Main Street," Frost said. "One of the men was Andy Treece. I don't know if—"

Taya looked up at Frost with wet red eyes. "*Andy* killed him?"

Frost nodded.

Taya's eyes flashed. "That son of a bitch. That hogshit-gargling waste of carbon. I'm going to bury him in so many pieces, the devil's gonna need a fucking IKEA catalog to put him back together. How could he?"

Frost paused. He hadn't been expecting that. Particularly not from someone related to Lincoln or Brakespeare. But, he thought, remembering her holding him up with a box cutter, she had run with some dangerous people. It seemed she had picked up some habits to match.

"That's what I'm trying to understand," Frost said. "You were seeing Silver, right?"

"Mhm. I was his girlfriend. *Am* his girlfriend."

"Is he the father?" Frost said, gesturing to her belly.

Taya nodded. "Do you know Silver?"

"Not yet, but that's why I'm asking," Frost said. "Taya, why would Andy Treece kill your brother? Was Lincoln involved in drugs? In debt in some way with Silver or—"

"No," Taya said. "It was nothing like that. He—"

She leaned forward and picked up her tea and blew on it. She took a small sip and set it back down again.

"Lincoln didn't know what Silver and Treece were up to," Taya said. "I mean, not like that. He knew they were into sketchy shit—everybody does—but he didn't *know*. You know what I mean? He wasn't involved."

"Did you know?" Frost asked.

"I had a pretty bad problem back then. One night I got invited to a party in this mansion out in the woods, and why would I say no? I was gonna score, and I was gonna finally have some fun in this nowhere town." Taya met Frost's gaze straight-backed and fearless. If she was ever ashamed of her addiction, she wasn't now.

"And Silver got you hooked?"

"Silver actually helped me get clean. Forced me, more like. Said he didn't want his woman wanting him for his product."

"So you owed him. And he must have treated you like his queen," Frost said.

"Of course," Taya said. "Dinners, clothes, apartments—whatever he wanted, he could get for me in a little backwater like Clear Rock. Anything he couldn't, he sent for. It was intoxicating, at first. Better than the drugs were, so I didn't even mind losing them. And then my head began to clear. I saw what he was doing to the town."

"Right."

"As we kept seeing each other," Taya said, "it just started to weigh heavier on my conscience. And I didn't know what to do. I went to church, even. You believe that? Hadn't been back since Sunday school. And yet I just couldn't leave him, you know? I couldn't stop."

"Were you in love with him?" Frost asked.

Taya nodded. A muscle in her jaw tensed, and she looked to Frost as though she were holding back tears. She took a breath and another sip of tea. Yet Frost saw in the way her face was set that she was still holding onto something. Something that wanted out. It quivered at the edges of her eyes, aching for release.

He placed his hand over top of hers.

"What changed, Taya?"

———

The dark blue Chevelle crept up the long farm driveway, only its headlights visible in the velvet darkness. The flatland was cloaked by the baldachin of soundless storm clouds above that hid the moon and stars from sight.

Taya awoke in the farmhouse bedroom. She glanced over at Silver in the bed beside her, and his phone vibrating angrily on the nightstand. It buzzed three times before Silver's hand lashed out and snatched the phone from the nightstand.

"Hello?" he said. He listened. "Good. I'll be right out."

He hung up and pulled on a pair of gray sweatpants.

"What is it?" Taya said.

"Just business, babe. Go back to sleep. I'll be back soon."

Silver grabbed the leather double-shoulder holster hung over the bedpost and looped his arms through it. A silver .357 Magnum hung in the left holster, while the right holster was empty.

"What's going on?" Taya asked, eyeing the gun.

Silver turned and flashed her a smile. "No need to worry. Just the nature of the beast. Sometimes, you gotta work the graveyard shift."

Taya heard the wooden stairs creak beneath him as he went down to the first floor of the house. The squeak of the patio door hinge as it opened and slammed shut against the threshold behind him.

Taya lay still, staring at the grayed ceiling above her. Soon the headlights of the Chevelle reached the farmhouse and cast panning silhouettes across the ceiling, flooding her room with twirling shadows. She heard the car leave the dirt drive and pass onto the grass lawn beside the farmhouse.

Curiosity got the better of Taya and she moved to the window, sticking to the shadows. The Chevelle turned a half-circle on the grass and stopped, pointed out towards the rural road, the way it had come in. The engine cut but the headlights remained on. Silver stepped off the wooden porch of the farmhouse and walked in front of the car, staring through its windshield. He stood with his hands on his hips, his silhouette sharp and tall behind him on the lawn.

The car doors of the Chevelle opened and shut, and Taya tried to see the new arrivals. She recognized Andy Treece, stepping out of the driver's seat, but she wasn't familiar enough with the other two to recognize them in the moonlight. Treece strode around the car to pop the trunk, and the other two lifted something heavy from within. It was a man, bound and gagged.

Taya grabbed her phone from the dresser top. She made sure the flash was off and began recording video, capturing the men below. Taya recognized the prisoner immediately as Sheriff Gomez, still in his beige police uniform, now covered in grease and dried blood. His hands were bound in front of his body, and there was a bandana tied tightly around his mouth. His graying hair was damp with sweat, and dried blood from a gash over one eye had crusted across his cheek in a brown-black mask.

Treece and the two others set the Sheriff on his knees in front of Silver. Taya caught a better glimpse of the other two now—one burly, the other slight. They set the Sheriff down and backed away into the darkness. Treece removed the Sheriff's gag and did the same.

Sheriff Gomez looked up at the bare-chested man in front of him, his hands held before him with like a penitent praying for forgiveness before an apparition of Christ. He began to speak, but then Silver drew his Magnum and shot the Sheriff in the head.

The discharge echoed out over the farmland and Sheriff Gomez's body crumpled sideways to the ground. She kept the camera rolling and kept her hand steady.

Silver stood over the dead Sheriff, replacing his Magnum in its holster and his hands on his hips as though he'd never moved at all. Treece emerged from the darkness. Silver said something, gesturing to the farmhouse, and Treece looked up at the bedroom window.

Taya pulled her phone away from the window and withdrew into the darkness of the room behind her. Her heart thumped inside her chest. She wasn't sure if Treece had seen her phone. She wasn't sure it would make a difference. She considered hiding somewhere in the room and ambushing Treece when he came up, but the barren farmhouse left very few places to hide. Relenting, she stuck her phone in her underwear and threw herself into bed, climbing under the covers.

She heard the patio door open and shut beneath her. Footsteps climbing the creaky staircase. A hard knock upon the bedroom door. And then a voice. It was Andy.

"Taya, get up," he said.

She didn't move or speak.

"I know you're not sleeping. Get up and get downstairs. You've got exactly one minute."

She heard him retreat down the stairs and go outside again. Silver was the kind of man who made things easy if you obeyed, and she got away with more than most. She couldn't run, and she couldn't stay where she was. She only had one choice. She got up and quickly put on her socks and a hoodie and went downstairs.

She emerged onto the wooden porch and saw Silver sitting in the rocking chair. He rocked gently back and forth, completely at ease. He spoke without looking at her.

"Andy's going to take you back to town," he said. "I've got a little extra work to do tonight."

And that was it. Taya knew better than to argue and she nodded. Andy was already in the driver's seat of the Chevelle. She stepped down off the porch and onto the grass, and was struck by the sudden intense fear that she would instead be led to the trunk. But nobody stopped her when she went to the passenger seat of the car and opened the door.

For a split second, she glanced back beyond the rear of the car. She saw the two men walking away from her in the pale light of the moon, dragging the dead man through the grass. They were headed towards the shadowed limbs of a tall, skeletal apple tree. One of the men held a shovel.

Taya climbed into the Chevelle and slowly looked over at Treece. He looked over at her but didn't say a word. He drove away from the farmhouse and stopped the car in front of the barn. He got out, leaving it running, and went inside the barn.

Taya's mind scrambled, searching for anything she could use to keep herself safe. She looked over at the barn beside her, at the barn quilt near the hayloft. She grabbed her phone from her underwear and quickly snapped a photo of the quilt. She sent it to the first person she thought of, Lincoln, and tucked the phone away again just as Treece emerged from the barn and climbed back into the driver's seat. And then they were off, parting the velvet night once more with those dual points of light.

Taya looked over at Frost and took another sip of her tea. Where once she had seemed stalwart and self-assured, now she seemed small. "Silver, Treece—they must've thought Lincoln knew about Sheriff Gomez's murder," she said. "That's why they killed him. They must have thought I told him about it."

"But you didn't?" Frost asked.

"No."

"You didn't send him the video?" Frost said.

"No. Just the photo," Taya said. "I wanted to keep the video. I thought maybe I could use it as blackmail, to keep myself safe."

"Why the barn quilt?" Frost said.

Taya shrugged. "If I died, Lincoln might at least know where to go looking for me. But if I sent him the video, I would risk myself and Lincoln and ruin my chance at blackmailing Silver. Lincoln would go straight to the police with that information, and he'd blow my last hope at bargaining for my life."

"I think I understand," Frost said.

"It didn't make a difference. He's still dead because of me."

"What happened to the video?" Frost said, to prevent her from following that train of thought. "Did you send it to *anyone*?"

"No," Taya said. "After Andy dropped me off, I stashed my phone. Turned it off so it couldn't be tracked or anything."

"Where'd you stash it?" Frost said.

"At my apartment," she said. "Right after Andy dropped me off that night. It needed to be somewhere safe, but not where it could lead straight to me. Then I packed a bag and left. Didn't tell anyone.

Walked down to Tick's and asked if I could stay here for a while. Hide out until... I don't know. Until the baby was born, at least."

She rubbed her belly and looked down at it. "Supposed to be any day now."

"So, you stashed your phone and took off without telling anyone?" Frost said. An unsupervised home birth. Frost was no OB, but that was hardly the safest option for her or the baby.

"Yeah," Taya said. "I mean, I genuinely thought Andy was going to kill me. The whole drive home I thought he would. He certainly would have if he knew what I had on me."

"And no one knows you're here?" Frost said. "You two haven't told anyone else?

"No," Taya said.

"No," Tick added.

"No one? Not a single soul?" Frost said.

"We kept our friendship a secret even before all this shit happened," Taya said. "Silver would never have allowed it. He's possessive to the point of lunacy. Everything that's his is his. Only Lincoln knew that Tick and I hung out."

Frost nodded. He took a moment.

"You really think Silver will kill you if he finds you?" he said. "Despite you carrying his child?"

Taya nodded. "No matter how much he claims he loves me, at the end of the day I'm just... his. Not quite property, but not a person. He might value what's his, but something is worse than worthless if it threatens his empire."

Tick shook his head and stared through the coffee table. "What the hell are we going to do?"

"Dismantle it," Frost said. "Every inch of it. There's nothing else *to* do."

"You have no idea who you're going up against," Tick said.

"He's right," Taya said. "Silver's a goddamn psychopath."

"Yeah, well, I've had my run-ins with them before," Frost said. "Now where'd you stash your phone?"

"In the paneling beneath the fireplace," Taya said.

"Fireplace? I didn't see a fireplace," Frost said.

"You were at my apartment?"

Frost nodded. "Today. Twice, actually."

"Which one?" Taya said.

"Which *one*? The brownstone," Frost said. "You've got more than one apartment?"

Taya nodded. "I've got the brownstone and a studio on the southside. I used to live there before I met Silver, and I didn't want to break the lease."

"I'm going to guess he's got that place surveilled too?" Frost said.

"Yeah. It's why I haven't been back," Taya said. "But Silver's thugs aren't getting in either, unless they go in shooting. It's a nice place with private security, and it's one of the few buildings that Silver doesn't own. That's why I left it behind—didn't want to put all my eggs in one basket, in case he caught up with me. I never got the owner to admit it, but I think he refuses to sell because he hates Silver's guts. Old man overheard Silver talking down to me one time when we were fighting, and he nearly took off his belt right there. Nobody affiliated with Silver has been let up to see me since. I thought it was hilarious, but Silver almost called for the old man's head."

Frost felt a growing apprehension at something Taya had said. "How many properties does Silver own in Clear Rock?"

"Dozens," Tick said. "Been buying up as much as he can. Even made me an offer on the bar."

"It really is a company town," Taya said. "He's a control freak—has to control as much of everything as he can. Soon it'll be all of Silver Rock."

Frost nodded and looked off. Glanced up at the flat-screen still playing *The Public Enemy*. Donald Cook opened his front door to greet James Cagney, only to watch his brother collapse dead on his face in their family's foyer. With all that money, all that power, all that cruelty, Frost wondered if he'd be able to best Silver when all was said and done. He'd faced his fair share of psychopaths and come out alive. But maybe these were the days when his luck finally ran dry, and he was indeed heading towards his own anonymous apple tree.

TWENTY

F rost's head began to throb. He rubbed his eyes and tried to shake off his incredible fatigue, but it was no use. The longest day was coming to an end, whether he was on board with its retirement or not. Discovering that Taya was safe—that she was alive —had released a wave of pent-up adrenaline within him, but now the wave was crashing upon a stony shore.

Frost drew in a deep breath. His brain felt like it didn't fit inside his skull. "Sixteen Huntington?"

"That's right," she said.

"Beneath the fireplace paneling," Frost said slowly, repeating as much for the opportunity to stay still just a moment longer as he was for the sake of his memory.

"Mm-hmm," Taya said. "Tick, you seen my purse?"

"Yeah, are we heading out?" Tick said, rising from the sofa and walking to the front hall closet.

"I'd say it's best you both stay put," Frost said. "Seems to be working so far."

"Well, *you* found us," Tick said. He opened the front hall closet and grabbed a small purse from the top shelf.

"I asked you if you'd seen my purse, Tick, not if you'd get it for me. The baby didn't break my legs," Taya said. Tick brought the purse to her anyway, and she pulled it from his hands. Tick looked unperturbed, and Frost guessed that he must be used to Taya's rougher edges by now.

"I devoted the past two days to tracking you down," Frost said, trying to maintain his train of thought.

"And I've got a murdered brother suggesting that Silver's similarly determined," Taya said, digging through her purse. "And if I remember right, you said that you found me by accident. I'm not taking my chances."

Frost stood, ignoring his brain's protests to remain seated. "Maybe so. But there's danger in moving, too. Plan a place to go to ground and take the quickest route possible there."

"Not like I was gonna grab a burger or anything on the way," Taya said. She pulled out a cluttered ring of keys from her purse. After a struggle, she removed a fob and unit key from the thicket of metal and handed them to Frost.

"It's 305," she said.

Frost took them. "Thanks. I'll get these back to you."

Taya smiled thinly. "Can't imagine I'll ever need them again."

She made to get up. Tick moved to her side to assist, but she pulled away from him. "Legs unbroken, remember?"

Tick shrugged and stepped away. Frost couldn't help but wonder exactly how their friendship worked. Tick would have seemed almost browbeaten, if Taya's growling had seemed to bother him in the least. Instead, he seemed just as relaxed as ever.

"It's all right," Frost said. "I'll let myself out."

Taya reached over and used Tick's shoulder to haul herself upward. Tick rolled his eyes. "I should get back down to bed anyway," she said.

"I'll get back to you once I've got more information. Just keep your heads low."

Taya nodded. "Thank you for your help, Mr. Johnson." She looked Frost in the eyes once, and even through his exhaustion, he saw that Taya carried with her a fearsome weariness in her soul. He had seen the same look in the military—men and women with souls so calloused that they expected no good and took the bad head-on. Lincoln's death was not game over for her. She couldn't let it be.

Frost surprised himself by holding out his hand for her to shake it. Judging by her arched eyebrow, Taya was surprised, too. She still took his hand and shook. Her hand was small but her grip was firm.

"We were starting to think just about everyone in this town had gone mad," Tick said. "Nice to see someone still knows which way is up."

Frost saw himself out, but not without first getting Tick's phone number. When he climbed into his truck, he took one long last look at Tick's house, still astounded that he'd had the good fortune of finding Taya before Silver or Treece. He hoped that good luck would hold, and that the two would keep themselves safe in the meantime. Then he gunned the ignition and drove away.

Clear Rock crouched beneath that most lonesome time of night—an hour of dead streets and absolute silence. Traffic lights turned for no one, signaling only to the breeze and the dark. Frost drove on and fought off sleep, struggling to keep his thoughts in order.

His tired mind blended his memories together, mixing past and present. He thought of the hawk picking at the roadkill, but the corpse in the road belonged to Lincoln Dane. He thought of the self-storage unit, where Taya waited inside with a mug of tea and a box cutter while Treece prepared to raise the massive metal door and discover her. He thought of Sarah, dead of an overdose, a tattoo needle in her arm still buzzing and struggling to inscribe the hopeless painting from her wall into her skin.

Frost turned on the radio to try to wake himself up a little more. Ozzy Osbourne launched from his car stereo mid-verse, and although it did few favors for his already aching head, "War Pigs" shook him back to reality. He turned his mind to the present. Silver was a monster, Taya had said. Frost considered the monsters he'd crossed in the past. Zahir, Crane. They hadn't defeated Frost yet, though God knew they'd tried. But he couldn't keep moving with the weight of their gaze on his shoulders. Taya's apartment would have to wait. He needed to sleep.

Frost parked behind the Black Lotus and pulled the spare key from the mailbox. He entered the darkened shop and climbed to the second floor. Frost opened her door as slowly and silently as possible.

Inside, Sarah lay asleep on the Murphy bed. The moonlight shone through the open curtains, parting the dim blue shadows with a soft light. Frost took his shoes off and slipped out of his jacket as quietly as he could. He walked to the bed and stared down at Sarah, whose sides rose and fell gently as she slept.

Frost knew that there was something he should feel for her. She was haunted, but her past had made her capable. She was bright despite her demons, and she responded to injustice by meeting it head-on. She was beautiful, dangerous, and full of life. Frost knew it and knew it should make him feel for her. But he could barely feel as it was.

And once Taya was safe, she would be in his rearview mirror whether he liked it or not.

He looked at her. In this moment, the withering day was behind them both. The softness of Sarah's bed lay before. The promise of rest alongside Sarah's warmth swept aside her regrets. Frost took off his clothes and climbed in bed in his undershirt and Jockeys. He moved across the bed and put his arm over Sarah from behind. She gave a small, pleased moan and reached for his hand.

"Wasn't sure you'd come," she whispered, her eyes still closed.

"Sorry to keep you waiting," Frost murmured.

"You must be exhausted," she said.

"Mm. I'm practically sleepwalking."

"Then take a load off, slugger. Rest your weary head. There'll be work aplenty in the morning."

Frost waited for her to say something else, but she had fallen asleep holding his hand. He was left to think on the warmth he couldn't return in the last moments before joining her in sleep.

―――――

The water fell hot and hard on Frost's back, the pressurized nozzle kneading out knots in his shoulders. He stood with one hand against the shower tile, leaning his head down, letting the water run over him for several minutes. It'd been a while since he'd had a proper shower, and he relished the luxury. He scrubbed deep and massaged his tight muscles where he could reach them. He did his best to keep his stitches dry, angling the showerhead so as not to douse Sarah's handiwork.

He finished showering, brushed his teeth, and indulged in a quick shave. He threw on some clean clothes from his truck and went out to greet Sarah.

She'd just finished making breakfast: Scrambled eggs, crisp bacon, and thick Texas toast which awaited a plate of butter and a jar of preserves. Two cups of black coffee steamed beside each plate. Frost set his bag down near the door and took a seat on one of the counter barstools.

"Smells great," he said. Nobody had made him a meal in quite some time.

"Thanks. You take milk or sugar?" Sarah asked.

"No, black's great," Frost said. "Hot sauce, maybe?"

"Sure," Sarah said.

She turned and went to the cabinet and pulled out a small bottle of Tabasco. She set it down in front of Frost and he shook a few dabs onto his eggs.

"How'd last night go with Tick?" Sarah asked, before taking a bite of toast.

"Well, it seems you're not the only girl in town he's got a soft spot for."

Sarah's eyes went wide. "You're kidding. Taya was there?"

Frost nodded. "He's been hiding her. You were right about the pregnancy—that's one of the reasons why she ran. He lied about the drinking to throw us off." He proceeded to fill Sarah in on everything he'd learned the previous night.

Sarah set her fork down when Frost stopped speaking and sat back for a minute. She didn't say anything for a long time. Frost let her set her own pace. He knew how overwhelming this all was to hear, especially for someone who'd lived in Clear Rock her whole life. To have a drug cartel enter your quiet town and within short order make it a hub for national distribution, all the while murdering good people who'd simply learned too much.

"Shit," Sarah said, almost under her breath.

It sounded like a resignation to Frost and it surprised him. It was as if she'd quelled the anger inside of her before it even had a chance to escape. As the clues fell into place, the reality of the situation seemed to be weighing down on her. Frost hoped that he wouldn't let it smother her.

"Okay, what's our first step?" Sarah asked after a deep breath. "What's the first thing we can do to start dismantling Silver?"

"Get Taya's phone," Frost said. "She hid it in her apartment. Her *other* apartment."

Sarah laughed and shook her head.

"It's sixteen Huntington. Do you know it?"

"Yeah, I know it. A girlfriend of mine lives there." She took a bite of toast.

Frost nodded. "Good. Taya gave me her keys, but she says the place is crawling with Silver's men. He doesn't own the place, but they're staked out and waiting for her to come back."

"Of course they are," Sarah said. "Well, I should be able to slip in just fine."

Frost sighed and Sarah narrowed her eyes.

"What's up? You suddenly find Tabasco particularly exasperating?" she asked.

"Sarah, I just—"

"Nope. Sorry, bud. I made breakfast, I get to break into the building. Front desk knows me, security guards know me. Nobody's going to bat an eye. You think you'll do any better?"

Frost didn't say anything.

"Didn't think so," Sarah said. "Eat your damn eggs."

TWENTY-ONE

The condo complex on Sixteen Huntington was a striking mid-rise building. Embossed with a pearl-colored exterior contoured by black window trimming, the five-story apartment stood out like a sore thumb against Clear Rock's squat skyline. The building boasted an outdoor park, an impressive fountain, and broad glass walls on its main floor that revealed an expansive foyer with a marble surveillance desk housing three security guards. For all the talk about Clear Rock being a small town, Frost thought, there sure were a lot of recent upscale developments. Silver's recent investments must have brought in a few housing interests.

Frost and Sarah sat parked across the street, taking in the property. Three men already stood at the security desk. One of them was Treece, flanked by two of his subordinates. The guards watched the three men impassively, their faces flat with disinterest.

Frost turned to Sarah, who was still staring at Treece.

"You said Treece doesn't know about the phone?" she asked.

"Taya didn't think so," Frost said.

"Hell of a coincidence that they show up here at the same time we do," Sarah muttered.

"They're probably trying to find us. We raided Taya's other apartment yesterday, and I was there twice. They know someone else is looking for her. For all they know, we might have information they don't."

"I mean, we do. But what do we do about the guys at the desk?"

"They're probably in the best situation we could ask for," Frost said. "If they're at the desk, they can't confront you until you're already inside the building. The guards can stop them while you're inside, and I can keep them busy once they leave. On the other hand, if they leave the desk, Treece and his goons go back to their stakeout position and can stop you from even entering the building."

"They might not even recognize me from the photo they took."

"Don't count on that. Treece, at least, knows about you from his relationship with your fiancé, and he could probably make you out from a decent enough description." Frost gestured to Sarah's tattoos. "You've got several distinguishing marks for his goons to report, even if the photo was bad. If he sees you, just keep walking. If he acts suspicious, I'll make a distraction while you look for the phone. With any luck, the security guards will help me clear them out."

Sarah nodded. "Okay, how about this: put your phone on vibrate. I'll call when I have the phone. If you don't answer, I'll assume something's wrong and either come down the back way or grab security. If not, we get away scot free and plan our next move."

Frost nodded, impressed. He hadn't realized how much he missed working in a team since he went into hiding.

"All right, it's settled. No risks, nothing reckless. Just in and out, if we can manage it."

169

Sarah stepped out of the car and strode toward the condos. Frost retrieved his binoculars and watched her walk in. As she opened the door, it seemed as though nobody took notice of her—the security guards and Treece's thugs were too busy arguing with one another. By Frost's guess, things were becoming heated, as one of the guards had risen from his seat. Frost's blood ran cold when he watched the guard gesture at the door in an attempt to get the thugs to leave, but relaxed when none of them turned in the direction he pointed to see Sarah crossing the lobby.

Sarah made her way for the elevator, and for a moment Frost thought that she was home free. But when she passed the security desk, one of the guards least invested in the conversation looked at her. Treece turned as he followed the guard's gaze, almost as an afterthought, but as he turned back to the conversation, his head snapped back in an obvious double-take. He nudged one of his men and gestured to Sarah, shouting something. Sarah didn't turn, and to her credit she kept a steady pace, but she knew it as well as Frost did: they had been made.

The elevator doors opened to admit her. One of the guards moved closer to the elevator in case Treece or his men decided to make a run for it. Frost took one last look at Sarah as the elevator doors closed, and he caught an uninterrupted glimpse of her widened eyes. The doors slid shut as she stared straight at Frost, willing him into action.

Frost was out of the car and running. As he had suspected, Treece's men started walking toward the lobby door. The best place to wait for Sarah would either be in their car or at the edge of the building nearest the parking lot, where the mostly-windowed lobby was shrouded by a wall of bushes. Frost could intercept them at either destination if he went to the bushes, and he pushed himself to cross the lawn before the men noticed him. He made it before all of them were even out the door, which gave him a moment to catch his breath.

"You sure that's her?" one of Treece's men asked.

"You're damn right I am," Treece snapped. "What, you think we'd go to all this trouble if I weren't? I think her man bought a bad dose from me a while back. She's probably trying to get me back by playing Nancy Drew to fuck me over."

"What a bitch," the other voice muttered.

"No fuckin' kiddin'," Treece growled.

Frost stepped as far back into the recesses of the bush as he could and crouched. He felt his handgun, pressed against his ribs at its proper place in his underarm holster and concealed beneath his jacket. Three against one. He might have given Treece a beating last time, but those odds were still long. If he couldn't make the most of the element of surprise again, he might have to draw on them.

Treece passed first, and he was too concentrated on the way forward to notice Frost. He was heading to his car. His henchmen, on the other hand, stopped at the corner, not two feet from where Frost crouched. Frost held his breath and didn't dare move a muscle. He wasn't going to budge until he saw Treece drive away.

"When do you think Silver's gonna buy this eyesore?" the first man asked.

"Dunno. I think the bigger question is how quick can he put those fuckers behind the front desk underground."

"Assholes."

"Yeah."

In the distance, the sound of a car door. Frost turned and watched the blue Chevelle that had haunted him throughout his stay in Clear Rock come to life. Frost shifted his weight on his feet.

"When do you think she's coming out?" the first man asked. He turned his head slightly toward his companion, and Frost saw the edge of a thick mustache jutting out over the man's lips.

"I dunno, maybe you can call and ask," the other man growled. Frost couldn't make out his face, but bright gold chains hanging from his neck and wrists were enough of an identifier.

Treece's car began to pull away. Frost prepared to attack Mustachio, who was slightly farther away but would be the most likely to see Frost coming. That would give him more time to strike at Goldilocks before the other man could retaliate. Just as soon as Treece left the parking lot.

And then Frost's phone vibrated.

"What was that?" Mustachio asked, turning to Frost. Before he could shift all the way around, Frost was up and moving. He planted a fist in the man's solar plexus, and he dropped to the ground, wheezing.

Goldilocks turned, but before he could, Frost planted a foot in the back of the man's knee with a crunch. The man howled and fell to the concrete, clutching at his leg. Frost turned back to Mustachio, who had regained his breath, and drove his fist into the man's throat. He wheezed, gasping at his windpipe. Frost almost felt bad about taking a page from Sarah's brutal fighting playbook. Almost. He dropped the man with one last blow to the temple, and then turned and drove his boot into Goldilock's stomach, twice, and once into his rib cage, where Frost heard cracking bone.

Then came the sound of tires, and Treece's car was driving straight for Frost. Frost drew his Glock, sucked in a breath, and squeezed the trigger. The bullet would have taken Treece straight through the nose if he hadn't swerved his car when he saw the gun. The bullet pierced the windshield, but Treece himself came away unharmed. The car peeled away, taking off down the road.

Frost patted the front of Mustachio's jacket for a cell phone, which he found in the inner pocket. He pulled the phone out and slipped it into his own jacket, while Goldilocks looked on in stunned horror.

"You follow me and I'm putting a bullet between your eyes," Frost snarled. Goldilocks could only reply with a terrified, pained gargle. Frost doubted he could. Whatever sound Goldilocks's knee had made, it wasn't the kind of sound that would let a man keep pace with someone like Frost. He reached over and searched through Goldilocks's pockets as well, retrieved the man's phone at gunpoint, and backed away.

Frost ran across the street and hopped into his truck. He watched Goldilocks try to shake Mustachio awake, but to no avail. After a moment, he dragged himself further into the parking lot and out of sight. Inside, the security guards tried to stop Sarah leaving the lobby, waving wildly in an attempt to convince her that it wasn't safe outside. She ignored them, having seen Frost in his truck, and strode confidently onto the manicured condo lawn.

"Piece of cake," she said, when she climbed into the car beside him.

Ten minutes later the two of them sat parked inconspicuously in a giant Walmart lot. They sat close together in the truck, scrolling through Taya's photo album on her phone. Frost stopped on the photograph of the barn quilt.

"That's the barn at the farmhouse," he said. "Where they're storing the shipments."

Frost scrolled over and landed on a video file. He looked over at Sarah. They both knew this was it. Frost hit play. They saw Silver blow the Sheriff away before Taya retreated from the window and the video abruptly ended. But Frost had noticed something that Taya had neglected to mention—something that she might not have noticed in the heat of the moment.

"Did you see who that was?" Frost said.

"You mean besides Andy and the Sheriff?" Sarah asked.

"Yeah, but I meant did you see who was with him?"

Sarah shook her head and looked back at the phone. Frost played the video file again and fast-forwarded to where Treece and the two men emerged with the bound Sheriff. He paused the video.

"There," Frost said.

He pointed to a face only partially obscured by the nighttime darkness, whom he had originally thought belonged to a man with a slim build.

"Jesus Christ," Sarah whispered. "She was *there*."

The figure wasn't a man at all. The slight frame in the video belonged to a woman, her cocksure face unmistakable. It was Sheriff Puck.

Sarah looked over at Frost and he could see her anger had returned anew. Her jaw was set and her eyes were narrow. Her fists balled around the fringe of her leather jacket.

Frost had had an inkling that Sheriff Puck had taken part in orchestrating her own promotion. But the confirmation—Puck's smiling face looking down over the former Sheriff's corpse—was still chilling. The grim reality had wrapped its bony fingers around them. It was a cruel, dark truth that Frost wished wasn't true. But there it was.

Clear Rock really was possessed in absolute. Silver owned the businesses, he owned the crime, and he owned the law. He could kill with impunity, whether it was a potential witness like Lincoln or the lead lawman like Sheriff Gomez. Or even a mistress like Taya and her unborn child.

"This doesn't change anything," Sarah whispered. "We're still gonna get these bastards. Right?"

"Right," Frost said.

The police were their enemies. Even if there were decent cops on the force—even if, say, Deputy Kim was on their side—it wouldn't matter. Silver, Treece, and Puck would silence any officer they thought might get in their way. And Frost couldn't risk reaching farther up the ladder to the state police or the FBI. If Crane got tipped off to where he was, he'd be dead within twelve hours, and no use to anyone. Especially not Taya or Sarah, whose death warrant would have already been signed.

Frost remembered the black town car that had pulled up beside him in front of Taya's brownstone, and wondered if Crane wasn't onto him already.

But they had the phone. They had Treece running scared. They had tools, a lead, and bargaining chips. Frost was reminded of something that Brakespeare had said to him a few times when the pressure of endless combat zones far from home had begun to wear on them both. It was supposed to be a quote from Churchill, but even that might have been apocryphal. Still, it was just as good a guiding star as ever.

If you're going through hell, you might as well keep going.

TWENTY-TWO

Frost and Sarah pulled up in front of Tick's house. The afternoon sun had sunk lower on the horizon, casting stark lonely shadows upon the neighborhood. Sunrays fell through the elm trees that lined the street, its thinned autumnal foliage pleasingly backlit like descending spirits. The calmness of the late summer belied the town's murky underbelly.

Now that they had her phone, they needed to get Taya to safety. With Silver and Treece and the local police all stacked against her, hiding out at Tick's was no longer an option. Since their parting, he hoped they had taken his advice and gotten the hell out of Dodge.

Frost and Sarah looked towards the house. The front door was open, hanging off its bottom hinge, the wood trim around the lock faceplate splintered.

"Oh, God," Taya whispered.

Frost said nothing. He pulled his Glock from its holster, withdrew the magazine, and thumbed in the missing bullet from the earlier firefight. He returned the magazine, pulled the slide, and released it when he saw brass in the chamber.

He looked over at Sarah. If the gun bothered her, she gave no sign. Instead, her gaze kept wandering to the shattered door. Frost thought about how he could reassure her, but realized that there might not be anything to reassure her about. He could walk into Tick's place and find both Tick and Taya laid out with bullets in their skulls.

"I'll be right back," he said.

Frost got out of the truck and ran towards the house, keeping low. He raised his gun as he reached the front door, approaching the doorway at an angle. A loud pop rang out and Frost jumped to the side to flatten himself against the façade of the house.

He shook his head, disappointed with himself. The noise had come from the television. Tick must've been watching some old western on Turner Classic Movies. Frost could hear more shots from the TV now: horses galloping, men whooping, and the masculine boom of Gary Cooper.

Frost leaned back and glanced into the living room. He expected to see the place turned over like Lincoln and Taya's apartments, but it wasn't. It was as neat and tidy as it had always been, but for one jarring difference.

Tick lay dead on the living room floor, a halo of blood pooled around him from a ragged bullet wound in his head. *You expected this,* Frost thought, his gaze lingering a moment too long on the dead bartender. *You were ready for it. Don't let it overtake you. Forward, soldier.*

Frost swept through the house as quickly as he dared, checking his corners and watching for movement. Eventually his search took him downstairs, to Taya's room in the basement.

The basement was a carpeted den with a sofa and television. A double bed sat in the corner next to an old chifforobe. Bowls and food packets were scattered across every surface, along with a number of weapons—a bat leaning against the bed, her box cutter on the sofa, and a can of mace on the television. There were two doors on the far side of the room, and Frost checked both before examining the room further. One was a bathroom with a small shower. The other was a concrete cold storage room with a full shelf of nonperishables and a large boiler. They were both empty. Further exploration only confirmed what Frost had suspected.

Taya was gone.

Frost came back into the main room and looked over it. The television was still on, its volume low. A number of drawers of the chifforobe were open, and clothes were spread all over the bed and floor. She'd left in a hurry. Yet Frost couldn't tell if she'd done so of her own volition or if she'd been taken.

He thought of the last words she'd said to him. *Can't imagine I'll ever return.*

Frost heard footsteps upstairs. He hadn't yet checked the master bedroom or the bathroom. He ran upstairs with his gun drawn, but saw that it wasn't Taya. It was Sarah. She stood in the threshold of the front door, staring down at Tick's dead body.

Frost thought to comfort her, but he turned and went down the hallway first. He swept the bedroom and the bathroom before returning to Sarah. He lowered his gun and pulled her in with his free arm and hugged her tight.

"Come on," he said. "Taya's gone."

Frost looked at the television. The classic western *Garden of Evil* was playing. He wondered why he could concentrate more on the film than the corpse of a man who had traded friendly words with him not even a day ago.

"They took her," Sarah said.

"Seems like the most likely option," Frost said.

Sarah looked at Tick again, hardening herself to the grisly image.

"First Lincoln, now Tick. We can't let them get away with this," she said.

"We won't," Frost said, holding her tighter, hoping that she couldn't feel his numbness through the tightness of their embrace. "But there's nothing more to be done here."

"We can't just leave him like this," Sarah said.

"I'm sorry," Frost said, "but what else can we do? We can't call the police."

She drew in a hesitant breath, but nodded after a moment. "Okay," she said.

"We'll find Taya," Frost said. "Either Silver has her, or she's on the run."

"Or she's…" Sarah said, looking at Tick again.

"We don't know that yet," Frost said. "There's no blood and no sign of a struggle downstairs. There's a slim chance, but she might well have run off. Maybe she left and Tick stayed, and he got a bullet for his troubles. But if she's alive, any speculation to the contrary won't do anything for her. We need to operate on the assumption that she's alive and work on finding her until we know otherwise."

"Okay," Sarah said, shaking her head as though to clear it. "How are we going to find her?"

Frost stared down at Tick.

"We work the angles we've got."

TWENTY-THREE

Frost and Sarah crossed Tick's front lawn and walked towards the Ranger. A crow cawed from a telephone line and Sarah looked up at it. Frost followed her gaze. It sat perched upon the wire, staring down at them. *It knows that we're leaving Tick's body behind,* Frost thought. *It knows we both think his corpse is just another piece of meat.*

"When I was a kid, sometimes I thought that cawing crows were trying to hex me. Like they were a witch in disguise, or something," Sarah said, her voice distant.

"Only a little weirder than what I was thinking," Frost said. Sarah smiled a little. Frost did too. He didn't think that either of them meant it.

Frost opened the passenger door for Sarah and shut it behind her as she got in. He walked around the front of the truck to get his own door. As soon as he wrapped his fingers around the handle, the window exploded.

The nighttime calm shattered with it, the empty suburban street echoing with the sound of the gunshot. Sarah flattened herself below the edge of the window, forcing her body into a smaller target. Frost jumped inside the truck, using the door for cover as another shot rang out. It sure as hell wasn't a Turner Classic Movie this time. The bullet pelted the steel siding of the Ranger, but didn't punch through the door. Frost reached out for the handle and slammed the door shut behind him as another shot embedded itself in the frame of the truck. Frost dug his keys into the ignition, threw the truck in drive, and slammed on the gas.

"Keep your head down," Frost said, speeding off down the street.

"Who's shooting?" Sarah asked, unexpectedly calm.

Frost looked into his rearview mirror and saw a smaller gray car pull out from a line of parked cars. A coupe, maybe. Frost took a right corner fast and the Ranger nearly lifted off its passenger-side wheels as it turned the street. He checked his mirror and saw the car take the corner just as hard as he had. It was right on top of them.

Sarah turned carefully and looked through the camper shell at the street behind them.

"Is it Andy?" she said.

"I don't know," Frost said, "but it ain't his Chevelle. Keep your head down."

Frost took another sharp corner. Checked his mirror. The coupe was gaining on them.

Whoever was in that car had been waiting for them. Whether or not Taya had gotten away or been captured herself, someone still cared enough to set a trap and kill them. It wasn't the best trap, to be sure —Zahir's sniper would have to give the guy some trade secrets on ambush marksmanship when they both met in hell—but Silver had spent time and manpower on the bet that Sarah and Frost would come back. Seemed like they had gotten under the man's skin.

Frost turned his mind to how he'd lose the tail. He was leaving the suburbs and approaching downtown Clear Rock. He glanced in the rearview mirror. He couldn't outrun the car. It was only closing the gap on him now. Maybe he could take the chase off-road? His 4x4 could create some distance over rougher terrain. He could have Sarah direct him, but with the coupe gaining on them, he couldn't bank his hopes that they would find favorable terrain before they were caught.

"What part of downtown are we headed into? Anywhere we can lose this guy?" Frost asked.

There was a pause, and the only sound was Frost's revving engine and the sound of the coupe behind them.

"Sarah?" he asked, gritting his teeth.

"Yeah. Yeah, there's gonna be an alleyway on your left, right off of Main, between a Dairy Queen and an antique shop. Take that, and I'll show you where to go from there."

He skidded around another corner onto Main Street and saw the narrow access alleyway Sarah had described. Frost took it, his Ranger bouncing up over the uneven lip as they entered. Frost kept the car steady, grimacing as the side mirror on his truck scraped against the wall. It was a tight fit. Losing their pursuer wasn't a guarantee. He might have to find a way to take the car out.

He checked the rearview once more. The coupe slowed ever so slightly to take the corner into the alley. Frost had gained a few dozen yards in the interim. He needed every inch he could get.

"There," Sarah said, pointing forward. Frost looked towards the end of the alleyway up ahead to see a wall of dense woodland lining the opposite side of the street that they alley emptied into. He floored it. It was now or never.

Frost burst out of the alley and slammed his brakes and skidded sideways onto the two-lane road. He had two choices: he could take his chances with continuing the pursuit, or he could take an even bigger risk and stop this quickly.

"Sarah, do you trust me?" Frost asked.

"Yeah," Sarah said, her eyes forward and her jaw set.

"Then I'm gonna need you to run."

———

The gray coupe pulled up just in time for the driver to catch Sarah disappearing into the woods. The driver stepped out and nearly lost his balance as he put his weight on his injured leg. As he did so, a gold chain on his wrist caught the light of a nearby streetlamp. Goldilocks looked into the woods and cursed to himself. He laid his right hand, still holding his handgun, on the roof of the car and retrieved a brand-new phone from his jacket.

When the screen lit up for him to dial in a call, two gunshots barked out into the night. The bullets struck Goldilocks center mass, dropping him beside his coupe.

Frost rose up from the ditch on the opposite side of the road. He sprinted across the asphalt to the prone man, who looked up at Frost with terror in his eyes for the second time that day. He reached feebly for the Sig Sauer that lay on the gravel beside him. Frost put a bullet in his head.

Frost went back to his truck.

"Are you all right?" he called out.

"You just up and executed him, huh? We doing that now?" Sarah's voice drifted back. She walked out from behind a tree not five yards from where Goldilocks had lost her in the tree line and strode back to the truck.

"Is that an issue?" Frost asked.

She cast a dead-eyed look down at the dead thug. "Fella working for the guy who killed my fiancé and the guy poisoning my hometown? I'll get over it."

Frost winced at her reaction, but only because he saw some of his own coldness in her. He wouldn't wish his hollowness on anyone, and especially not Sarah. He slipped wordlessly into the driver's seat and shut the door as Sarah climbed in beside him. He reversed the truck to give himself some room, drove around the body, and sped off down the street. The corpse and abandoned car glowed red in the taillights, derelict on the side of the road. In time the light faded, and they were only vague silhouettes in Frost's rearview.

It would be fine. Surely, the local Sheriff's Department would take care of it.

TWENTY-FOUR

They drove in silence for a long time. Frost felt like he should say something to Sarah about killing a man in front of her, but he didn't know what to say. He wasn't sure what he could offer, by way of comfort or even explanation. He wasn't even sure if she needed any. This was what she had signed up for, wasn't it?

"Are you hungry?" he asked, finally breaking the silence.

Sarah looked over at him, her brow furrowed, apparently confused by his question.

"What?"

"Are you hungry?"

"It honestly hadn't occurred to me."

"What's on your mind?" Frost asked.

"I'm honestly not sure. It's all… kind of a blur. Today's a blur. Tick and Taya and that other guy are a blur, too. I'm not really sure how you can be thinking about food right now."

"Less about food and more about eating, if that makes sense," Frost said. "We haven't eaten since this morning, and I figured it might be a good idea. Until this is over, we might not have much spare time to maintain ourselves or our tools. We have to take the opportunity when we can."

Sarah nodded and looked back out the driver's side window. Frost hoped that she wasn't losing her determination. Her motivations had been noble, and nobility hardly intersected with doing what needed to be done. Like shooting wounded men, for example. She had been an invaluable partner up to this point, and losing her to apathy would put them both in danger.

The woodland passed by outside, and Frost was buffeted by tree-scented wind through his shattered window. Sarah straightened in her seat and pointed ahead, toward the upcoming Hognose River.

"Pull over up here," Sarah said, without looking at him. "Just before the bridge. There's a public lot."

Frost pulled off onto the short access road before the bridge. It led to a small parking lot beside the river that had been set up with a few picnic tables and trash bins. A polished wooden sign crediting the Clear Rock Conservation Society for the nearby trails stood by the entrance. Closer to the bank, separate biking and walking paths lead away from the lot in opposite directions. Unlike the condominiums and brownstones, this little lot with its community-maintained nature trails and well-worn charcoal grill felt like the true heart and soul of Clear Rock.

Frost parked in a space at the far end of the lot and turned off the truck. There were only two other vehicles parked in the lot, and both seemed empty. He looked over at Sarah. She stared down at her lap, still silent.

Frost put his hand on her shoulder. Her back stiffened, as though uncomfortable. Frost removed his hand. After a moment, Sarah turned and got out of the truck and shut the door behind her. Frost did the same.

He found her leaning against the rear of the truck, staring out over the river. She was shaking slightly. After a minute, Frost got out of the truck and walked around to her side, but making sure to give her plenty of room. He didn't say anything to her, hoping that she would lead the conversation.

"Just... talk to me?" Sarah said, finally. So much for that hope.

"About what?" Frost said.

"About anything."

Frost breathed in, trying to think of what to say. So much of his personal interaction since the accident had just been other people taking the lead. Even Lincoln, his first pleasant conversation since he had taken to the road, had filled the gaps in the silence for him. The only thing he could think of to distract her was telling her about one of his own coping mechanisms.

"I have a system. When I was in the Army, it was how I dealt with crises. They say that adrenaline can poison you—when you come down from an adrenaline high, the chemicals in your body that try to de-escalate you literally rot your brain. It destroys your memory and your ability for reasoning. Once upon a time, those were more important to me than anything else in the world. So I resolved to analyze my crises before my mind could blow them out of proportion and send me into unnecessary spirals of fight-or-flight."

Sarah looked over at him. She didn't seem concerned or confused, just contemplative.

"So I tried to categorize each situation using the information at hand. I used a scale from one to five, with one being the least threatening and five being the most likely to get me killed."

"What level were we back there?" Sarah asked.

"Probably about a Four."

"A *Four?*" she asked, scoffing in disbelief. "You almost caught a bullet, Kevin."

"I've been in tighter spots. The shooter was practically an amateur, even though he got the drop on us. Honestly, the biggest danger was a vehicle collision during the chase."

Sarah nodded, but her raised eyebrows still suggested that she was incredulous.

"You spend years overseas in a Spec Ops fireteam and you get some confusing new perspectives on just what it means to be in danger," Frost said, shrugging.

"Spec Ops?" she asked. "Is that how you got those scars?"

Frost nodded. "Bomb disposal."

Sarah stayed silent for a moment, and Frost heard the peace of nature around them both. The rush of the river, the wind through the trees, the insects and nocturnal fauna all blended into a nightly countryside ceremony that he had missed from his time as a child.

"Kevin, you asked me before if I trusted you," she said.

"I did."

"Do you trust me?"

Frost thought for a moment, considering everything. He had trusted her in plenty of tight spots over the past few days. It was the most trust he had afforded anyone in quite some time.

"I do."

A cold breeze shifted over the river water and washed over them, blowing wisps of Sarah's hair across her face. She brushed them back with her hand and met Frost's gaze.

"Then tell me your real name," she said.

Frost stared back for a moment before breaking eye contact. He thought about lying to her. Again. Telling her his name really was Kevin Johnson or giving her another fake identity. But he knew she'd be able to tell the difference. She couldn't possibly endanger him more with the knowledge of his real name than he was endangering himself day by day. And, as she had made him state himself, he trusted her.

Frost looked back at her.

"All right."

———

The bullet-scarred Ranger sat in an inconspicuous spot around the side of Rocky's Diner, a real greasy spoon with all-day breakfast, bottomless coffee, and the scent of fresh-baked cherry pie wafting through its interior. Frost and Sarah sat across from one another in a maroon vinyl booth, menus on the table, steaming mugs in front of them.

Frost stared down into his black coffee.

"Don't think your name's hiding in there," Sarah said.

Frost looked up and smiled thinly. He had distracted her enough by suggesting again that they get something to eat while he told his story. Time to rip off the bandage.

"Look, it's hard. I haven't spoken to anyone who knows my real name for a long time. Giving it out isn't exactly second nature anymore."

"Are you on the lam or something? Or do you tangle with people like Silver on a regular basis?" she asked. Her voice was low, but Frost still checked to see if anyone in the bar had heard her use Silver's name.

"More the former than the latter," said Frost. "I've been using a fake name because Silver ain't the only psycho I've crossed paths with. I don't say that to brag—I say that because you knowing my name is a real and present danger to us both, all right? Even after this conversation, I'm still Kevin Johnson."

"Of course."

Frost exhaled and nodded to himself. He stared into Sarah's eyes, steeling himself for the leap of faith.

"My real name is Marion Frost," he said.

Sarah looked at him and nodded and blew on her tea. After a moment she responded.

"Marion, huh?" She stared at him, her expression illegibly casual. "Well, at least I know you're not lying. Nobody would choose a name like Marion as an alias."

Frost shrugged defensively. Of all the reactions he was expecting from Sarah, he probably should have guessed she would rib him— even at a time like this.

"Jesus. You going to bust my balls about it?"

"I didn't say anything," Sarah said, using her mug of tea to hide a smile.

"Yeah, well, now you might see why I go by Ion," Frost said, pronouncing the word as *Ian*. "Going to school with a name like Marion was hell on earth."

"I bet."

Frost took a sip of his coffee. He felt compelled to share more, emboldened by Sarah's reaction.

"My father Harry was a huge Cleveland Browns fan," he continued. "Ever since he was a kid. The guy worshipped their fullback, Marion Motley. Thought he was God's gift to football. And if the name was good enough for Motley, it was good enough for me."

Sarah nodded. "Are you close with your parents?"

Frost shook his head. "No. You?"

Sarah shrugged. "My mom's over on the Wind River reservation. Her and my stepfather moved there years ago. We're all right, I guess. See each other on holidays."

"Is your mother Native American?" Frost asked.

"My stepfather is," Sarah said, sipping her tea. "Arapaho."

"Hard life," Frost said, remembering a fellow Cadet's stories of growing up on a Navajo reservation in Arizona without running water.

"They make a hard life good, despite how the government treats them. You always know you have a family." She paused. "You still talk to your mom?"

Frost shook his head. "Died of cancer."

"Sorry to hear. My father passed, too," Sarah said. "Liver disease. You still speak to your father?"

Frost shook his head. "He died in a bar fight years ago."

"Jesus."

"Yeah. Six months after I enlisted," Frost said. He shrugged. "I suppose it was poetic, though, in a way. He died how he lived."

"Fighting?" Sarah said.

"Drunk," Frost said.

The waitress returned to their table, pen and pad in hand. Frost was thankful for the break in conversation, as talking about his past and his family had almost left him feeling winded. He didn't know if it was his isolation or his brain injury, but emotional disclosure seemed to take more energy than the fistfight. Frost ordered a BLT with fries, and Sarah ordered a chicken fried steak with hash browns and extra gravy. The waitress gave Sarah a judgmental cock of one eyebrow at her order, took their menus, and was off again. Sarah flipped the waitress off as soon as she turned her back, and Frost couldn't help but laugh.

"So, these people who are after you," Sarah said. "Is that why you live out of your truck? And why you're in such a hurry to get out of Clear Rock?"

"Partly. I've never stayed in the same town more than a day or two, if I can help it. Always been restless."

Sarah nodded and took a sip of tea. Then her head jerked back up, as though she had suddenly remembered something.

"Oh! I meant to show you," she said, setting down her mug. She pulled out Taya's phone from her pocket and began scrolling through a few of her old photos. "I was looking through Taya's phone in front of Tick's place, and I think I found something."

She stopped scrolling and handed the phone to Frost.

"Look at that," she said.

Frost looked at the photo. It was a slightly blurred picture taken at an odd angle, showing a dark desk with a closed laptop and papers spread across it. In the background, he could make out a blurry cabinet. What looked like maybe a wet bar in the corner.

"Look at the desk," Sarah said. "The map."

Frost rotated the photo upside down and zoomed in to get a better look. A large map of Clear Rock sat unfolded on the desk. A red marker line zig-zagged down a dozen conjoined streets.

"Taya obviously snapped that in secret, right? The angle and everything," Sarah said. "It's gotta be something important."

"Might be Silver's office, or another distribution center," Frost said. "And what's this route?"

Sarah smiled. "That's the route for the Clear Rock Founding Day Parade," she said.

The two of them paused as the waitress returned with their plates. Frost poured some ketchup on his fries and Sarah buried her hash browns in black pepper in silence as they waited for her to walk away.

"So, tell me about the parade," he said when the waitress was out of earshot.

"It happens every year," Sarah said. "A big deal for the town. There's a small music festival, food trucks, carnival rides. Even some tourists coming in and spending money. People from all over—Idaho, Colorado, Utah."

"How many people attend?" Frost asked.

"A lot. Thousands, on a good year. Sheriff Gomez would always get a few of the surrounding municipalities to lend him officers for the weekend to handle the drunks and direct traffic. Why, what are you thinking?"

Frost took a sip of coffee. "The town's biggest attraction, thousands of outsiders coming in from all over? Out of state vehicles and plates? I think this is what we're looking for."

"The parade?"

"It's his golden opportunity to offload a massive shipment. And it's our chance to take him apart."

TWENTY-FIVE

Frost leaned forward in his seat, feeling more excited than he had in a week. "It's Little Chicago, like you said. Only Chicago distributers can offload their product with relative ease, under the radar, because it's a city of the world. Trucks and drivers coming in from all over the country. The amount of product Silver's got sitting in that barn, the seeming regularity of the shipments he and Treece talked about in their emails—this is a giant wholesale deal."

"But if Silver's got all of Clear Rock on his payroll, why would he care either way?" Sarah asked.

"There's the FBI and the Wyoming Highway Patrol, for one. There's a weigh station at nearly every interstate border. Trucks are required to check in. The influx of out-of-state trucks headed for little Clear Rock would raise red flags."

"But not if they've got a parade festival to attend."

Frost nodded. "Exactly. And if I were Silver, I'd just have the buyers register legitimate businesses for the parade. Mainway attractions, carnival rides, food trucks. Just seal things up that much tighter."

Frost took another bite of his sandwich and washed it down with another sip of his coffee.

"So when is the parade?" he asked.

"Tomorrow," Sarah said.

"*Tomorrow?*" Frost said. "Jesus Christ."

"I know."

Frost stared out the window. A brilliant red sun ignited the darkened horizon. Cirrus wisps of heliotrope, tangerine, and baby pink bled into the retreating night sky.

He had one day to learn what he could about the festival and how Silver had gotten his claws into its workings. All he had to do was work at the problem piece by piece and item by item. He could sever supply lines, remove important operators, and sabotage areas of operation. But he was solely lacking in tools and manpower.

One massive loose end was Taya and her unborn child. If she had truly been kidnapped by Silver, they were either dead or in severe danger. Just as bad, Taya—as an objective—was completely perpendicular to any plans Frost could make to stop Silver's distribution plan. Unless Frost got fantastically lucky, he could only choose one: save Taya, or stop the deal. Even then, he might not accomplish either.

You walked out of that desert alive, he told himself. *Plenty of people would have called that impossible*. There was still time to do a few more impossible things.

"Right. So, Silver has Taya," Frost said. "It's safe to assume that. If he doesn't, she's safe anyway. And we know he's going to be in town for the deal tomorrow. So, he's either at the farmhouse or his mansion. Taya's already compromised the farmhouse in multiple ways. It makes the most sense for Silver to keep her in the mansion."

"Okay, that makes sense. I know the mansion's apparently up in the mountainside backwoods, but I don't know where exactly," Sarah said.

"Taya said it was on Lafayette Drive. You know it?"

Sarah raised her eyebrows. "Huh. Yeah, I know it. It's a winding mountain road. Spans the entire range. I don't recall ever seeing any houses, but I haven't spent a whole lot of time up there."

"We'll make the mansion our priority, then. Scout it out and make a plan once we know the lay of the land. It won't be easy, and we may need to play this by the seat of our pants, but I think that we can do this." Frost wasn't at all sure that they could pull this off, but he wanted to be confident for Sarah's sake.

Sarah smiled. "Okay. Awesome," she said, wiping her mouth with her napkin. "I'm just going to run to the washroom, and we'll get out of here."

"Great. I'll settle up and wait in the truck," Frost said.

Sarah rose and disappeared into the back washroom. Frost finished the last of his lunch, paid their bill, and went outside to his truck. No sooner had he opened the driver's side door than a familiar voice called out.

"Mr. Johnson."

Frost turned to see Sheriff Puck walking across the parking lot towards the diner entrance, flanked by Officers Burr and Warren. Her dark Interceptor and their officers' patrol car were parked across several rows of spaces. Frost tensed, wondering just what a crooked sheriff could get away with in broad daylight.

"Hope you got a chance to try some of Rocky's famous apple pie," Sheriff Puck said. She walked up to Frost and squared her shoulders, her hands on her hips. The cocksure gesture would have been laughable due to the difference in their sizes, but she could have her officers on him in a moment. "Best in the state, if you ask me," she said.

Frost examined Burr and Warren, noting their stiff shoulders and the slight bend to their elbows. The duo was poised to draw their weapons if necessary. Frost assessed the scene as a Level Three, Crapshoot, only because there was a chance they wouldn't kill him right there in the parking lot in broad daylight.

"What can I do for you?" Frost said.

"You can tell me what the fuck you're still doing in my town," Sheriff Puck said. "I told you if you kept sniffing around the Danes, there'd be trouble. So, why did you take that as permission to get in a brawl outside of Taya's studio?"

Frost wondered how she'd found him. There was either a tracer on his truck, or she had tracked him down from Goldilocks's body with some uncharacteristically thorough detective work. Frost suspected the former.

"I was just on my way out," Frost said, turning towards his truck. "Stopped for a bite."

"Hold on there, pal," Sheriff Puck said.

Frost's body tensed, preparing for what might happen next. He turned back to face her.

"You ain't going anywhere, you hear me?" Sheriff Puck said. "You had your chance for that, and you pissed it down the drain. Now, you turn your back on me again, and you're going to wish you hadn't."

"So, what?" Frost said. "You going to arrest me for loitering?"

Sheriff Puck smiled and looked him over. "Those head-breakers at Rawlins are going to love that pretty mouth of yours."

Frost stared into her eyes. She was savoring this. She had big plans for him.

"Tell me, Mr. Johnson, do you know a Gordon Howard?"

"I don't," Frost said.

"Folks round here call him Tick."

They were going to pin Tick's murder on him. They could take him into custody, likely have him killed before he even reached the county lock-up. Bury him somewhere out on the plains beneath another anonymous tree.

The grim reality of his situation began to sink in. He couldn't simply fight them all off. Burr and Warren were practically ready to draw. They'd shoot him dead if he made the slightest aggressive move. He'd have to actually kill them if he was going to escape. All three of them, right there, right then. The deck was certainly stacked against him, but he could do it, his Glock still with three live rounds in the magazine. He'd need to be perfect, but he could do it.

But he wouldn't. If he killed three police officers, he'd have the entire state police force on top of him within an hour. The FBI, too. And even if he somehow extricated himself from that mess, Crane would follow soon after. Besides, even if Sheriff Puck had well-proven herself to be cold-blooded and vile beyond measure, that didn't necessarily mean Burr and Warren shared her guilt.

Frost decided to go quietly. He looked at the two officers and then back at Sheriff Puck.

"You even going to bother with the Miranda rights?" he said.

"Turn around," Sheriff Puck said, "and place your hands behind your back."

Frost did, and Puck pulled her handcuffs from her utility belt.

"He makes one move," she said to Officers Burr and Warren, "and you make sure to put a bullet in his head."

Sheriff Puck stepped towards Frost and handcuffed him. She shoved him hard against his truck and began patting him down.

"Mr. Johnson, I'm placing you under arrest for the murder of Gordon 'Tick' Howard."

She patted down Frost's ankles and legs and soon came across his gun tucked into its holster. She held it up for the other officers to see. "Burr?"

Officer Burr stepped forward and took the gun from Sheriff Puck. He walked to the back of the truck to disassemble it for safe transport. Puck turned Frost around to face her.

She smiled at him, evidently enjoying every minute of his defeat. "Non-residents require a license to carry a concealed weapon, Mr. Johnson," Sheriff Puck said.

"Still smells like gunpowder," Officer Burr said from the back of the Ranger. Sheriff Puck glanced over. "Been discharged recently."

Sheriff Puck whistled and smiled at Frost. "A recently discharged nine-millimeter handgun, Mr. Johnson?"

Frost didn't answer. He wouldn't give her anything else to use against him.

"Mr. Howard was found with a nine-millimeter bullet in his skull. And my money's on the county coroner retrieving the same ammunition from Lincoln Dane's body during his autopsy."

Frost nodded. Of course, he thought. If they were going to pin one murder on him, why not all of them? He wondered where Sarah was, and if she had elected to stay hidden. If so, it was the smartest move. There wasn't anything stopping Puck from implicating Sarah, too.

"Now, I sure hope we don't find Taya Dane dead, too, Mr. Johnson," Sheriff Puck said. "I mean, you've already got two possible murder charges hanging over your head. So, if you know where Taya is, know anything at all about her whereabouts, then it'd be a lot better for you if you just saved us the trouble and told us outright."

Frost stared at Puck. He didn't say a word. He'd do what he could to keep her on the line, and maybe she'd keep him alive long enough to make a difference.

"All right, Mr. Johnson. Have it your way." Sheriff Puck grabbed Frost under his forearm and marched him across the lot towards their parked police vehicles. Her officers followed in their wake, and Frost felt their glares boring holes in the back of his skull.

TWENTY-SIX

The Clear Rock Sheriff's Department station sat silhouetted against an iris-colored sky. The shadows bruised, the air growing cold, the lonesome howl of a coyote somewhere far out inside all that dark. Sheriff Puck ushered Frost into the back of the jailhouse connected to the broader station office on its west side. She walked him in past the small booking area with its single desk and few chairs and marched him down the short hallway towards the detention area. Inside were three identical empty cells, each separated by a concrete wall. They had a concrete floor with a concrete bed, a toilet and sink, and steel bars at their front. A thin pillow and wool blanket had been tossed on the bed as an apparent afterthought.

Sheriff Puck took Frost to the cell at the furthest end of the hallway. Frost saw that there didn't seem to be any cameras in the cells, nor even in this entire jailhouse section of the station. It seemed like a cartoonishly stupid security oversight, but he theorized that Puck probably enjoyed the carte blanche to toy with her prisoners.

Puck stopped Frost and searched her retractable keyring until she found the right key. She opened the door, ushered Frost into the cell, and locked it once more.

"Hands," she said.

Frost turned around and backed up towards the cell door and fed his handcuffed hands through the small slot set in the steel bars. Sheriff Puck fetched another key from her ring and removed his handcuffs.

Frost rubbed his wrists and looked at her. Belly of the beast. At least he had his hands back. Puck smiled.

"You're not even going to question me? Not even going to bother with the charade at all, are you?"

"Here's a question for you: on a scale of one to ten, how fucked do you think you are right now?" Sheriff Puck said.

"Is ten super safe, or super fucked?" Frost asked. Puck couldn't hate him much more than she already did, he figured.

But she didn't say a thing. She just stared Frost in the eyes and kept her cool.

"I'd get as comfortable as possible if I were you," she said. "These walls are going to be your world for a long while."

And without another word, she turned and walked back down the hallway. He heard Sheriff Puck give orders that he couldn't make out to an officer he couldn't identify. And then the backdoor opened and closed again. Frost wasn't sure how many remained in the office. Frost guessed it was likely Officer Burr and Warren that had remained. The Sheriff would be off finalizing arrangements for the parade. For the shipment.

Frost turned around and went to the concrete bed and sat upon it. His cell was windowless, but there was a single glass pane set high in the wall across the hallway from him. It offered a little light from the moon outside. Otherwise, the only light in the place came from the dim glow of a trio of overhead fixtures lining the hall.

Frost tuned his mind to Sarah. He hoped she'd keep a level head and not come anywhere near the station. Yet he hoped she wouldn't go anywhere near the farmhouse or the mansion either. He knew it would be suicide if she went there alone. These were very serious people, with tens of millions of dollars at stake. Hundreds, maybe.

Frost stood up and began pacing his cell. After all the adrenaline and action of the last two days, it was torturous to be tethered inside this small, dark box. Boxed in with nowhere to go, the running clock of the approaching parade ticking down in his mind like some grim metronome. Thoughts of Sarah and Taya bounced around in his head. Images of them being hurt, tortured, murdered, all while he stood powerless inside this gray room.

It reminded him of Afghanistan. Long days, weeks, sometimes even months of dull nothingness punctuated by brief bursts of life-and-death violence. The nothingness, the anticipation, was always the more torturous of the two scenarios—just the smooth highway before the inevitable nail in the road, and the anticipation ruined any peace he might have found.

Frost needed the action, the agency. He couldn't just be a passenger waiting for the next catastrophe. Frost could never stand the waiting, the nothingness. The helplessness to sit back and wait for chaos to come crashing down on you. It felt like being forced to stare at the blinking light on an IED receiver. Just waiting helplessly for it to go off in his face. Even if he tried and failed, the reality that he couldn't try weighed heavier on him than failure ever could.

Frost thought about the attempted murder in Zangabad. About Anderson and Dean and Peña. About Captain Robert Crane, the architect of all his suffering. He remembered the night at the barracks.

Frost sat awake in his shared second-floor room in the barracks headquarters at the Kandahar Airfield. He was reading David Butler's *The Fall of Saigon* by the faint light of a reading lamp clipped to the book's back cover. The warm night air flowed through the grated window beside him, creating a pleasant cross breeze.

Elsewhere, his new team was off getting drunk on the airfield boardwalk, a sprawling wooden promenade that at its height featured a KFC, a Nathan's World Famous, and a T.G.I. Fridays. Now, however, it had been reduced to a Kabob House, a coffee shop, and a generic Irish-style pub among a few other paltry offerings. The thirty-thousand servicemen that once populated the airfield had dwindled to fewer than three thousand.

Frost checked his wristwatch. It was nearly two in the morning. He'd typically have fallen asleep hours ago, but he couldn't stop thinking about what Brakespeare had said to him on their last mission together. The Zahir bounty on his head, the ambush at the adobe compound, the likelihood of a leak somewhere in the chain of command. Frost hadn't been able to get a decent night's sleep since. He knew there was a leak. Knew it to a certainty. He and Brakespeare were not meant to survive that night.

Two voices came from outside his window—the loud, self-assured, tumbling voices of the inebriated. Frost recognized them. It was Dean and Peña, back from the bar. Frost shut his book and set it down on the nightstand beside him.

"What time is it?" Peña asked.

Dean took a second. Checked his wristwatch, Frost assumed.

"Two," Dean said, laughing.

"Christ," Peña said. "We've only got three hours before Anderson picks us up."

"No point in heading to bed then, is there? You got any more of those amphetamines?"

"Fuck it," Peña asked. "It's nine hours to Gardez. We'll catch up on winks on the way. Pop a couple addys when we get there."

Frost heard something sloshing against glass.

"*Nine hours?* Jesus," Dean said. "You'd figure Anderson would've just secured us a chopper. Or the captain could have."

"Yeah, real bright. Very subtle. Dumbass."

"I ain't saying we announce our business," Dean said. He paused, and when he spoke again, his voice was unsteady with hesitation. "You think we'll run into any Taliban up there?"

"Captain said we're escorting the package to the Pakistani border outside Khost. So yeah, I'd say it's likely to get hairy. Fuckin' Tally town out there. Crane says they've probably gotten wise to the route by now, too."

Frost's brow furrowed. What package? He hadn't heard anything about Khost.

"Think we should ask the new guy along?" Dean said. "Extra firepower?"

"Fuck no," Peña said. "You know what the main man would do if he found out we brought the guy who killed his kid in our squad?"

Frost's blood ran cold.

"Wait, that's who the FNG is? Our bargaining chip?" Dean asked.

"None other. Or did you think that we got him transferred for his companionship? Fucker looks at us like we're the scum of the earth," Peña said.

Frost couldn't help but feel in this moment that a judgment like that was justified.

"Well, at least we're not diluting the take," Dean said, and went on slightly too loudly in his inebriated voice. "After all this, I'm gonna lay on a beach and fuck all day. I'm gonna buy a mansion, a-and designer clothes, and designer cars—if that's even a thing, I'm gonna get one. No, at least five, man. At least five. You hear me?"

"That's the spirit. C'mon, I got some stuff in my room that'll be good for taking the edge off for the next few hours."

Frost heard the two make their way to the main floor barracks entrance. He folded his reading light—he didn't want to have to engage the two when they came up to their shared room—but as he went to close it, the clip slipped from the book's back cover and dropped to the floor with a light clatter. Frost heard the footsteps outside halt, then a few indiscernible whispers. Then the footsteps continued onward once more.

Frost picked up the clip from the floor and set it back on the nightstand. He turned over and set his back to the room and pretended that he was sleeping, silently chastising himself for his error.

His new team was working for Zahir, the warlord who wanted him dead. Something clicked about the ambush at the deserted village near the Hindu Kush mountains. Dean and Peña wouldn't have had the resources to leak Frost's whereabouts. Crane, on the other hand, just might have had enough knowledge of troop deployments and special ops to pull it off.

An Army captain working for a local warlord? That would have been alarming enough on its own. But now he was Frost's direct superior, in bed with a man who wanted him dead. What could he do, accuse a United States Captain of being involved in such a far-reaching conspiracy with no evidence but hearsay? No, he'd be bound, gagged, and left for dead somewhere if he did that.

He needed to tread lightly if he was going to live through his time in this squad. He was evidently a bargaining chip for Crane, which implied that he had value alive. There was a chance Frost could quietly find a way to get transferred to another unit before the bounty on his head became more tempting than his worth as a bargaining chip. He'd need a damn good reason, and a very discreet CO.

He'd need to do it soon. They'd been scheduled to travel to Lashkar Gah on a slow sweeping patrol mission the day after tomorrow, searching for Taliban forces and sympathizers up and down the riverbed along the way. He couldn't give them time to make their move. Then, after he was out from under their thumb, he'd get payback for Holt, Gage, and Noonan. Until then, he was nothing but a helpless man with a price on his head, waiting for the bullet he'd never hear coming.

————

The sound of approaching footsteps echoed through the jail hallway. Frost sat up straight and stared out the front of his cell and saw Sheriff Puck emerge. She stared through the steel bars at him.

"We ran your name through the database," she said.

Frost wasn't too worried yet. They only had a fake name and his description. That couldn't possibly alert Crane to his position, even if he was constantly scanning state databases. They hadn't yet taken his mugshot.

"It appears you're a ghost, Mr. Johnson," Sheriff Puck said. "Unless of course your ID, your name, are bullshit."

"Any chance I can get that phone call?" Frost asked. It was a stupid question, but he'd been locked up too long. He was going insane wondering if Sarah was okay.

Sheriff Puck laughed. "You might have a chance if you were in a fuckin' movie, sport," she said. "Now why don't you tell me how much you know?"

"I know a dozen ways to kill a man without making a sound," Frost said, his expression flat.

"See, that information is less than useful to *anyone*, because you're stuck in a cage!" Sheriff Puck said. She turned and began back down the hallway to the booking area. "You holler when you have something worth my time, and I might consider giving you a phone call," she said.

Frost stood up and began pacing the room again. Every second he was stuck in this cell was a second wasted. He knew Sheriff Puck was keeping him here at least until the parade was over. And after that, who knew?

It was all too much. Every what-if scenario was driving him mad. Frost hoped Sarah had fled town after he was arrested. That she'd gotten as far away from Clear Rock as she possibly could. But he knew she hadn't. If she didn't stick around to personally run Treece or Silver down with her car, she'd do it to try to save Frost and Taya.

He laid down on the concrete bed, folded up his jacket and placed it over his practically wafer-thin pillow. Worrying about the eventualities was useless. He needed rest. He was going to get out of this cell, and when he did, those who stood against him would find him sharp-eyed and clear-minded.

TWENTY-SEVEN

Officer Ashley Warren stood outside, leaning against the façade of the jailhouse. She took a long drag from her cigarette and stared out over the prairie flatland beyond the back parking lot. She glanced up at the sparkling constellations above her, the hazy spread of the Milky Way laid out before her like a diamond-studded roadmap.

As much as she hated it, she thought about her mom at times like this. Leticia Warren, God love her, had always told her daughter that she could do anything—that the world was wide, the universe was wider, and all that stood in the way of Ashley's potential was her own doubts. Those doubts had never faded, but they had bought and furnished a fine new condo downtown. All she had to do was turn her back on a few things that her mother, a firm believer in the great and all-loving universe, would have considered unforgivable. And now, here came just one more unforgivable thing.

A pair of headlights bounced into the lot, cutting through the deepening darkness. Andy Treece parked his dark blue Chevelle beside Warren and stepped out. Warren finished her cigarette and tossed it to the pavement, where she butted it out with her boot.

"You the only one here?" Treece asked.

Officer Warren nodded. "In the booking office here, yeah," she said. "Three or four officers ought to be in the main building still. They'll be there all night."

Treece glanced over at the broader Sheriff's Department station attached to the jailhouse. The front foyer was lit brightly at the end of the building, but the few office windows leading up to it remained black.

"Keys?" Treece said, holding out his hand like an impatient parent.

Officer Warren removed the cell door key from her retractable keyring and handed it to Treece.

"Third cell. End of the hallway," she said.

Treece took the key and made to go inside.

"So, what's the story?" Warren asked. She didn't particularly want to know, but she needed to if she was going to corroborate the story. On-duty officers who lied under oath needed to be good at that.

Treece turned back and looked at her. He must have seen the apathy in her eyes, and the smile that crept across his face told her that he was getting off on it. He owned her, after all, but owning didn't guarantee agreement. But that's what he saw in her expression. One more cop on his payroll, ready to look the other way just for him.

"*You* are going to have another cigarette, take a drive, and resume your post in fifteen minutes," he said. "Check on the prisoner after. I think you'll find that, tragically, the poor soul inside got his hands on your service weapon and took his own life. Speaking of which, I'll need that pistol when you get back."

He turned and went inside. Officer Ashley Warren stared back over the flatland. After a moment, she pulled out her pack of cigarettes and lit a new one. Leticia Warren would still be rolling in her grave, if they'd still had money for the family plot when she passed. But that's what trusting in the goodness of the universe got you: a wailing death in a backwater hospital and a dusty urn on your kid's mantelpiece. Warren wouldn't be another of the great, wide universe's victims. She climbed into her cruiser and gunned the ignition, shutting out the stars above her. She went for a drive.

––––––

Andy Treece entered the back of the booking office and glanced beyond, down the dark narrow hallway. He pulled his Beretta 92 from his shoulder holster, grinning in anticipation. Carefully, almost reverently, he threaded a titanium silencer into the Beretta's barrel. Ready and eager, he advanced upon the cells.

Treece walked the hall slowly, glancing inside the first and then the second cell as he passed by. The digs were far from ideal, what with all the bare concrete. After being a pain in his ass the past couple days, this fucker was trapped in a cement cage and waiting to be put down like a stupid, useless dog.

Treece reached the final cell and looked beyond the steel bars. It was difficult to make out in the dark, but Treece saw him there. Sleeping on the concrete bed with his back to the hallway, with the wool blanket pulled over him.

Treece smiled again. He raised his pistol at Johnson's back. He frowned. Something was wrong, but he couldn't—

A hand darted out of the shadowed corner of the jail cell and grabbed the Beretta's barrel. The hand yanked forward, hard, and Treece was so focused on maintaining his grip on the gun that he was sent sprawling forward. His heart seized in terror as a second hand wrapped around his wrist and pulled backward with the resounding *crack* of breaking bone.

———

Frost snatched the gun from Treece's hand before he could pull the trigger and hauled on the man's broken arm. Treece was dragged, howling, to his knees, his shoulder pressed against the bar as his feet scrabbled on the concrete floor for purchase. Frost reversed the Beretta and fit his finger through the trigger guard. Treece's wide eyes rolled in the moonlight, his mouth frothing with insensate pain.

"P-please," Treece grunted. "Please just let me go. I can give you—"

The gun coughed once, and Treece slumped wordlessly to the floor. Frost reached beyond the bars and riffled through Treece's pockets until he found the cell keys. He unlocked the door and kicked Treece's arm away to slide the bars aside. He glanced down the hall, and when he felt sure that no help was coming, he recovered his bundled jacket from beneath the thin wool blanket. Then he stepped over Treece's body and out of the cell.

As he did, however, a glint caught Frost's eye. Brakespeare's dog tags glimmered in the moonlight, shaken free in the struggle. Frost knelt, ripped the tags from Treece's neck, and put them in his pocket. Then he grabbed Treece's car keys and phone for good measure before dragging the dealer's body back into the jail cell and shutting the door behind him.

Nobody remained in the jailhouse, the booking area, or the parking lot beyond. Frost went to Treece's Chevelle, unlocked it, and climbed inside. He allowed himself a small smile as he gunned the Chevelle's engine and peeled out of the parking lot.

TWENTY-EIGHT

F rost pulled out of the station backlot and turned onto the main road. He wished he remembered Sarah's number off the top of his head. He needed to make sure that she was all right. He was snapped from his reverie by the sight of approaching headlights.

Frost froze. The oncoming car was none other than Sheriff Puck's Interceptor, likely on her way to help clean up the evidence. There was nothing else for it. He couldn't turn. He just had to keep driving, keep his head down and hope that the officer didn't notice it wasn't Treece behind the wheel of Treece's car.

It was dark, so maybe he'd get lucky, he thought. The officer would just see the Chevelle, assume that the job was done, and drive on none the wiser until she found Treece.

The Interceptor and the Chevelle passed one another. Frost looked straight ahead, hoping the dark of the night might conceal his face. After a moment, Frost checked his side mirror, watching for a reaction. The Interceptor approached the police station in the distance and slowed to turn into the parking lot.

Frost breathed a sigh of relief. But just for a moment. Because as he checked his side mirror again, he saw the two headlights of the Interceptor swing back into view, having turned around in the station parking lot. The vehicle drove back out onto the main road and accelerated. Its red-and-blue lights flashed to life.

Frost floored the gas and the Chevelle lurched forward. He wouldn't go quietly this time. This time, the Sheriff would kill him the second she got the chance. He glanced in his rearview. The Interceptor was gaining on him, its customized horsepower keeping pace with the heavy Chevelle.

Frost cursed. He tried to calm himself. To stay focused and vigilant. He looked towards the horizon. With another car chase ahead and the sheriff bearing down on him, Frost realized that the situation might warrant his first Level Five in quite some time.

Not quite, a voice in his head thought. *You've survived worse.*

———

Sweat trickled onto the cracked earth. The droplets hit the sandy clay and disappeared as if they'd never been. Frost hobbled forward, the mottled trail of blood behind him already dried by the desert sun, the IED shrapnel embedded in his left side shining red-black with his blood in the harsh daylight. He wiped his brow with the back of his sleeve and squinted towards the horizon. The jagged and grayed granite of the Chagai Hills loomed in the distance a half mile ahead, blown out and distorted in his swimming vision like a soaked oil painting.

A stabbing migraine set in behind his eyes again like a thousand bayonets. Frost gritted his teeth and shut his eyes to the world and continued onward. Just a few steps onward, and then a few more. Then he could rest. He reached under his thin DCU jacket and felt his left side. His lower abdomen and upper leg were slathered in gore, soaked all through the thin bandages that he'd hastily wrapped himself in.

He began up the graduated slope of the hillside and took shelter behind a formation of jutted black shale that provided a few feet of shade. He took pains to lower himself and sat with his back against the rock. The shaded earth was no cooler than the unshaded, but the dimmed light allowed Frost to open his eyes with less pain. He checked his wounds. His uniform was torn and caked in dried blood, and his feet squelched in his boots where undried blood had pooled, but nothing had gotten worse. Not yet.

He pulled out his canteen and shook it. Barely anything left. He took a small sip and set it back in its holster on his belt before glancing up the rocky hillside, stretching upward for miles. He'd never make it.

A deathstalker scorpion emerged from under the rocks a few feet away. It scurried forth into the hot sunlight and turned to face Frost. He twisted his head to the side and stared down at it. The venom of the scorpion contained chlorotoxin, a peptide used to treat brain tumors. Frost wondered if it could do anything for a bad case of brain shrapnel. Just pour a little on like WD-40, and you're good to go. He laughed to himself, but something in his chest made even that hurt. The pain brought him back to the present.

He had been slipping. Had slipped. He focused his thoughts and returned them to the mission in front of him. He'd only slip further the longer he stayed still. Maybe he'd make it through the mountains. Maybe not. But he knew for sure that he was dead right there if he didn't get up and get moving.

The deathstalker scurried an inch towards Frost and he slowly rose to his feet. He grimaced in pain as he did, sliding his back against the rock to support himself. He took one last look at the scorpion and kicked it down the hillside.

He squinted and looked back toward the way he'd come, over the desaturated red sands of the Registan Desert. Miles off in the distance, vaporous in the hazed heat, a plume of dust rose from the narrow road. Some car or truck. A military Humvee, perhaps, or just Balochi nomads. They'd be able to help, if he could get to them. Drive him to a clinic or the village doctor, if they were friendlies. Or maybe it was his team or Zahir's men, ready to finish him off. Deathstalkers of an entirely different kind.

Frost ran the system in his head, calculating every conceivable possibility. Weighing every statistic, every variable, examining his death or survival with increasingly cold detachment. Each micro-decision committed to accomplishing his simple objective of staying alive. The program finished and the system read its answer: Level Three.

Crapshoot, Frost said to himself. Not worth the risk.

He turned around to face the slope of the black Chagai Hills. His chosen opponent, the terrain before him, would be hostile to him in its own way. Alone and without resources, the mountains would test him at every turn. Frost steeled his resolve, gritted his teeth against the blinding haze, and drew his last stationary breath, vowing to not stop again until he was safe or dead. Taking a final look, he began up through the hills, continuing his slow and arduous journey across the undefended border into Pakistan.

———

The Chevelle raced through the night down the rural route road, the Interceptor right on top of it. The Interceptor's headlights glared white in Frost's rearview mirror, the howl of its siren wailing out into the night. Frost flew over a small concrete hill and his car smashed down hard against the road. He couldn't outrun the Interceptor, but maybe he could outmaneuver it. The Chevelle's lower center of gravity would allow it to take corners at faster speeds than the Interceptor. With any luck, Puck would roll the SUV trying to keep up with him.

Frost checked his mirror again. He drew his seatbelt down over his chest and clicked it into its holster. He stared ahead and charged onward towards greater downtown Clear Rock.

Just a few steps onward, then a few steps more.

TWENTY-NINE

Tape blocked off parking spots all over downtown, reserving them for the parade food trucks. Signs plastered all over the downtown businesses let people know where they could park, where they couldn't, gave directions to the parade route, and proclaimed the schedule for the weekend's festivities. A child-sized Ferris Wheel had been erected in the middle of the small city park. Few cars and fewer pedestrians rode the streets. The night was cold and still and quiet.

The sharp squeal of brakes shattered the peace as Frost took a corner hard and fast, flying into the downtown district. He burned rubber, leaving harsh skid marks in his wake. He sped onward and checked his rearview. The Interceptor was close behind. He'd created some distance, but he hadn't lost her.

Just as he peeled out onto Main Street, the light ahead of him turned red. With no time to brake, Frost blew through the red light just as a large flatbed truck passed through on his legal green, and the truck clipped the back end of the Chevelle as it passed. The car swerved and Frost cut the wheel in an attempt to right it, but he'd only turned into the momentum. The Chevelle skidded, swung about, slammed its tail into a parked car and flipped over onto its passenger side. It slid for ten feet or so, the metal and glass grinding horribly upon the concrete as it did before, finally, it came to rest in the middle of the street.

Frost sat suspended in the driver seat, his seatbelt holding him tightly in place, digging into his side. He forced down the incredible pain coursing through his skull. Sheriff Puck would be on him any second. Frost glanced down at the passenger side window below him. It would be a hard fall, but he had to free himself. He held onto the back of his seat to relieve the tension of his weight on the seatbelt and unbuckled it, lowering himself to the passenger side door when the buckle reeled back into place.

Frost turned in the seat and donkey-kicked the loosened windshield free. He squeezed his body through the opening and crawled out onto the street. From the cover of the car, he picked out a nearby alley too narrow for Puck's bulky Interceptor to follow him.

He heard the rev of an engine and Frost peered around the upended Chevelle to see Puck's SUV roaring across the intersection toward him. Frost wasted no time and sprinted from behind his cover, beelining for the alleyway.

Puck's Interceptor slammed into the Chevelle, sending it skidding on its side across the asphalt. By the time she had turned the Interceptor about again, Frost was already past the mouth of the alley, ducking between dumpsters for cover. Frost expected to hear her fire at him, but when he turned, he saw that she and her car were already gone. She would be driving around to meet him where the alley ended—he could either double back or keep going. Then, he saw it: a wall of aspens and Douglas firs on the other side of the opposite parking lot, stretching into the foothills of the mountains around Clear Rock.

Frost emerged from the alley and sprinted across the parking lot towards the woods. Behind him, tires screeched in the distance as the Interceptor burst into the parking lot. Headlights illuminated Frost from the rear as he ran. He made it to the tree line with time to spare. If Puck wanted him, she would have to ditch her precious SUV.

He kept running, deeper and deeper into the woods. The orange glow of the parking lot's high-pressure sodium lamps grew dimmer as he did. The contrasting darkness bled in all around him now.

He ran behind a thick whitebark pine and stopped to catch his breath. If the crash had injured him, the adrenaline rush wasn't letting him know. But now he had time to gather himself and prepare for Puck's pursuit.

At the edge of the tree line, the Interceptor headlights cut out, and the woodland fell almost completely black. Frost heard Sheriff Puck step out of the vehicle and slam her door shut. There was a faint click as she opened and reloaded her revolver, another as the cylinder was set back in place. Then, the opening of her trunk and the rack of a shotgun.

Only one of them was leaving these woods alive.

THIRTY

Frost peered around the whitebark at Sheriff Puck. He saw her silhouette slip down the shallow ditch behind the lot and disappear into the velvet darkness of the woods. The dim glow of the parking lot sodium lamps cast a sickly canary-yellow behind her like a cancerous, radioactive fog.

"Give it up, Johnson!" Sheriff Puck called from the shadows. "I'll have you dead in a jail cell or dead in a woodland ditch, but I *will* have you dead."

Frost held the Beretta at his side. There was no use aiming it into the darkness. He couldn't see a thing from where he stood. Nothing that moved, at least. Just the shallow dim bleed of the burnt-honey light at the woodland's edge. He squinted and glanced at what little of the foliage he could see in front of him. He couldn't move without disturbing the undergrowth and alerting Sheriff Puck to his position.

"You come out without a fuss, and I just might give you that phone call!" Sheriff Puck said. Frost could feel her smirking. "Not that anyone's left to pick up."

Frost's body went cold, like his heart was pumping liquid nitrogen. Sarah had been alone in Clear Rock, on a drug lord's radar, for an entire day. There was too much Puck and Silver could have done to her in that time. Frost buried the thought for the time being. Right now, it didn't matter whether Sarah was alive or not. Right now the only thing that mattered was for Frost himself to stay alive. All else would follow, or else nothing would.

He heard a branch snap nearby. Judging by the sound, Puck was maybe twenty or thirty feet away. He considered peering out from behind the whitebark again to see if he could track her, but decided against it. The motion might catch in the hazed glow of the lamps, and Puck was making mistakes that Frost had resolved to avoid by moving over the dry brush. She was giving away her position in conditions that would otherwise render her unpredictable. Frost was wounded and Puck had him trumped on firepower, but as long as he was patient, he could get the upper hand.

Frost consciously slowed his breath. The air hung heavy and cold now that night had settled in. A few degrees lower and his breath would start showing. He could barely hear Puck's faint breathing beyond. Just barely. But there was something else, too. Something out in the darkness in the opposite direction. A very low, almost inaudible whooshing, like heavy rain.

The river. With the chase and the crash, he hadn't realized he was so close.

Frost knelt as smoothly as he could and grabbed a rock, barely visible in the half-light. He whipped the rock in the opposite direction of the river, and heard Puck turn when the rock hit the ground. Frost broke from the tree, rolling his steps to keep from making noise, and as soon as he had put a few more meters between himself and Puck, he broke into a run.

He knew the Hognose River flowed southbound. If he could get to it, he could reorient himself and follow the river south to the public lot he and Sarah had stopped in. From there he could get to Rocky's Diner and his truck, if the police hadn't towed it already.

Behind him, Frost heard Puck hiss a curse into the night air. She would pursue in a moment, but even with Frost's injuries, he wagered he could still outrun her. At last, he broke the tree line at the riverbank.

Puck arrived soon after, following but not breaking the tree line. She dropped to one knee, the butt of the shotgun pressed to her shoulder. Frost had to hand it to her—she hadn't made the same mistake Goldilocks had. But she still suffered from some dangerously two-dimensional thinking.

The Berretta barked twice, blowing two bloodless holes in the back of Sheriff Puck's coat and knocking the crooked cop onto her stomach. Frost dropped down from the tree, got a firm grip on her shotgun, and tossed it toward the riverbank. Judging by the bullet holes, she was wearing a vest, but at that range the rounds would still have broken a few ribs. If Puck were still conscious, she would be in intense pain.

Then the sheriff rolled on her back, pistol in hand, and put a nine-millimeter round through Frost's left shoulder. Evidently, Frost thought, she handled pain fairly well. He bit back the pain and stomped on her hand, then kicked her sidearm away as well.

"Country boy gonna kill an unarmed lady?" she coughed. She smiled between pained spasms, and her teeth gleamed dark and wet with blood in the scant moonlight. "Some hometown hero."

"I'm sure your predecessor will sympathize," Frost grunted.

Puck rolled her eyes. "Gomez? If incontinence took the shape of a man, it would have looked tougher than Sheriff Gomez. Taking his office was an act of charity."

"What do you know about Sarah? What did you do to her?" He didn't have time to spare exchanging barbs with Puck. It was almost a guarantee that her men would be on their way soon, following the crash on Main Street. If he was particularly unlucky, they would have heard the gunshots, as well.

"I'm not the one you need to worry about where she's concerned, Mr. Johnson," Puck said. "Taking care of you was my job. Well, mine and Treece's. How's Andy, by the way?"

Frost put his boot on Puck's chest, and she wheezed at the pressure.

"All right, that's all the answer I need. So, do you really want to draw this out, hero?"

Puck didn't know anything about Sarah. She would send more men after him if he left her alive. And after everything, what was one more body in his wake?

"You're wrong about one thing, Puck. I'm no hero," Frost said. "But you're right about another. I've wasted enough time on you."

The Beretta barked one more time. There was a moment of silence, then the gentle crack of underbrush beneath a pair of sturdy boots. Frost walked back the way he came, toward the hazed light of the parking lot. He walked alone.

THIRTY-ONE

Frost climbed into Puck's Interceptor and started it up with her keys. The headlights came to life and shot out into the woodland, slicing through the darkness. Frost found the AC dial on the dashboard console and cranked the heat as high as it would go, waiting for it to melt away the Colorado cold.

Puck's phone lay on the passenger's seat. Frost had searched for it on her body and come up empty. He grabbed it, and for the second time in as many days wished he had memorized the number to call Sarah. He dropped the phone and put the SUV in reverse, carefully watching that the push-bumper grill guard or the front tires didn't get caught on the mangled chain-link fence.

Frost grabbed the phone again. He searched through Sheriff Puck's contacts and found Donald Kim. He called the number and waited.

Treece was right when he'd called this whole operation a giant machine, and Frost would need others helping him if the machine was going to be dismantled. If he was truly going to stop Silver and keep Taya safe.

The call went to Deputy Kim's voicemail.

"Deputy Kim, this is Sarah Albany's friend, Kevin Johnson," Frost said. "This is all going to sound incredibly strange to you, but I just witnessed Sheriff Puck's murder. Someone who claimed to be working for Silver incapacitated her and executed her. Said something about her not being useful anymore. Her body can be found on the east riverbank of the Hognose River, on the opposite side of the woods that sits between the river and—"

Frost glanced over at the strip mall on the far side of the parking lot. Read the nameplate marquee that hung over the front entrance.

"—the Pinewood Mall parking lot. But that's just part of the problem. Silver's done something to Sarah, and I don't know if she's alive or dead. And in just a few hours, Silver will be meeting with national buyers to offload a massive shipment of imported heroin. It will take place during the Founding Day Parade tomorrow. I can't find a way to stay safe and give you the evidence, so I'm asking you to trust me. I know it for a certainty. Puck and Silver and Treece were all working together, and they were all involved in the murder of Sheriff Gomez. I need you to call the DEA, the FBI. Tell them to look for any out-of-state trucks entering Clear Rock in the next forty-eight hours. I promise you this will all make sense soon enough, but... right now Sarah and I need your help."

Frost went to hang up, but paused. He put the phone back to his ear.

"And watch your back, Deputy," he said. "Your office is crawling with cops working for Silver."

Frost hung up, tossed the phone back onto the passenger's seat, and put the accelerator to the floor. He tore out of the parking lot through downtown Clear Rock on the quickest route to Rocky's Diner. He knew Sarah wouldn't be there, but he needed to retrieve his truck. His Ranger wouldn't exactly be inconspicuous any longer, but neither was the Sheriff's Interceptor, and it had his supplies.

That was, of course, assuming his truck was still waiting for him in the lot.

It was. Frost pulled into the Rocky's Diner and was relieved to see his Ranger. It was the only vehicle in the small lot, the diner having closed for the night. Frost found a gap in the trees on the opposite side of the road from Rocky's and slipped the Interceptor between them, as far off the road as he could manage.

He jogged back to the parking lot and climbed into the Ranger. He breathed a sigh of relief. It felt like home. Frost removed the Beretta from his back waistband and checked the magazine. There were four bullets left. He shoved the magazine back into the well and put the gun on the passenger's seat.

He leaned back and winced in pain as his wound brushed against the seat. He glanced down at his shoulder. He couldn't see how bad it was, just the hole in his jacket and the blood around its edges. The pain was manageable as long as he continued to compartmentalize it, and his mobility was only somewhat hindered. He guessed it was just a flesh wound, but he'd still need to take a look.

Frost opened his glove box and retrieved his flip phone. He checked his missed calls and found none. Not one call from Sarah. Another pang of worry, one he'd been fighting back, shot through him. Maybe she was dead at Silver's hand. Maybe she really wasn't in danger, and had gone to ground. Frost had no way of knowing. He started up the Ranger and drove out of Rocky's lot.

Fifteen minutes later, Frost was parked in front of the Black Lotus. He stared at the front windows. The shop was dark, as to be expected. He glanced up at Sarah's second-floor apartment. Dark as well. If this was a trap, he had walked away from worse. All he had to do was tread lightly.

He drove his truck through the alley and parked in the lot behind the parlor. He got out and retrieved the key from the mailbox. One hand gripping the Beretta, he unlocked the door and crept inside.

No one waited in the Black Lotus's lobby. He shut the door behind him, leaving the light off. He slowly made his way through the shop and down the hallway. He heard a faint crash upstairs, from Sarah's apartment.

Frost ignored the urge to storm up the back stairs, instead taking measured steps two at a time. The keylock mechanism on the apartment door had been broken, jagged splinters showing beneath the metal plate. Frost opened the door as gingerly as he could, checking his corners as he stepped inside with his gun raised.

The apartment was empty. Frost searched the bathroom and the closet, but the place was abandoned. Yet it was clear that someone had been there, because the unit was completely trashed—barstools upturned, papers and paraphernalia everywhere, Sarah's laptop on the floor. The Murphy bed was down, its mattress and bedding loosed. Sarah's paintings were haphazardly strewn about the room, some completely destroyed. Her master easel lay overturned, her oil paints bleeding out on the floor.

Frost tried to discern if they'd trashed the place in Sarah's absence or while struggling to subdue her. The mess seemed systematic: objects were thrown from shelves and surfaces in piles, shifted aside to make room for searching eyes and hands. He looked around, shuffling the papers on the kitchen counter to see if anything was underneath them. If he found her keys or wallet, it would suggest that she'd returned home and had been taken afterwards. He found something else instead, drifting to the floor from between two of the scattered papers.

It was the receipt for their meal at Rocky's. He then saw her cellphone, propping up the edge of an overturned fruit bowl.

So she had been home, and now she was gone. Frost tried to remind himself that she might have come home and left before the men had arrived and trashed the place. Or after, even. But he knew how unlikely that was. They'd grabbed her. He could feel it.

Another light crash startled Frost and he turned to the noise. It was Sarah's cat, Sid. She'd knocked a plastic cup off the counter as she darted away from her hiding spot to a second bolt-hole beneath the couch. Her bright yellow eyes peered out at Frost from the new vantage point.

Frost looked around the kitchen and found Sid's two hand-painted ceramic bowls on the floor. He picked up one and filled it with water and set it back. The cat crept out from under the couch, her eyes on Frost as she moved, until she arrived at the bowl where she lapped up the fresh water. Frost then looked through a few cupboards before finding the bag of dry cat food. He poured some out into the second bowl. Sid flinched at first, but begrudgingly allowed him to finish pouring the food. Frost sighed and knelt beside the cat, staring at the ruined apartment while she ate.

THIRTY-TWO

F rost stood in the bathroom in front of Sarah's vanity mirror. He removed his jacket and waffle sweatshirt and was relieved to see, despite the blood, that the bullet had merely grazed his left shoulder. He fetched a few of Sarah's clean towels and wetted one with warm water and wiped his shoulder clean. The cleaning removed the clotted blood from the wound, and it began to bleed once more, running down his arm.

Frost opened the cabinet under the sink and found Sarah's Tupperware container full of medical supplies. He grabbed it and set it down on top of the toilet seat and opened it up. He wiped the wound dry again and patched it up with a large elastic bandage and wrapped it with medical gauze, taping himself off afterwards.

He stared at himself in the mirror. As ever, he found it hard to recognize the scarred face that stared back. He ran the water again and splashed some on his face, as though the rinse would restore his features to the way they were before he went overseas—alive, young, and able to feel. One last look into the mirror and the cold eyes on the other side told him everything he needed: no dice.

He needed to get back on the road. If Sarah was alive at all, she would either be at the farmhouse or at Silver's mansion. Frost left the bathroom and set his bloodied sweatshirt on the kitchen counter and pulled on his jacket. He'd have to grab a change of clothes from his truck. He glanced at Sid a final time, now grooming herself on the bed, and turned to leave.

But something stopped him. A twinge, like irritation that he couldn't identify. Something in the living room was off among all that mess. He moved into the living room. His instincts led him towards the mantlepiece around the electric fireplace. A single framed photograph sat facedown atop it. The half dozen other frames that once surrounded it now scattered about the floor, knocked down during the melee.

Frost went to the photograph frame and picked it up. It was a photograph of Sarah and what looked like her mother. Same eyes, same smile. They sat on a porch, laughing, blurred mountains in the background beyond a flat prairieland. Could be the Wind River reservation, thought Frost. Perhaps it was Sarah's stepfather who took the photo. Though it could just as well have been taken here in Clear Rock.

It brought Frost to thoughts of his own mother; a rare flash of who she'd been before the cancer. Her long hair, deep black and tied in a ponytail so that it looked like a painter's brush immersed in an inkwell, still wet.

Frost set the photograph back down on the mantle. It wasn't what his instincts had flagged, but he knew there was *something* here. Something his gut told him to pursue.

He looked to the floor, where one of Sarah's paintings leaned against the mantlepiece in front of the electric fireplace. Frost tilted his head to get a better look. It was another abstract piece, grim and foreboding in the same style as the painting they had discussed the first time Frost had come up to Sarah's apartment. The base was predominantly black, streaked with shades of ash and charcoal, with a lighter silver base at the bottom of the frame. Half a dozen slashes of golden rectangles emanated from the center. And at its focal point, a marooned rectangular shape, crude and somehow unsettling.

But then he realized it. It wasn't the painting he was drawn to. It was the electric fireplace it was leaning against, and the mantlepiece where the photograph had been set. Frost picked the painting up, moved it aside, and saw what had drawn him to this corner of the apartment.

Beneath the electric fireplace of the mantlepiece was a shallow hearth, not more than two inches from the floor, with a long piece of wooden trim covering its front. One end hung loose, and as Frost knelt to examine it, something inside the small alcove glinted in the light. He yanked the trim away and found its source: set on the dusted floor beneath the hearth lay Taya's phone, its screen facing up and just barely catching the light from the kitchen. Frost had seen it just as he walked by, the glare irritating his photosensitivity and engaging his interest.

Frost couldn't help but smile. Sarah must have heard the men enter the shop beneath her and realized very quickly that she'd need to hide the phone, or else the evidence of Sheriff Gomez's murder would be lost forever. So she'd taken a page from Taya's book and shoved the phone beneath a fireplace, where maybe, just maybe, Frost might know to look for it.

He scrolled through the phone to be sure it was in fact Taya's, and indeed it was. The video of the murder still burned a hole in her photo gallery. He had the smoking gun. Now he needed to decide what to do with it.

Frost picked up Sarah's laptop from the floor and set it upright on the kitchen counter. The screen came to life and Frost was relieved to see the computer had not been broken in the commotion. He opened her desktop browser and created a secure Proton Mail email address. He emailed the murder video and the few photos taken at the farmhouse from Taya's phone to his account. He created a Dropbox account with the same email and uploaded the files there as a backup. Frost then opened Sarah's Contacts app on her laptop, found Deputy Kim's number and, using Taya's phone, sent the files to him.

He cleared Sarah's browsing history and pocketed Taya's phone. He stood up and realized just how exhausted he was. Fatigue falling upon him as if it were a dense wave of humidity. He shook it off and slapped himself lightly in the face and made to leave the apartment.

But he stopped. He'd heard something again, and it wasn't Sid this time. It was coming from downstairs in the shop. A second noise followed. It was the front door opening and closing as someone entered the parlor. He had locked the front door behind himself— whoever was here either had a key or picked the lock. He cursed and made for the stairs, Beretta drawn.

He opened the apartment door as quietly as he could and glanced down the back stairwell. The wooden steps would creak beneath him as he went down, but he couldn't wait at the top. He began his descent. Sure enough, upon only the second step from the top, the wood creaked beneath him like the shifting hull of a ship and Frost froze to discern if the intruder had indeed heard it.

Nothing. Silence hung in the air like a foul scent. Then quick footsteps broke the silence, and Frost heard the swift tug at the shop's front door, the hinges squealing as it flew open. Frost flew down the stairwell as fast as he could and ran through the short hallway towards the front of the shop. He emerged in the waiting area of the parlor with his Beretta level. He glanced through the front picture window and saw a shadow climbing into the driver's seat of an idling car. Frost ran out the front door into the street and raised his Beretta, but it was already peeling out into the night. He watched as the car's red taillights disappeared into the darkness. Soon he was alone again, standing in the street beneath the soft falling snow.

But Frost had caught the make of the car through the picture window: a black Lincoln Town Car. The same car that had shadowed him outside of Taya's brownstone apartment.

THIRTY-THREE

Frost needed to get moving. Before he did, however, he wanted to sweep the shop for any clues he might have missed. He looked over the parlor's waiting area. He could faintly smell the intruder's cologne still lingering in the air. It was an older man's scent, thought Frost. A kind of vanillic sandalwood, classy and sophisticated. Whoever it was, they had good taste.

The town car pursuer wasn't one of Silver's men, thought Frost. It wasn't just the scent that led him to that conclusion, but the interaction as well—Silver's men would have tried to kill Frost the moment they heard a creak on the steps. They would have come out firing.

Frost considered the possibility that the man might have belonged to Crane, but discarded the theory for similar reasons. Crane would be sending professional assassins, and while they would put up a better fight than Silver's thugs, they certainly wouldn't have run either.

So then who was this man that had been inside the shop, and what did he want? He had already followed Frost once, and he had retreated then as well. Between the town car and the cologne, he was too well-off to be interested in robbing Frost, and he'd waived the chance to kill him multiple times. The detail that confused Frost the most was the man's investigation of the Black Lotus, which was subtle but not particularly invasive.

Frost turned his mind towards the town car. First in front of Taya's brownstone and now here. He and Sarah were the only connections that he could see at the moment.

The town car. A Lincoln. Frost inevitably turned to thoughts of the kid. Thoughts about Brakespeare. He reached into his pocket, remembering, and pulled out the recovered dog tags. He'd nearly forgotten he had taken them back. He cradled the tags, staring into them as if they hid answers to the future within their home in the past.

———

Frost and Brakespeare sat on the tailgate of a beige Toyota Tacoma well behind the protection of Bagram Airfield's security walls. They stared out at the snow-covered mountains far off in the distance, passing a bottle of Bushmill's between them, the magic hour light casting soft oranges and purples and pinks over their faces. It was their last night at the base before shipping out on a ten-day mission to sweep easterly villages for enemy forces. The Tacoma, a combat technical fitted with a M240 machine gun on its roof, was intended to be their ride during the expedition.

Frost took a swig of whiskey and passed the bottle back to Brakespeare. He glanced over his shoulder at the machine gun behind them.

"Ever fired one of those?" Frost said.

"What, a machine gun?" Brakespeare said.

"One mounted to a technical, specifically."

"Nah," Brakespeare said. "You?"

"Nuh-uh. But who knows—maybe this week. Valley's supposed to be heavy with ISIL," Frost said.

"The whole border is."

"Well, you better promise to turn that thing on me if we get surrounded. I've heard the stories. I ain't getting taken."

"You really want *me* popping my cherry like that, under that kind of pressure?" Brakespeare said. "Well, all right, but don't go blaming me if I go through a whole belt of ammo before landing the kill shot."

"Better than me showing up on LiveLeak. Another Mary, Queen of Scots," Frost said.

Brakespeare chuckled dryly and handed the bottle over to Frost.

"We got Gage and Noonan with us and they're solid," Brakespeare said. "And MSG Holt seems all right, from what I've seen of him so far. It'll be fine."

Frost took another swig. "You say that as if it were some certainty."

"It is a certainty. I'm clairvoyant. Didn't I tell you?"

"Can't say that you did."

"Oh yeah. I bet I could figure out where you're from in less than three questions," Brakespeare said.

"You already know where I'm from."

"Just like I said. Better than the best."

Frost laughed and handed the bottle back. He stared off at the distant mountainscape. Dark shadows crept across the lower peaks as the sun slipped away.

"You religious?" Frost said.

"Oh, so we're *drinking*-drinking, huh?"

Frost laughed.

"Nah, I'm not," Brakespeare said. "You? Wait—let me guess." He glanced over at Frost, squinting at him. "Lutheran?"

Frost smiled. "You really are a fuckin' clairvoyant."

Brakespeare shrugged. "Good ol' boy from Oklahoma like you? What else you going to be?"

"Can't really say I'm much of a practitioner, though," Frost said. "Haven't set foot in a church in years."

"But you still think of yourself as Lutheran?"

Frost shrugged. "Just something you say, I guess. Something to put on the forms."

"You don't believe it?" Brakespeare said, taking a swig of whiskey.

"I don't know," Frost said. "Don't really think about it. It's really just something I was born into. And even then, it was only ever *weekend* Christianity, you know? Church on Sundays. Grace at dinner. That's about it."

"Your parents into it?"

"My old man was. Well, he picked and chose what he was into and what he wasn't. He liked the merciful God bit, the forgiveness. It helped him get away with himself when he was sober enough to feel regret. Oh, and the water into wine. Would have loved for that bit to be true. Especially when he ran out of Pabst. Really, though, I think he just figured it was something you were supposed to do. An obligation. Something you were supposed to pass on to your kids. And that maybe if *I* turned out to be a decent Christian it might help absolve him."

"Imagine his disappointment," Brakespeare said.

"You ain't kidding." Frost smiled. "Now there's something he never ran out of."

"Whosoever believeth in him shall not perish, but have everlasting life."

Frost made a show of rolling his eyes, and Brakespeare handed the bottle over again.

"He gone, your old man?" Brakespeare said.

Frost took a swig and nodded. "Yeah."

"Mine too," Brakespeare said. "Sucks, though. I actually liked my dad."

Frost laughed. Brakespeare didn't.

Brakespeare looked out towards the mountains again. The evening had darkened to where a handful of stars were now visible. Half a dozen gemstones strewn across the dioxazine sky.

"You ever wonder what they'd make of us now?" Brakespeare said.

"No," Frost said. "They're dead."

"Don't mean you can't still seek their approval."

"Of the dead?"

"Sure. What the hell do you think Christianity's based on?" Brakespeare said.

"I don't know. I don't really care what my old man might think of me now," Frost said. He felt odd. Normally, he hated talking about his father. Tonight seemed different. "Any connection I might've had to him disappeared when he passed."

"Oh yeah?" Brakespeare said. "I bet you ten-to-one you got *Protestant* engraved right there on your tags."

Frost glanced down and pictured the dog tags beneath his shirt. He smiled. *Protestant* was indeed carved under his name, Social Security number, and blood type.

"So, tell me then," Brakespeare said, "since you ain't a believer, who's *that* for?"

"You know, you really ought to play the Powerball with that talent of yours," Frost said.

Brakespeare laughed, grabbing the bottle from Frost. "You know a *talent* is actually a unit of measurement in the Old Testament?"

"The fuck are you talking about?" Frost said.

"Yeah. A *talent* is a measure of weight. I think one talent is like a hundred pounds or something. So they'd really only ever use it to weigh gigantic sums of gold. I mean, they talk about twenty, thirty talents worth of gold in the Bible. You imagine that? Thirty-thousand *pounds* worth of gold? That's over a metric ton."

"How the hell do you know this shit?" Frost said. "I thought you weren't religious."

"I'm not," Brakespeare said. He reached beneath his shirt and pulled out his own dog tags. "See? *No preference.*"

"Yet you've read the Bible?" Frost said.

"Not all of it. I kind of crashed hard after my old man went. Rudderless, you know? So I started grasping at anything I could get my hands on. Philosophy, religion, literature. So, yeah, I read me some Bible."

"Didn't take?" Frost said.

"I wouldn't say that exactly," Brakespeare said. "I might disagree with the overall thesis, but there's plenty of wisdom in there. And I mean, really, it's all the same thing, no matter where you're looking. Everyone's just trying to make sense of this giant mess."

"You think there's any sense to be had?"

"This world's always going to be cruel, Snowman. No getting around it. But that don't mean you need to lose your head with the rest of them."

"So to speak," Frost said.

Brakespeare chuckled. "Yeah, so to speak. Look, if nothing else, I know that there is a compass in me. I don't always follow it, but it's there. Always will be. If I shut up long enough, it points me the right way, no matter how far I've wandered. So, let others be malevolent and lawless and wrathful. Fuck 'em. They're not gonna lead me astray. I've got my compass, and it's pointing me home."

"And where exactly is home?" Frost asked.

"Standing in the way of the malevolent and lawless and wrathful." Brakespeare grinned, evidently pleased with himself, and took another pull from the Bushmill's.

"And that's enough for you?" Frost said. "That sustains?"

Brakespeare shrugged and jerked a thumb back to the truck-mounted M240. "Gonna have to be. What else is there for guys like you and me?"

Frost stared at Brakespeare for a moment, glancing over at his dog tags. He took another swig of whiskey and stared out towards the distant, towering mountains.

"Maybe I ought to try seeing things that way," Frost said.

"May-be, Snowman," Brakespeare said. "I wouldn't complain. Better to stand against the malevolent when you're shoulder to shoulder with good company."

Frost said nothing. The mountains had swallowed the sun to make way for night. Brakespeare offered him the bottle, and he took it. It was a long while before Frost took another swig, captivated as he was by the stars above him and the possibilities before him.

———

Frost closed his fist around the dog tags and shoved them back into his pocket. It was time to go. He felt his pocket and made sure he'd collected Taya's cell phone. He had. Satisfied, Frost turned to leave, but scanned the room one more time before he did. And then he saw it.

There on top of the glass display case, set beside the till and nearly indiscernible in the parlor's dim lighting, lay a black baronial envelope. Frost knew it had not been there when he had walked into the Lotus earlier. Yet more startling than its mere appearance was what was written on its face.

In a clean and elegant hand, the face of the envelope simply read: Frost.

THIRTY-FOUR

Frost picked up the envelope and stared at his name. His *real* name. It sent a cold vibration down his spine. What the hell was going on? Nobody from Silver's crew should know Frost's name, and nobody Crane would hire would prefer leaving a letter over a bullet in Frost's head. They could be playing games with him, but that was highly unlikely.

He opened the envelope. Inside was a single baronial panel card, cream-colored with the same tidy handwriting on it, written in black ink. It read: Silver Fitzgerald, 1210 Lafayette Drive. And at the bottom, simply the initials: BB.

Frost spun around and glanced out the shop's front window. He felt as though he was being watched again. He knew that he wasn't—that the feeling was only a result of the intrusion into his private thoughts, into his internal mind—but it was a felt presence nonetheless. Like he was a piece in some larger chess match, ready to be removed from the board once he'd fulfilled his purpose.

Could this possibly be some ally? They'd provided Frost with a crucial piece of information. Then again, it might very well still be a trap.

The letter raised more questions than it answered. But Frost didn't have time to spare deliberating on so many unknowns. Let them try to spring a trap—he had survived more than his fair share. Taya and Sarah's lives were on the line, and he was going to get them to safety come hell or high water.

Frost steeled himself to the task in front of him and shook hands with it. Hardened himself to the grim violence that he knew awaited him further on up on the road.

He locked the door behind him and returned the key to the mailbox. He climbed into his Ranger, started it up, and pulled around onto the main road.

The snow fell heavier now, slicking the streets with a thin layer of white. Frost headed north and pulled into a truck stop just before the highway. A dozen or so semi-trailers slumbered in an even row next to the filling stations. A mini-van squatted beneath the buzzing neon canopy, its yawning owner pumping gas into its tank. Nearby, there loomed a convenience store with an adjoining coffee shop and public restrooms.

Frost parked his Ranger in the back of the dark parking lot and got out. He looked around. No one watched him, and no one stood close by. He looked back towards the station and gauged that he was likely out of the sight line of the mounted CCTV cameras.

He went to the rear of his truck and opened the tailgate and affixed the hinge of the camper shell door so that it hung open. He removed the Beretta from his back waistband and set it on the tailgate. He tossed his jacket into the back of the truck and opened a side compartment. There were several changes of clothes stowed away. Frost reached to the bottom of the compartment and pulled out a black BW pullover, thermal top, and tactical pants. He then opened the center compartment set into the bed of the truck, revealing a hard-shelled tactical case. Frost hoisted it out and opened it.

The case held an HK416 assault rifle and magazine with a suppressor. The gun set snugly inside charcoal-colored polyurethane molding alongside an HK45 pistol with an extra magazine, nylon belt-holsters for both, and a sheathed Marine Raider bowie knife. Frost checked the cartridges in the clip. He replaced the magazine and chambered a round before setting the rifle down and doing the same thing with the pistol.

Frost reached into the inset center compartment again and pulled out a small plastic tackle box. Inside the box were five small Semtex explosive bricks individually wrapped in cellophane. Frost retrieved two bricks and two homemade detonators made from Timex watches.

He shut the tailgate and the camper and walked back to the driver's seat. He reached into the glove box and retrieved a small cardboard box of ammonia inhalants. He broke one under his nose and the irritant flooded into his nasal membranes to shock him into a state of hypervigilance. His lungs responded, and he began breathing faster to send more oxygen to his brain. Stimulated and focused, he started his truck and headed for the highway.

Frost's Ranger flew down the highway, reaching the exit that led to the farmhouse. He cut his headlights and drove onward, toward the prairieland valley. In the moonlight, the freshly fallen snow seemed to glow on the flatland, as though it were lit by something beneath. The pockets of woodland burst like bouquets of giant black flowers through the alabaster.

Frost saw the barbed-wire fenceposts of Silver's farmland property up ahead and took the dirt pass that flanked its east side. He again parked behind the small copse of dense birch trees and cut the engine. He went to the shallow ditch that lined the pass and glassed the landscape with his binoculars.

He was struck then by just how much the scene reminded him of the painting in Sarah's apartment. The vista, predominantly black with shades of charcoal and ash. The silvered field of moonlit snow before him. The marooned rectangle barn at the center of everything. It was if the universe were indeed trying to tell him something. To warn him, perhaps. His own *Ides of March*.

Frost looked the property over. The farmhouse sat dead, not a single light on inside. The barn, on the other hand, was buzzing. Frost could see a number of vehicles parked in front, all dimly lit by flood lamps inside. There were half a dozen cars and a sixteen-wheel truck with Pete's Storage decaled on the side. Several men exited the barn with skids of stacked brown packages, running them up the ramps onto the trucks before returning for more. Frost clocked holstered pistols on several of them, others with weapons tucked into their waistbands. Frost counted twelve men total, with two or three inside the barn that he couldn't see.

He fetched a pair of wire cutters from a side compartment in his truck and went back to the barbed-wire fenceposts beside the ditch. Frost cut the top and bottom lines of the fence and pushed it back and went back to his truck to retrieve his assault rifle. He slung it over his shoulder before closing the tailgate once more.

Frost walked back to where he'd cut the fence and stopped. He reached into his pocket and pulled out the small Semtex bricks, peeling away their cellophane wrappers and pressing the detonator wires into the pliable clay. He now held two functional homemade bombs, each only about the size of a sunglasses case.

Frost placed the primed explosives back into his pocket and shouldered his rifle. Black clouds had crept across the sky, casting the field in darkness. He pushed past the fence and toward the farmhouse.

THIRTY-FIVE

Frost crossed over the snowy flatland at a crouched sprint. He headed towards the apple tree across from the farmhouse, away from the light bleeding out the front of the barn. He hoped to stay inside the shadows of the darkened home and the tree's thick limbs, wary that he could lose cloud cover at any moment.

He brought himself flush against the tree and peered around the side, toward the rear of the barn. A man emerged from the side paddock door and looked out over the property. He walked around to the rear of the barn and turned away from Frost to continue his patrol. Frost moved out from behind the tree and moved as silently as he could manage, his rifle trained on the guard as he moved. He reached the farmhouse and continued behind the ambling man, maintaining around ten feet of distance between them.

When the guard rounded the corner, Frost closed the gap and waited a moment before peering after him. There was no one there, the guard having continued around the other side of the barn. The back of the barn was a shallow ten-foot pass between the side of the barn and the deeper greenwoods that dominated the property. Frost straightened up and took a step back and looked at the rear wall of the barn. Horizontal slat pallets embossed the vertical wood paneling.

He set one foot on the first slat and his hand on another and pulled downward, testing to see whether they would hold his weight. The wood held firm. He hoisted himself up and mounted the broad shed roof. From the rear to the front, the roof was white with untouched snow. Frost took care to watch his step as he crossed it, as the wet snow atop the metal sheeting would make for poor footing. Worse, if anyone looked at the side of the roof he had ascended, they would notice his tracks in the powder.

Frost doubted that anyone inside, even the patrols, would have much reason to look at the roof, but someone walking toward the barn might see it on approach. At this point, relying on probability was asking for disaster—he would need to be quick. He climbed the roof's shallow incline towards the clerestory windows of the barn proper and peered through one at the middle.

The window looked over the barn loft, which spanned the length of the building. There was a wooden desk in the corner with an opened laptop on it, green Excel spreadsheets visible on its screen, a single desk lamp the only light source. A cheap leather couch and loveseat slumped on the far side of the loft. A ceiling fan hung motionless overhead, awaiting summer. And in the corner of the room, a wooden bannister and staircase that led down to the barn floor.

Frost slid the window open and slipped inside the loft. He stepped carefully, knowing men stood right below him. He could hear men shifting in and out of the broader barn below: pallets being loaded, skids moving around, small talk above a low-volume portable stereo.

He crept to the edge of the loft and peered over, as slowly as he dared. He counted seven men below him walking from point to point throughout the room—five were loading packages onto pallets, while one stood leaning against a back wall watching them and another sat at a forklift participating in small talk with the package haulers. Above them and across from Frost, two long fluorescent lights hung slapdash from crooked nails in the wooden beams.

What interested Frost was in the corner: the hastily packed components for a narcotics lab, only partially shoved into crates and covered with tarps in anticipation of distribution day. He pulled one of the Semtex bombs from his pocket and set the timer on the watch to twenty seconds. Drug production created a massive amount of toxic waste even when done successfully, and the components used to do so were hardly less volatile. With some luck, Frost might not even need the second explosive.

He watched the men and their patrol routes for a moment longer. When three of the five men had their backs turned from his position in the loft, he activated the watch wired to the bomb's detonator and pitched it into the crates. One of the two men hauling packages stopped and cocked his head. Frost brought his rifle to bear, exhaled, and squeezed the trigger. The suppressed rifle coughed and the man's head snapped back, a chunk of his skull tearing away as the round opened a cavernous exit wound. Another burst from Frost's rifle, and the second forward-facing man dropped beside him.

Frost turned the rifle barrel upward and blew out the lights above him. He turned on his heel and ran as confused voices barked below, confused men struggling to identify the source of the gunshots. Frost ran back towards the clerestory window he'd entered and dove out feet first, tucking his assault rifle in close to his body. He flew out of the window onto the slicked metal sheeting of the shed roof just as the bomb exploded. The lab must have contained more materials than Frost had seen from his vantage point, because the explosion ripped through the bowels of the barn and launched him forward.

He flew from the side of the barn and crashed to the ground below, turning his momentum into a roll through the snow. He gritted his teeth and hoped that if he kept moving, he could ignore the head-splitting ache from his aggravated brain trauma. He brought himself upright into a kneel and swung the barrel toward the front of the barn. The open door belched flames and smoke, but nothing else emerged from the inferno. He charged toward the front of the barn as a secondary explosion sent flaming pieces of metal sheeting and shards of cedar arcing upward into the night sky.

Frost reached the sixteen-wheeler and pressed his shoulder against the side of the trailer, using his new position as a vantage point to see into the barn. A few men were attempting to stagger out, their clothes ablaze and their skin charring. He could hear their agonized screams as the flames ate at their flesh. He crept closer, resolving to kill them quicker if he could get a clear shot. All things equal, nobody deserved to die that way.

He stopped when two men ran forward from the back of the truck toward their comrades. Frost crept forward to the back where the men had emerged and peered around to see a stunned man staring at the blaze in horror, frozen in place. Frost ducked back. The two thugs aiding the burning men eventually gave up, drew their guns and fired. The screaming stopped. Now that the deed was done, Frost drew a bead on them both and put two three-round bursts through the men's chests. He heard a yelp of surprise from inside the truck, and he spun inward to see the stunned man trying to pull his gun from a clasped holster at his hip. Frost put two rounds through the thug's chest, who fell heavily to the floor of the trailer, unmoving.

"Mark? Tony? Did someone start shooting?" sounded another man's voice from the opposite side of the truck.

Frost doubled back the way he came, rounding the front of the truck to come upon the driver. He treaded carefully toward the back of the trailer, gun drawn.

"Fuck, guys, get back in the truck! Silver can take care of this mess."

Frost had heard enough. He fired three times, and the man twitched and fell into the snow.

No sound came but the whistling wind, the roaring barn fire, and the sizzling of the metal and cedar debris falling upon the lawn. Then there was a loud cracking of wood as the roof above the loft caved in and the cupola collapsed, engulfed by the flames beneath it, releasing a massive black cloud of smoke flecked with a swarm of dancing sparks.

Frost walked back around to the open trailer. Even with the barn in flames, there were still multiple crates worth of narcotics already packed inside. He couldn't just let them sit there to be salvaged by Silver. He looked around the driveway for anything he could use and saw a hefty piece of two-by-four debris with a small fire burning at its end.

Frost walked back to the truck's cab and climbed inside. He opened the glove box and found a pile of miscellaneous license and registry papers, some napkins, and a user's manual for the truck. He rolled together the available materials into a cylinder and climbed back down.

He went to the fuel cap at the rear of the vehicle and unscrewed it. He crammed the rolled-up papers into the fuel filler neck, leaving them half protruding from the tank. Using the flaming two-by-four from the driveway, he lit the end of the paper manual sticking out of the filler neck.

Frost tossed the two-by-four aside and began jogging back across the snowy farmland property, heading towards his truck. He hadn't gone thirty yards before the truck exploded with a tremendous bellow behind him, sending twisted metal high into the air—luckily, he was far enough away that the sound didn't bother him. The burning barn and the truck now cast a flickering golden light out onto the silvered field, and Frost's shadow walked tall over the expanse.

THIRTY-SIX

The shifting winds of the coming storm stirred up flurries on the empty highway in front of Frost's headlights. He looked towards the horizon as the Ranger flew back towards broader Clear Rock. It was still a few hours until sunrise, the early morning still dark, but the storm had created a kind of heather-colored firmament above him. An uncanny, almost surreal vista, hallucinatory and hypnotic.

Frost clicked open his glove box as he drove on. He removed Taya's phone from inside and scrolled through and typed in *1210 Lafayette Drive* into her Maps application. He wasn't far off. The app directed him to the exit just before Clear Rock, leading up the mountainside hills that overlooked the town.

Lafayette Drive was a winding two-lane strip of asphalt that snaked through the woods lining the side of the mountains. The Ranger's headlights played off the thin steel guardrail running along the road's south side, protecting vehicles from plummeting off the steep drop below. Frost continued to glance over at the woods on the northside as he ascended the road. The app indicated that he was approaching 1210, but there were no visible road markers peering out from among the trees and no indicators of a hidden homestead whatsoever.

But then he saw it. He'd have missed it for sure if he wasn't looking. On the northside of the road, near the top of one of the lower range plateaus, was a very narrow drive set back into the wooded hillside. It was wide enough for only one vehicle at a time and cocooned by a dense tree line on both sides that hid it nearly completely from the road.

Frost slowed his Ranger and glanced up the driveway as he passed. He saw a mechanized chain-link gate at its front connecting to a broader fence that Frost assumed lined the entire property. The gate and fence were both bedecked with a faux-foliage camouflage to further hide the home from prying eyes.

Frost kept on driving and headed a little further up the mountainside to its flattened plateau. There he found a shallow shoulder on the south side, the guardrail extended outward with it, that served as a roadside turnaround. The little land shelf could function as a makeshift observation point, though Frost couldn't imagine it attracted many tourists. There was only room for two, maybe three cars at most. He pulled onto the shoulder of the turnaround and cut the Ranger's engine.

Frost re-armed, reloading the HK14, holstering his pistol and strapping his binoculars to his hip. He jogged away from the truck, crossing the two-lane road and hopping over the short ditch to enter the thick woods lining the mountainside. The incline was only slight at the plateau, but he could see it rising sharply to the north alongside the mountain. The woods hissed with wind coursing through rustling branches of ponderosa, whitebark and aspen. The snow that had accumulated on the forest floor dampened all sound. Frost trekked through the woods until he found the mansion.

As he'd guessed, the entire perimeter of the property was lined with a camouflaged chain-link fence. He looked towards the top of the fence line and swept its horizon, scanning the canopies of the trees around which the fence weaved. There weren't any security cameras that he could see, but they'd be on the exterior of the mansion for sure.

He clipped the chain-link fence vertically with his wire cutters and pulled the severed portion back. He slipped through the hole and made his way towards the house, the snowy woodland continuing uninterrupted for another hundred yards or so in front of him. But he trudged onward and soon the tree line thinned. There it was, its silhouette obscured by the denser snow flurries which now blew nearly sideways. Frost took out his binoculars and glassed the house.

The mansion was contemporarily styled, with an exterior of maple wood, stone veneer, and steel in strong geometrical masses of curated asymmetry. Large floor-to-ceiling windows of dark black SmartGlass mirrored the woodland around it, its opacity able to shift from transparent to opaque at the flick of a switch. A long driveway sprawled below, with several vehicles parked in it next to a large frosted reflecting pool. A few ambered porch lights glowed hazily in the worsening storm. And as he'd guessed, half a dozen globe CCTV cameras hung beneath the cornices of the façade.

The storm was certainly a welcome blessing. It might shroud any guards on the property, preventing him from seeing Silver's men before they saw him, but he had the element of surprise and the advantage of preparation. As long as he chose a clear path forward now and stuck to it as he advanced, he could enter unnoticed.

He turned his attention back to the front of the house. The golden floodlights above the three-car garage suddenly burst to life above the driveway. Moments later the front door opened and seven men exited the home. They hurried up the steps to their vehicles, shouting as they went. Frost watched one man striding imperiously among the others as he made his way into the passenger side of a black Escalade. Frost recognized the imposing figure from the grainy nighttime video on Taya's phone, in command and larger than life: Silver. Dressed in an all-black suit fitted to his broad-shouldered, six-foot-five frame, his men scurried around him like honeybees around the queen, motivated by awe and terror.

Frost watched Silver's driver and two passengers hurry into the Escalade to join him. Soon the handful of vehicles pulled out and began down the driveway to the road proper. The property fell silent again, but for the violent hissing wind.

They must have gotten word of the barn. Frost was surprised it had taken this long. The fire would certainly be visible from a great distance, so perhaps one of Silver's men had driven by it and alerted his boss. Or maybe a neighbor had called the police.

Frost turned his focus back to the mansion. The vehicles leaving the property didn't mean the house would be empty. Silver would have left at least a few men behind to guard Taya and Sarah, if they were still alive.

He returned the binoculars to his pocket and stood. He began trudging sideways through the woods, making his way towards the backyard of the mansion. He saw now that the property line valleyed in the back, revealing the entire basement floor of the house. The main floor above it was encased in black opaque SmartGlass as well, gleaming like a wall of wet obsidian.

Frost took a knee at the edge of the woodland and scanned the property again. The backyard featured a giant lagoon-shaped swimming pool, not yet tarped for the season, and a soft-covered in-ground Jacuzzi. There was a large sheltered cabana bar and stone deck leading to an inset fireplace towards the back of the yard. A separate guesthouse with a stone patio and small gardening shed lined the westerly side. The whole ensemble was tidily hidden from the broader outside world by the tall pines edging the property line and the mountain range rising tall at the back of the sprawling yard.

Frost looked for his area of ingress. At the side of the house, where the property began to slope towards the back, was a wide two-sectioned sliding window set into the exposed stone veneer. The window would be locked and rigged with a shatter alarm, but he could work his way around that if necessary. He memorized the terrain between him and the house, including areas where the snow was deepest and where he could find the best footing.

He spotted the nearest two security cameras and watched them rotate on their motorized fixtures. As far as he could tell, they covered one another's blind spots as they turned, leaving Frost without a practical window to approach unseen. Still, the wind blew thick sheets of snow around him. If he picked his moment, he would be able to use the weather as cover.

A high wind stirred up a flurry of snow before him. Frost moved, using the sheet of snow and the howling wind as a shroud. He emerged from the woods and crossed the property at a careful run, using what he had memorized of the terrain to steal safely over the snow-covered ground. He came up against the façade of the house and peered inside the window. It was nearly opaque, but he could barely make out the darkened room inside. There didn't seem to be anyone inside.

Frost placed his hands against the windowpane and pulled upward. The lock caught it, but he shifted the sliding window toward the latch and jimmied the window up and down. After a tense few moments of bobbing the window in place, the latch clicked upward with the movement of the window and Frost was able to slide it aside.

He bent down and peered inside alongside his rifle barrel. There nobody awaited him, and no audible alarm or commotion sounded within. Not wanting to push his luck further with the cameras, Frost slid the window upward and climbed inside.

THIRTY-SEVEN

Frost closed the window behind him and took in his surroundings. He was in a large laundry room with a washer and dryer, ironing area, and linen shelf. He went to the door of the room and slowly opened it to peer out. The hallway beyond was dark, lit only by a few overhead pin lights, and Frost emerged with his rifle up and his finger on the trigger. He moved slowly down the short hallway, his rolling footsteps silent on the carpeted floor.

He listened. Still nothing. No alarm, no voices, no sound of any kind that he could hear beyond the faint whistling of the wind coming from outside. He emerged into the broader den of the basement, an elegant and masculine room with dark, rich colors. A broad plasma screen TV hung from the wall, and a billiard table sat beside a fully stocked wet bar. French patio doors that opened out onto the backyard, the deck and swimming pool partially visible past the striated snowfall.

Frost approached the stairwell to the main floor. The basement had too many easy entrances and exits for Taya and Sarah to be held within. Special Forces training included hostage rescue, and the best place to keep a captive was always the places that offered the fewest opportunities for ingress or egress possible; which is to say, not a basement man cave. He then had two priorities for his search: an upper floor, or a second basement. Beyond that, he would search for a panic room or any specifically built holding areas.

Frost climbed the staircase and arrived in the sleek modular kitchen on the main floor. It was dominated by charcoal, steel, and bone-white. The floor-to-ceiling SmartGlass windows offered a panoramic view of the front property and the woodland where Frost had scouted the house. He wondered if anyone had been watching him the whole time, or if they might be watching him now.

He glanced over at the large living room on the opposite side of the house. Two lamps glowed atop separate end tables, but other than that, there were no signs of life. Frost turned and glanced out the front windows again. He wondered if the two women weren't already buried somewhere out in those dark, cold woods.

He moved further through the house, his rifle tight against his shoulder, his aim ready. He came upon the living room, handsome in its minimalism and earthy dark color palette. Frost glanced at the front foyer beside the living room. There was the door to the garage and a separate hallway that led to the west wing. Frost made towards the hallway when he heard something upstairs. Someone speaking. A television, perhaps, but a sign of life. He began up the stairs.

The landing of the second floor opened to a hallway on both sides with several doors. Frost heard noise coming from a bedroom at the end of the hallway to his left. He could tell it was a television now as he heard the frantic analysis of a sports announcer, backed by the faint roar of a stadium audience. Frost went to the right. He wanted to clear the rest of the floor quickly, so that there were no surprises when he took out whoever was in the bedroom.

He went to the end of the hallway to his right and opened the door to the last room, checking the corners as he entered. With a king-sized bed dominating the space, a leather fainting couch at its foot, and a small chandelier above, the room seemed to be the master bedroom. Frost cleared the room and then the master bathroom attached to it, and turned back to the hallway again. But approaching the bedroom door, he heard someone speaking out in the hallway.

Frost glanced out into the hallway through the doorway sliver. A man emerged at the top of the steps. Against all probability, it was Andy Treece. A bloodstained bandage was wrapped around his skull where Frost's bullet must have glanced off and knocked him unconscious, unbeknownst to Frost in the quiet frenzy of their jailhouse confrontation. And, true to form, Treece was once again on his phone.

"Don't worry, I'm grabbing them now," Treece said. "How far you want me to go to get them to spill? Mm. Got it."

He hung up and turned down the hallway to the left, away from Frost. Yet he hesitated. He stopped walking and turned around, lowering himself to his knees to pick something up off the hallway floor. He held it in front of himself. It was a single wet gravel stone. Frost must've tracked it inside, lodged in one of his boot treads. Treece looked at the stone for a second and then looked straight ahead at the door to the master bedroom. Frost stared back at him over the barrel of his HK416.

"Don't move," Frost said.

The color left Treece's face. The dealer rose to his feet, his hand drifting towards his Beretta.

"Your hand touches that pistol, and you're the first one dead tonight. You cooperate, maybe you're the last. Or maybe you make one last miraculous getaway." Frost was half-whispering, careful not to alert any other men inside the house.

"You're not going to shoot me here," Treece said, his voice trembling. "You fire, and them boys downstairs are going to be on top of us in seconds."

"I plan to deal with them, too. In time. But you're first. Do you want to meet God now, or later?" Frost asked.

"L-look, you shoot me and it's not just your life on the line. Before I even hit the floor, those two women will be executed."

"So they're alive? That's awfully good to know. I was just here to put a bullet in your boss's brain. Seemed like the thing to do after burning his barn to the ground."

Treece's face slackened further. Frost didn't know how good the dealer's poker face was, but he supposed that everyone's charisma faltered when staring down the barrel of a man that already shot them in the head once today.

Frost flew through his options. Was Treece bluffing? Frost didn't yet know exactly where Sarah and Taya were in the house, though he'd guessed they were in the bedroom at the end of the hall. From the sound of the television, by what Treece had just said on the phone and where he'd been headed. But were they guarded? If they *were*, any gunfire might indeed sign their death warrant.

"Hey now," Treece said. "I ain't fucking around here. Lower that fucking gun if you want to keep them women alive."

Frost hadn't come this far to let a lowlife like Andy Treece get him by the balls.

"Come here, Treece. You play your cards right, and we just might make it through this night together."

Treece paused and looked again from the gun to Frost's eyes. He took one step forward. Then another. Frost took his hand off the barrel of his rifle to open the door wider. As soon as he did, Treece ran.

The dealer set off at a stumbling sprint toward the staircase downstairs, screaming for help from the rest of the house. Frost stepped out into the hallway and steadied his rifle, but Treece was already in the stairwell. Frost bolted after him, weighed down by his rifle but calmer and more sure-footed. He made the top of the staircase just as Treece spun around, pistol in hand. A shot rang out, and Frost felt a searing pain in his thigh as the bullet tore through his leg. Frost felt a lurch in his center of balance as his forward momentum carried him over the first stair, but he was able to turn the fall into a leap straight at Treece. The dealer was too surprised to get another shot off at Frost before the two collided.

The two toppled off the floating stairs and hit the hardwood floor below with a loud thud. Frost had both the wind and his assault rifle knocked from him. Treece had his Beretta knocked from his hands as well, but Frost had landed on him and gotten the worst of the impact. The man held the injured side of his head and howled in animalistic pain. Frost didn't miss his chance again. He drew his sidearm, turned, and sent a bullet through Andy Treece's head. The man lay still, and this time Frost could see that there wasn't nearly enough left of the man to get him up again.

Frost heard two sets of heavy footsteps pounding down the west wing hallway. He struggled to stand, hobbled by the wound in his thigh, but rose to one knee, steadying himself. He aimed and shot both men center-mass, one after the other, as they came around the corner. Charging blindly, they never even saw Frost. Amateurs.

Frost released the magazine from the well of his pistol and loaded the extra clip from his belt holster. He racked the slide and waited for the sounds of other men in the west wing, or from anywhere else in the house. But all was silent. Frost stayed there for a moment to make sure before he moved again.

With some difficulty and greater pain, Frost rose to both feet and picked up his assault rifle. He set his pistol back in its holster and stalked back up the staircase to the second floor. His thigh stung, but the wound wasn't dire. It hadn't hit any bones and wasn't bleeding enough to have struck an artery. He could keep compartmentalizing the pain for as long as it took to get Sarah and Taya safe. Hopefully, he wouldn't run out of compartments any time soon.

He went to the bedroom door on the left side of the hall. He could hear that the television had been shut off. He approached the door and leaned his ear towards it. Listened. There was no noise coming from inside at all. No shuffling, no heavy footsteps. Nothing.

Frost tried the knob. It was locked. He took a step back and brought the rifle butt down on the doorknob.

THIRTY-EIGHT

The room was large, albeit smaller than the master bedroom down the hall. There was a queen-sized bed, an elegant handcrafted dresser with a broken vanity mirror and makeup desk, and a large flat-screen television mounted on the wall. And there, crouching over a dead thug bleeding into the cream-colored carpet, were Sarah and Taya.

Sarah hauled Taya upright, the pregnant woman's hand bleeding from the shard of mirror she had plunged into their guard's throat. Both looked to Frost. Sarah seemed unharmed, but her eyes were wide and haunted. Taya just seemed angry, but her blood-soaked nightgown might have influenced that perception.

"Good, it's you," Taya said, exhaling. She jerked her thumb in Sarah's direction. "This one said that she recognized your voice, so we figured it would be a good time to make our move."

Sarah ran over and threw her arms around Frost.

"Oh my God," she said. "I can't believe it's you. I thought that Silver would have had you killed in jail for sure."

"He definitely tried," Frost said.

"Glad he failed, Slugger." Sarah buried her face in Frost's chest. Frost cradled the back of her head. Adrenaline bled away into relief, and relief into something else—another faint feeling that he couldn't quite grasp.

"The reunion's sweet, but we might have an extra complication here," Taya said. Her voice was more unsteady than it had been a moment ago.

"What's wrong?" Frost asked, releasing Sarah to ready his rifle.

"Oh, fuck," Sarah breathed.

Frost followed her stare. Beside the spreading bloodstain in the carpet was a second wet spot between Taya's bare feet.

"Oh, fuck," Frost said. Taya's water had broken. He could hardly have imagined a worse time or place.

"I don't suppose getting her to the hospital's going to be an easy order, is it?" Sarah asked.

"My truck's parked further up the road," Frost said. "At the observation spot. Too far for us to walk safely in this weather. We're better off taking one of the cars in the garage, if there are any left. Can you walk, Taya?"

Taya shot Frost a glare that, more than anything, told him that she was feeling as fine as she had been when they first met. "Yeah, I'm good to walk."

"She won't be far enough into contractions for the pain to be an issue. At least, not for a little while," Sarah said.

"We've still got a long way to go. Let's not waste any time."

Frost led the way out of the bedroom and down the hall. For all her bravado, Taya still moved significantly slower than Sarah or Frost.

Frost checked the staircase again as Sarah helped Taya keep pace.

"Did you find her phone?" Sarah called down the hallway to Frost.

"I did. I backed up the files and emailed them to Donny Kim. Thanks for putting it somewhere I'd find it."

"You got it. I'm just glad it worked."

Sarah smiled and helped Taya onward. Frost moved ahead and began down the staircase, hobbling with his bad leg, and reached the bottom. He stood guard, sweeping the living room and kitchen area with his rifle, as Sarah helped Taya down the stairs.

"Oh my God," Taya said as she saw the three men dead on the floor beside the stairs.

"It's all right," Frost said. "Don't look at it."

"What? Are you kidding?" Taya flipped Treece's corpse the bird. "I didn't think Andy would ever get what was coming to him. See you in hell, you fucking cockroach."

Sarah and Frost exchanged furtive glances. Sarah shrugged.

"What happened with Puck?" Sarah asked.

"She's dead. Tried to track me after I broke out of jail, and it didn't work out for her," Frost said. "Took out the barn, too."

"Damn," Sarah said. "You've been busy, huh?"

Frost was about to respond, but a loud *ding* cut through the front of the house and startled the three. Frost swiveled his rifle towards the sound. It had come from Treece's body. Frost knelt and pulled Treece's phone from his pocket. The home screen revealed that an encrypted text message had been sent from Silver two minutes ago. This was the second notification. Frost swiped the screen and read it. The text message said *Joey called. Shots at house? Report. Heading back now.*

"Fuck," Frost said, throwing the phone down.

"What is it?" Sarah said.

"Silver's on his way back," Frost said.

"What?" Sarah said. "I thought you said—"

"I burned down the farmland barn and part of their shipment. I think they were rushing to check the damage. But one of these heavies must've contacted Silver before I shot him."

"Jesus Christ, it doesn't end," Sarah muttered.

"Doesn't change anything. Let's go," Taya said, shuffling toward the garage.

"She's got the right idea, but now we know that we need to be careful," Frost said, walking briskly to get ahead of Taya.

Frost moved to the cabinet in the front foyer and yanked open the first drawer, hoping to find a set of car keys. He did: a Mercedes-Benz ignition key with remote keyless buttons on its face. He just prayed the matching car was still on the property.

Frost grabbed the key and handed it to Sarah.

"When we get outside, you just start slamming the unlock button until we find the right car," Frost said. "But stay behind me."

Sarah nodded and took the key from him. Frost turned to the door that led to the garage, but as he did, the door flew open.

THIRTY-NINE

A man in a suit—Silver recognized him as Silver's driver—stood in the doorway. Frost put a three-round burst through the man's chest before he could react. But before the body could drop, a massive hand reached out from beyond the doorframe and grabbed the body by the neck, keeping it upright and steady. A leviathan shadow shifted behind the body, and there came a brilliant flash and roar as a shotgun discharged.

Frost leapt away from the doorway, rolling back into the seating area near the kitchen. He fired another burst through the doorway, but the rounds only tore through the corpse, causing it to twitch grotesquely with each impact. A trio of distant metal pings sounded as the bullets buried themselves somewhere in the garage.

There came a clack of metal over metal as the unseen figure racked their shotgun one-handed. Frost dove for cover, but the girls couldn't move as quickly. Sarah stood between the door and Taya, the two left out in the open. Then the massive shadow moved into the room, holding the body before it like a full-sized puppet.

Frost hadn't seen Silver up close before, and the immediate effect of his presence was palpable. Tall and stout, he dominated the room the moment he stepped into the kitchen, carrying his driver's corpse with one hand. A copse of dark hair escaped above the neckline of his button-up and covered his thick forearms, otherwise sleeved in a dense cartography of tattoos both charnel and pornographic. He was tanned and well-groomed with a sculpted stubble line. He held a strapped six-shot Mossberg 590 in his other hand, and two silver Magnums hung from shoulder holsters beneath his sizeable arms.

Silver dropped the corpse to the floor with a thud and pointed his shotgun at Sarah.

"Toss your guns to my feet, or I'm putting one in her stomach," Silver said to Frost. "You have three seconds."

Frost wasn't about to call his bluff. He slid the rifle across the floor and unholstered his pistol to toss it at Silver's feet. His head throbbed from the gunshot in close quarters, and the pain from his leg and shoulder insisted on creeping back into reality.

"And the knife," Silver said. "Throw it into the kitchen."

Frost removed the bowie knife from his belt sheath and did so. It clanged into the dining room.

"Good," Silver said. "Now get up slow and sit on the sofa. No bullshit."

Frost got to his feet, wiping bits of shattered coffee table glass off of himself, and sat down on the couch. Silver watched him do so and then stared over at Taya.

"You go sit down, baby. You shouldn't be on your feet in your condition. And you," he said, turning to Sarah on the sofa, "you stay right where you are. You move, and we get to find out if the first bullet goes through you or your obnoxious boy toy."

Taya staggered to the sofa, her teeth gritted and her eyes ablaze. "I'm going into labor, you sonofabitch. I need to go to the hospital."

"Not another word," Silver said, his tone soft. "Don't make me do something we'll regret."

He was frightening in his solemnity, as though he never raised his voice. As though he never needed to. He had the air of a man entirely willing to follow up every single act of disobedience with a bullet.

Silver knelt down and laid his shotgun next to him on the floor and picked up Frost's pistol. He ejected the magazine and tossed it towards the front door and ejected the remaining round from the chamber before tossing the gun over his shoulder.

He glanced at the three dead men in his front foyer, then back at Frost.

"Shame Andy didn't make it through this. Not unusual for our line of work, but still. Pity. We go way back."

He and Frost stared at one another. Silver's eyes were dark, the irises black and lined with razor-thin layers of burnt umber, reminding Frost of twin solar eclipses.

"I'll make you feel that one, friend," Silver said, his voice soft and low as a sousaphone. "I promise you that."

Taya grunted as another contraction gripped her body. "Ronnie, this is your kid, too. I don't get to a hospital, we might both lose him," she said. Frost was surprised that she would try appealing to Silver's humanity, but she knew him better than Frost did.

"We need to go as soon as possible," Sarah said.

Without hesitation, Silver drew his Magnum and fired a bullet into the sofa directly between Sarah and Taya. The thunderstrike of the gunshot carried through the open living room. Sarah screamed and

Taya snarled, the bullet hole between them gently wafting smoke into the air.

"We're getting to that," Silver said.

He turned back to Frost.

"I didn't make it to the farm before I had to turn back," Silver said. "But it's gone, isn't it? The shipment, my men, the barn. It's okay, you can answer."

"Yeah," Frost said. "It's gone."

Silver nodded and looked to the floor. He shook his head. "That's not good. There's going to be a lot of pissed off people after me. Dangerous people. Buyers already on their way to Clear Rock as we speak. And these aren't people who take disappointment in stride." He looked up at Frost. "You see this?" he said, holding up his left hand.

His pinky finger was missing. Only a short stump remained, just beyond the knuckle. Frost looked over at the hand and nodded. Silver turned and looked at Sarah, showing her.

"My daddy took that. Caught me in his woodshop when I was a boy, where I didn't belong. But I went in anyway. It was the smell that did it for me. The wood chips. Intoxicating."

Sarah looked over at Frost. Uncertainty and fear were written across her features. She didn't know what to expect next. To Frost's growing unease, neither did he.

"I hadn't even touched anything. Hadn't messed up his tools or nothing. But still, there he stood. Then something shook in that pickled brain of his and he dragged me to his worktable and set my wrist in a vice. I screamed and screamed, but he didn't hear me. Daddy was miles away. Then he picked up his wood chisel and set to work on this here finger. I could smell the Johnny Red on his breath the whole time, mixing in with the woodchips."

272

Frost saw the tethered rage in Silver's black eyes as he spoke. Frost stared back, his back stiff. For as many times as he had told himself that he had gone toe-to-toe with psychopaths, this was the first time he had ever sat down with one at gunpoint. This was the most dangerous place he could possibly be, and he had no escape.

"Now, I passed out, naturally. But when I woke up that evening, the wound was soldered shut and I had time to think about what he'd done. Sure, it wasn't the first time he'd hurt me. It was actually pretty rare that he'd go a night without whooping my ass. But this was different. People would say he was just another evil drunk, mad at the world and taking it out on me. But that's just what people tell themselves to make them feel safe. But my daddy had been trespassed somewhere in his mind. Unmanned, you know? Somewhere beyond that mist of Johnny Red. And somewhere deeper —beyond him or me or anything that ever was—something had fated us to be in that same space at that same moment in time. An unknown catalyst in the cosmos, one action leading to a random but fated reaction. Cause and effect gone insane. The result was me. A man with the will to power."

Silver stared at Frost.

"You understand what I'm trying to say? You can't begrudge the way things went when they was never going to be another way. You destroyed my drug shipment. Set me up to be destroyed by these dangerous men. Well, all right then. That's about the worst news I could get. But no use weeping over it. No use raging against the night. Just the way it is, and never could be no other."

"So, then what?" Frost said.

"So, what you think? You're going to make this right for me the only way you possibly can. I'm going to empty this cylinder into your fuckin' head." Silver held up the revolver in his hands and dislodged the cylinder. He pulled out one of the five cartridges inside and held it up between his thumb and index finger. "You see that?"

273

"A silver bullet," Frost said.

"That's right," Silver said. "Ain't that nice? But no, what I'm really asking is, do you see what's written on the side of that bullet there?"

Frost looked at the cartridge but couldn't discern anything from across the room.

"No," he said.

"It's got your name there, carved right into it," Silver said, turning the bullet to catch the light. "All six of them do. F-R-O-S-T."

Frost's blood ran cold. He stared up at Silver.

Silver smirked back. "Oh, what? You didn't realize I knew, Mr. Frost? Or do you prefer Marion?"

Frost glanced to Sarah, whose eyes remained fixed on Silver. He found himself grateful that she didn't give off any obvious tells that Silver was right about Frost's name, or that she had known it all along. She was silent and cold, like she had been during their last car ride. He hoped she wouldn't put herself at risk for them—not if he could do the same for her first.

Beside her, Taya looked to be oscillating between fear and simmering rage. Frost could see how she might have caught Silver's eye, as they both shared a certain intensity. He was ice, and she was fire. Problem was that one eventually extinguished the other.

With that fury, Frost expected Taya to do something foolhardy more than he did Sarah, but he also couldn't fault Taya's instincts in a crisis. If Frost played his cards right, they would both be valuable in making it through the night in one piece.

"You been on the run for some time, haven't you?" Silver said. "And I've recently been told about your bounty. It seems that you know all about pissing off dangerous men, don't you?"

Frost felt his heart sink. If Silver knew about the bounty, then there was almost a guarantee that Crane knew where he was. Frost realized that his likelihood of surviving the night was dwindling with each passing minute. If he wanted to come out of this with his skull intact, his time was extremely limited.

"I've been given assurances that proof of death for Marion Frost will net me a cool penny," Silver said. "I was planning on killing you after the deal tomorrow anyway, because, well, why the fuck not—but since there won't be no deal tomorrow, I might as well step up the schedule. So you can start to see why I'm not *too* put out by your fuckery here. With the money I make off your head, I can spot the buyers for their lost time and inconvenience, fund a new shipment, and still walk away with a solid foundation for my business. Not as much cash as I'd initially planned, but there it is. Just the way things are."

Silver set the revolver back in his shoulder holster and hoisted the shotgun. "Now get up. All three of you."

"Why?" Taya snarled. "Just do it here, if you're gonna."

"Oh, Taya. I wish this could have gone another way. The cosmos should have had better plans for you, baby. Either way, despite the mess your friends have made of my house already, I don't want to risk one of these shotgun shells missing one of you and cracking that SmartGlass behind you. Shit costs a fortune. Plus, I've already got three bodies to scrub out of the flooring. Get moving."

Sarah began to sob into her hands. The sudden burst of emotion surprised Frost, considering her earlier coolness.

"Hey. Hey now," Silver said, looking over at her. He spoke with almost genuine consolation and sympathy. "What did I just say? There was never going to be another way, darling. So, no use fighting it. Now up. And help Taya, if you would. We're going to the steam room, Tay. Lead the way."

"Fuck you, Ronnie," Taya growled. "You better look me in the eyes when you pull that trigger, you batshit son of a bitch!"

"Of course. I owe you that much, baby. Now, come on. If you make me do it here, I'll make sure you die slow. If you lead us to the steam room, I'll make it quick. Easier for everybody."

Sarah continued to weep hysterically but got to her feet. Taya put her arm around her and shot another caustic scowl to Silver.

"You're prettier when you smile, dear. It'll be kinder to your memory. Now go on," he said. "You too, Marion."

Silver watched as Taya led Sarah and Frost towards the west wing of the house. Silver followed behind with his shotgun raised at their backs, making sure to keep a safe distance behind Frost.

Frost ran through the options in his head. If he turned, Silver would blow him away. If he did nothing, Silver would gun him down all the same. So, Frost reasoned, he should at least go down fighting. There wasn't any point waiting another minute for himself, Sarah, and Taya to be put down like dogs. Leaving Silver to collect the bounty and continue unimpeded with his drug empire. Leaving Lincoln unavenged, his last wishes unfulfilled.

Frost couldn't let that happen. Not like this. He'd been hoping to get out of this alive, but if he couldn't, then he would damn well drag Silver to hell with him. And he had the means to do it.

Reaching into his pocket, Frost grabbed the second Semtex bomb.

FORTY

"Something you wanna share with the class?" Silver drawled. He raised the shotgun up and aimed it at Frost's head, still maintaining his distance. "Take your hand out of your pocket. Slowly."

Sarah and Taya stopped walking and turned around to see what was going on.

With his hand still on the bomb in his pocket, Frost clicked the timer setting on the digital watch and hit Start. The timer would automatically set itself to sixty seconds, and would now be counting backwards to zero.

"Let me see that hand now, friend."

Frost slowly removed his hand from his pocket and revealed the plastic explosive in his grip.

"The fuck is that?" Silver said.

Frost raised the explosive in his hand and held it up for Silver to see. The sixty-second countdown had now breached the forties. Silver took a step forward, though still outside of Frost's reach, and gripped the shotgun with intent.

"Shut it off, now," he said.

But Frost simply looked at him and slowly, without a word, mushed the plastic against the SmartGlass wall beside him. The explosive now stuck upon the glass, the countdown continuing.

"I'll fuckin' kill you right here," Silver said, taking another step forward.

"No, you won't," Frost said. "Putting a round through me now won't do you any good, 'cause I'll just land right here, bleeding out on your floor until that Semtex turns my body to a smear on the floor. Good luck collecting a bounty on *that*."

"Shut it off!" Silver roared. His voice boomed imperiously, and Frost wondered how long it been since he last raised it like that.

"If you hit the wrong button on the timer, it'll blow. So go ahead," Frost said. "Figure it out, if you're so smart."

Silver stood still for a moment. "You're fucking bluffing."

"We'll find out, won't we?" Frost said, "In... twenty-four seconds."

Frost watched Silver's dark eyes weigh his options. He was right in that Frost was bluffing *a little*—the watch was not in fact rigged to blow if the wrong button was hit. The countdown would cease the second anyone hit the Stop/Reset button on the side of the case, like any other digital watch. But Frost hoped he'd get Silver to back off and buy himself some time. Then he could grab the explosive, stop the timer, and continue holding himself hostage until he and the women somehow made it off that fucking mountain.

Either that, or Silver would move forward and Frost would be left with option two: brute force. And if that didn't work, Frost was indeed prepared to die. He could even appreciate the morbid poetry of dying to one of his own homemade explosives after having disarmed so many in Afghanistan.

Silver looked at the watch face again. Fifteen seconds remained. He twitched, the ridge of his brow clenching. Then he called Frost's bluff. Silver, the man who had built a drug empire on the strength of his ironclad nerves, would have made no other choice but to charge toward the explosive to stop its timer himself. Frost was relegated to option two.

Silver had to put himself within Frost's reach to turn off the timer and as he did so, Frost made for the shotgun. He slammed his right hand against the barrel and swatted it aside, away from his body, towards the glass. Instinctively, Silver pulled the trigger and the entire panel of SmartGlass shattered under the hail of buckshot, raining shards down onto the stone patio deck below, taking the Semtex explosive with it.

The men wrestled for the shotgun as the blizzard rushed into the exposed hallway, the wind clawing in at them as if the airlock on a spacecraft had been breached. Frost felt the brunt of Silver's size and strength as they grappled for the gun. Given his injuries, Frost knew it wouldn't be long until Silver gained the upper hand.

"Cosmos shoulda had better plans for you, Ronnie!" Taya snarled as she slashed at one of Silver's thighs with a shard of SmartGlass. The cut ran jagged and vertical down Silver's thigh, slicing the leg of his pants and the muscles beneath to ribbons. Silver bellowed in pain, but before he could react, Sarah had thrown her full weight against him. Silver was off-balance, grievously wounded, and still wrestling with Frost. All Frost had to do was shift his weight, and Silver was over the edge of the window and toppling earthward. Frost felt Silver's massive hand close around his wrist, and soon Frost was tumbling, too.

They landed hard on the wet patio. Silver groaned and reached for one of his holstered Magnums. Frost glanced around him, cuts stinging all over his body from the shattered glass they'd landed on. Before Silver could regain his bearings, Frost found the Semtex bomb and hurled it past Silver and away from the house. Then he threw himself as far as he could in the opposite direction, crashing against the façade of the house. He ducked and shielded his head with his arms.

A split-second later it exploded in midair. The force blew a chunk from the cabana, leaving a large depression beneath the stone patio deck. The heat singed the nearby pinewoods, and set fire to the roof of the adjacent guesthouse. Wood and glass debris rained down into the pool as a charcoal plume of smoke rose and melded with the wash of alabaster snow. Any airborne debris was snatched up by the tempest and torn away.

Frost stood, coughing and covered in sweat from the heat of the blast, the side of his face smeared with dark soot. He looked for Silver among the snowy-smoked mist and saw the force of the blast had damaged a large portion of the mansion's easterly façade, the French doors of the den now black and blown inward. He found Silver, guided by the sound of the man's insensate growling, and saw that half of his face was now blistered over with second-degree burns.

Silver cried out like an injured animal and looked over at Frost. He struggled to his feet, still holding the Magnum he had unholstered before the Semtex detonated. Frost took off as fast as he could towards the back of the property, stumbling on his bad leg. A shot rang out, just missing him, and he pushed as hard as he could, past the end of the pool and into the broader yard.

Off in the distance behind him, beyond Silver and the mansion and above the din of the blizzard, Frost could have sworn he heard the sound of ringing police sirens. Silver's cavalry was coming to run him down.

FORTY-ONE

The shrieking storm quieted as Frost entered the tree line, but for the high whistling wind that wound around the wooden limbs. The Magnum thundered behind him, echoing out through the storm. Visibility increased slightly. Frost glanced at the terrain before him. The woodland rose sharply in tandem with the incline of the mountainside. Frost would never make it with his wounded leg as long as he had Silver on his tail, and he realized these sheltered woods would actually leave him worse off than the open blizzard.

He began sideways across the incline in order to flank around Silver and head back to the mansion. As he walked, he ducked down to retrieve a thick oak branch, partially covered in snowfall, from the forest floor.

Perhaps he could get back into the house to recover his rifle and finally finish Silver off. He wondered if Sarah and Taya had made it out of the mansion all right. As long as Silver kept chasing Frost, they would have a clear escape route. There was a good chance that he would. As angry as Silver was with Taya, he was also practical. Taya was personal, Frost was business.

Branches snapped beneath Frost's feet as he traversed the uneven ground. He glanced back to the foothill of the woods where he'd entered and saw Silver's silhouette emerge from the wash of snow before it. Frost stopped moving, backed himself up against the thick trunk of an oak tree, and waited.

Silver entered the wooded mountainside and pulled the second Magnum from his holster. He raised them both up towards the woods and scanned the hillside.

"It's over, Mr. Frost," he said. "We both got our share of scrapes, but I'm sure that of the two of us, I'm the true man of purpose. If you come out here and get on your knees, I promise not to make the girls suffer when I catch up with them. Give me the opportunity to be merciful."

Frost didn't answer. He waited for the sound of Silver's approach. And he kept waiting. To Frost's mounting alarm, he realized that Silver's approach was careful and quiet enough that even with the man's wounded leg, Frost couldn't hear his footsteps in the underbrush. Frost carefully hefted the oak branch and dared a glance around the other side of the tree. Silver was barely five paces away. The kingpin's eye rolled in its charred socket as he noticed Frost, but by then Frost had closed the gap and swung hard.

The branch struck Silver's wrist and knocked one of the Magnums from his hand. Silver pivoted to fire at Frost with the spare revolver, but Frost threw himself forward and tackled Silver to the ground. Silver brought the Magnum to bear and pulled the trigger, discharging it near Frost's ear. The gunshot tore through Frost's scarred brain like a heavyweight uppercut, sending his world end over end. He rolled in disorienting pain, but stopped when his hand landed on a heavy rock the size of a baseball.

Silver climbed unsteadily to his feet to shoot Frost, but Frost swung upward with the rock and smashed it into Silver's right hand. It struck hard and dislodged the revolver from his grip. Frost lunged forward again and connected the rock with the burned side of Silver's face, snapping his ghoulish features sideways with the force of the blow. He recovered swiftly and drove his fist into Frost's gut.

"Fighting with sticks and rocks?" Silver spat, his ruined lips drooling, "Weapons for a desperate man, Frost! Weapons for a man of lower means, for whom the world will never turn!"

A second fist plowed into Frost's temple, sending starlight across his vision. He dropped into the snow. Silver stooped down to pick up his dropped Magnum, and Frost lashed out with his boot at the man's wounded calf. Silver dropped to his hands and knees in the snow with a crazed snarl.

"Why would a man of your talent turn his ire toward my humble operation in the first place? To save a whore in distress?" Silver spat as he tried to regain his footing. Frost tried to kick at his leg again, but the drug lord's hand lashed out and caught Frost by the ankle. He heaved Frost as hard as his battered body could manage, sending Frost tumbling a meter through the snow. "Surely your path would have been much more prosperous running parallel to mine, not against it."

Frost reeled, his head still throbbing and his mind still disoriented. But something Silver said had stuck out to him.

"There was a boy," Frost said, pushing himself upright. He felt it again, for the first time since Lincoln died—that light in his chest, flickering into a building burn. "A boy with a dying wish. And his uncle, who taught both of us to stand between the malevolent and lawless and wrathful."

And Frost recognized the light for what it was. It wasn't vengeance, or even anger. It was Brakespeare's spark. The spark that cancer had extinguished in his friend, and evil had extinguished in Lincoln. Frost carried it with him, too. It wasn't as clear as Brakespeare's compass, or as bright as Lincoln's hope, but it was a guiding star. And Frost could carry it with him even when they no longer could.

"You're talkin' about justice? You should know as well as I that justice withers in the garden of Man. There is only the chaos of free will, and the power it can bring to those who are strong." Silver had recovered one of his fallen Magnums from the snow.

Frost could have said something that Brakespeare would have been proud of—something about standing against corrupted men with twisted views of the world like Silver's—but Frost wasn't Brakespeare. Frost was broken and lost, only borrowing Brakespeare's spark to guide him in a world he could no longer feel. So Frost said nothing and hurled the rock at Silver's head as hard as he could.

There was a crunch as Silver's nose broke. The kingpin howled and stumbled backward, and Frost took two quick steps forward. With one hand, he grabbed Silver's Magnum. With the other, Frost drove the heel of his palm into Silver's wrist, shattering the bones and loosening his grip on the revolver. Frost took the Magnum and, in a snap shot that would have made his father proud, blew out Silver's right knee. The drug lord howled and collapsed in the snow.

"How do you know my name?" Frost asked.

Silver seethed, his breath hissing in ragged gasps through his teeth. "The Oracles of Delphi, of course," he panted. "How the fuck do you think?"

Frost admired the man's ability to be a completely obtuse piece of shit even with his kneecap blown out. He decided to see if it would stay with the other gone. The Magnum roared again, tearing a bloody crater in Silver's other leg. Silver howled, his teeth gnashing. His eyes rolled like a frenzied horse's.

"Try that again," Frost growled.

"Crane, of course!"

"And I assume you know him through his heroin. Supplied wholesale from overseas, delivered straight to your doorstep?"

"Glad to see you were paying attention," Silver said.

Frost heard the police vehicles pulling up in front of the house, their sirens echoing out through the gathering dawn. Car doors slammed shut and footsteps sounded on the driveway pavement.

A queer thought entered his mind.

"Never thought I'd see the bullet with my name on it," said Frost. "Let alone use it on someone else."

He raised up the Magnum and put the final shot through Silver's head. It blew it near clean off, obliterating everything above the man's nose. The snow behind Silver was streaked red with spattered gore. The echo of the gunshot drifted away on the wind. Then came the sound of rushing bootsteps through the underbrush, and the calls for Frost to drop his weapon.

Frost took a deep breath and held the Magnum out at his side and dropped it into the snow. He raised his hands behind his head and dropped to his knees. In those final moments, he hoped he had done right by Brakespeare. That he'd carried his spark just far enough to make a difference.

FORTY-TWO

"Don't move. Not an inch," a man's voice instructed as an officer moved upon Frost from behind. Frost didn't, and kept his hands behind his head. The officer handcuffed Frost and lifted him to his feet. Then he spun Frost around to face him. "Are you Kevin Johnson?"

Frost looked at the man. He wasn't a police officer. He wore no uniform other than a blue windbreaker. Then Frost noticed the letters *DEA* in yellow above the heart.

"Sir, are you Kevin Johnson?" the agent asked again.

"Yes," Frost said. "I am."

The agent nodded. "This way."

He led Frost by the forearm around the side of the house, and Frost watched as the DEA agents got to work on the property. A tarp was placed over Silver's body to protect it from the snowfall. Police tape was put up, evidence markers littered throughout the house, firearms collected and rendered inoperable, electronics seized and removed.

Frost was led to the front driveway where a number of parked vehicles waited. Marked and unmarked agency sedans, a large white Crime Scene Unit van, and a few Clear Rock Sherriff's Department patrol cars. The DEA agent marched Frost to the back of one of these patrol cars.

"I'm going to remove those cuffs now," the agent said. "We're going to have a medic come by to look at that leg, all right?"

Frost nodded in silent agreement. The agent removed the cuffs, opened the back door, and Frost climbed inside. The agent ducked into the front seat and cranked the patrol car's heater before disappearing around the side of the house again. Frost stared out the window at the buzzing agents and officers in the driveway and wondered what the hell was going on. They'd just witnessed him execute someone in cold blood, but they didn't seem intent on arresting him. Not without the handcuffs or reading him his rights. The agent hadn't even patted him down to see if he had any other weapons on him.

Frost got the creeping feeling that this wasn't finished. The relief he'd initially felt upon seeing the DEA agents and not Clear Rock officers faded fast. They could still be corrupt. Just because they hadn't lit him up in the forest didn't mean they were straight.

Frost looked at the agents milling in and out of the front of the house. This was a real crime scene investigation and not some dust off, so at least the majority of the operation was legitimate. But maybe one officer would take their opportunity to hop in the driver's seat and steal him away, never to be seen again.

Frost looked out the window and up at the brightening sky. The blizzard was quieting down a little, the snow falling a bit lighter. The early morning sun now bled through the overcast clouds, turning the whitewashed sky a yellowed cream.

The same DEA agent returned from the backyard and to the patrol car, this time holding a thick wool blanket. To Frost, the man might as well have been holding a balloon animal. After the past few days, the idea of a lawman handing Frost a blanket seemed about as likely.

The agent opened the back door and handed the blanket to Frost. Frost took it and the agent went to shut the door again.

"Wait," Frost said, and the agent ducked his head back into the car. "There were two women—"

He cut Frost off. "They're safe. We caught them halfway down the hillside. They should have arrived at the hospital by now."

"But I... what the hell's going on here?" Frost said.

"An officer and a medic will be along soon," the agent said and he shut the door.

Frost wrapped himself tightly in the wool blanket and tried to get warm. He hung his head low, his adrenaline draining, his body now screaming with pain and exhaustion. He wondered if someone with the Sheriff's Department would kill him, or if the DEA would hand him over to Crane. Either way, Frost didn't think he could take another fight to the death right now. Even if he could summon the mental fortitude, his body wouldn't have it. He could feel it shutting down, and knew it would remain offline until someone saw to his injuries. Until he slept. He could barely even hold his head up.

The paramedic came and stitched up Frost's leg, but blanched at the various stitching jobs Frost and Sarah had done over the course of the past few days. Frost took the criticism in stride, but the medic demanded that Frost get to a hospital as soon as possible. Someone's voice called from outside the car, and the medic withdrew. The medic spoke briefly with a man whose voice Frost couldn't quite make out.

The driver door of the patrol car opened and a familiar officer climbed in and shut the door behind him. He started the car up and headed down the winding driveway towards Lafayette Drive. Frost glanced out of the window at the surrounding woodland, and the aspens where Silver had nearly killed him shuttered past. Slivers of sun cut through the overcast sky beyond them.

"You were right," Deputy Kim said from the front seat.

"Right about what?" Frost said, only half aware of the face in the rearview.

"It *was* incredibly strange receiving that voicemail from you."

Frost turned in time to catch Kim turning to wink at Frost in the rearview mirror. Frost could do nothing but sigh and let his head drop against the back of the seat.

"Thank God I was right about you being one of the good ones," Frost said.

Kim turned his eyes back to the road. "Hell, maybe one of the *only* good ones left in the Sheriff's Department," he said. "But it seems they still got a few in the DEA, huh?"

Frost exhaled deeply, flooded with relief. Nearly overwhelmed by it.

"You're safe now, Mr. Johnson," Deputy Kim said. "That agent that cuffed you back there? That's Hemsley. He's an old friend of mine. A good guy."

Deputy Kim reached Lafayette Drive and turned down the hillside towards Clear Rock.

"How the hell did you pull this off?" Frost said.

"I called Hemsley, an old college buddy of mine who I knew was over at the Cheyenne office, and told him what you told me. He couldn't have been happier to hear it. His office already had a file on the state's growing heroin problem, but no solid leads. And once I received your email with the video of Gomez's murder, the DEA had probable cause to do just about whatever the hell they wanted. So Hemsley got on the wire with his colleagues, hopped on a chopper, and headed straight here. He wasn't going to let his white whale slip through the cracks."

"But why'd the DEA let me go?" Frost said. "I mean, I roasted most of the evidence against Silver. And took his head off. Not much left for them to use at a trial."

Kim clucked his tongue. "The barn fire was a problem, but our boys down on the property say there was plenty of actionable evidence in the farmhouse. And Hemsley handed you over because I asked him to. Quid pro quo. Look, there ain't no love lost over Silver. Or any of his crew. This is the Cowboy State, after all, Mr. Johnson. As far as anyone cares, this was one part self-defense and two parts community service. The DEA used your leads to track a few mafioso buyers in-state that were preparing to purchase at the parade. So the DEA will likely be able to flip a few of them and make inroads into other organizations. I mean, they've got all of Silver's hard drives now. Plus, considering that you couldn't go through the Clear Rock Sheriff's Department, it's arguable that proper channels weren't available to you. It's in their interests to let you walk. And to be completely honest, even if it weren't, I don't think they'd want the truth of what you did here getting out."

"What do you mean?"

"You humiliated them." Deputy Kim laughed. "A single man with some stones and a lot of hard bark on him did what an entire federal agency couldn't? Especially after they let Silver corrupt an entire police department and rot an entire town from the inside without noticing? They might wanna keep this quiet. Chances are, they'll just claim the mansion and the barn were the result of in-fighting. Or Silver's deal going bad on him."

Frost grimaced. The idea of answering corruption with more corruption left a bad taste in his mouth, but he was hardly in a position to do anything about it. The patrol car reached the bottom of the hill, and Deputy Kim turned to drive further into town.

"Thank you, Donny," Frost said. "For everything."

"Hell, it's the least I can do, pal," Deputy Kim said. He stared out the front of his patrol car and looked at sleepy Clear Rock before him. "You saved my town."

FORTY-THREE

Taya sat in bed in her maternity ward recovery room at the Clear Rock Hospital, cradling her newborn girl in her arms. ID tag on her wrist, sweaty and exhausted, the fight in her eyes had subsided for just a moment as she touched her baby's face with a gentleness that Frost hadn't known she was capable of. Sarah stood beside them, staring down at the infant's scrunched face and sleepy eyes. Her posture seemed exhausted, but her face was serene.

Frost knocked on the open door from the hallway. He wore a hoodie and a pair of sweatpants that Deputy Kim had lent him from a gym bag in his trunk. They were small on Frost, but they had thankfully been recently washed. The lack of bullet holes was also a plus.

"Is it all right if I come in?" Frost said.

"Of course," Taya said.

"Donny dropped me off," Frost said. "Said he'd be by later."

Sarah stared over at Frost for a second. She stepped forward and stopped herself, as though worried that something might happen to

Frost if she touched him. Taya broke the tension by swatting Sarah on the ass to spur her forward.

"Y'both nearly died for this kid, Ink Girl, go stick your tongue in his mouth," the new mother said.

Sarah ran over and threw her arms around him and hugged him tight. He hugged her back, holding her close for a minute before letting go. He looked at her and saw she had misty eyes.

"I…" Sarah said, wiping her eyes. She couldn't finish.

"Yeah. Me too. It's over," Frost said. He felt a dull relief, but mostly exhaustion. The scars across his gray matter still locked whatever he felt for Sarah down tight.

"Have you been looked at?" Sarah asked, stepping back and taking in his cuts, bruises, and visible limp.

Frost nodded. "I just came from a nurse. Only needed a few stitches." That wasn't true. He was still due to meet with the nurse, and only standing thanks to the DEA medic's goodwill.

"Can't keep a good man down, can you?" Sarah asked.

Frost smiled. "Might be why I feel like dropping into a heap right now."

Sarah exhaled and turned her attention back to Taya and her newborn. The brightening morning cast dim sunshine through the window curtains beside the bed, bathing the child in light. Taya looked up at him.

"Thank you, Mr. Johnson, or whatever your name is," she said, with uncharacteristic gravity. "My daughter and I both owe you our lives."

"You don't owe me a thing," Frost said. "Your uncle saved my life more than once. I'm just keeping the scales balanced."

"I'm just—" said Taya. She looked away, as though what she was about to say was monumentally difficult for her. "I'm sorry."

"Sorry?" Frost said. "What do you have to be sorry about?"

"I fucked up bad, falling in with Silver. Lincoln paid for that with his life. You two almost did. I thought that fucking up that bad could only come back to bite me. I was so, so stupid."

Frost walked towards her and took her free hand. "Don't ever give that thought any credence. Nobody can predict the outcomes of their mistakes. Silver was a gargantuan mistake, but his doings aren't your responsibility. At least you and your baby are safe. You're a survivor, and an insane goddamn wolverine."

Taya smiled and squeezed his hand back. "I'd cut those men again in a heartbeat if it meant keeping this one safe. But thank you, Mr. Johnson. Sincerely."

Frost reached down the front of his collar and pulled a necklace up over his head with his free hand. It was Brakespeare's dog tags. He turned Taya's hand over and set the dog tags inside.

"These were your uncle's," he said.

Taya looked at them, and then back to Frost with a cocked eyebrow. "You sure? He was a good friend to you."

"Please," Frost said. "They're yours. Returning them to Brakespeare's kin was all I came here to do. It's what he wanted. It kept me going."

"But I really—"

Frost closed her hand into a fist around the tags and smiled. "Consider it a baby shower gift."

Taya took the dog tags. She held them dangling over her baby girl's tiny hands, and the newborn's pudgy fingers instinctively closed around one of the tags.

"Have you thought of any names?" Sarah said in a hushed voice.

"I was thinking Jamie. It was Lincoln's middle name," Taya said.

"Jamie Dane," Sarah said. "Sounds like an Old Hollywood movie star."

Taya smiled, staring down at her daughter. "None of them ever burned half as bright."

A knock came at the door, and they turned to see the nurse enter. She stared at Frost's battered body for a moment, distracted, before returning her attention to Taya.

"Taya, the doctor will be by in a minute to run the pediatric exams, all right?" she said briskly. "And we'll set her down for a nap in the nursery after that. Let you get some rest as well." The nurse moved on down the hallway to continue her rounds.

"I should get going, anyway," Frost said.

Sarah looked over at him, disappointment in her eyes. "You need a ride? The feds let me grab my car before I came here."

"That'd be great," Frost said. They needed a chance to talk privately. He knew the conversation would be difficult.

"I'll be back later tonight," Sarah said to Taya.

Frost leaned forward and squeezed her hand again. "Congratulations, Taya," he said.

The pediatrician announced himself as he entered the room with a new nurse, and Frost and Sarah took their leave. They exited the hospital and crossed the parking lot to Sarah's car without speaking. Once inside, Sarah sat there for a moment without starting it up, thumbing the car keys in her hand.

"You're leaving, aren't you? For good," she said, staring down at her keys.

Frost hesitated. She looked over at him.

"Yes," he said. "I'm leaving."

"The good ones never stay," she said, her mouth set in a grim line.

"I can't, Sarah," Frost said.

"What do you mean you can't? You said yourself this was all over."

"With Silver," he said. "Not with the other men on my tail. And as long as I'm around you, you'll always be in danger. I'm not going to do that to you."

"Do you at least want to?" she said. The question surprised Frost.

"Of course I do." Frost said. Again, only a half-truth. He couldn't feel for her in the way she felt for him, and his shattered brain would only end up breaking her heart. But he felt more around her than he had around any other person he'd met since his injury, and he wanted to be there to heal alongside her. It was too bad that he couldn't guarantee to either of them that he ever *would* heal enough to appreciate her heart.

"I'm sorry. It was selfish of me to get involved with you to begin with. But I did care for you. More than I thought I could care for anything."

Sarah looked up at him. Her eyes were still damp from earlier, but her mouth was drawn into a grin. "Really?" she asked.

"Knocked me to my knees," Frost said.

"Where you did some of your best work, though."

Frost laughed, and after a moment, Sarah did too. He leaned over and kissed her, cupping her cheek in his hand.

"I'm sorry this is how it has to be," he said.

"Me too," Sarah said. She kissed him again and let him go. Worse, Frost felt her letting him go in every way possible.

She wiped her eyes and set the key in the ignition.

"Where can I take you?"

They drove across town and headed back to Lafayette Drive to collect Frost's truck. The day was much brighter now. A light powdered snow danced down from the pale blue sky. Municipal snow plows cleared the roads of the blizzard's leavings. They drove up the mountainside in silence and peered over at Silver's driveway as they passed. A patrol cruiser parked horizontally across the access as the DEA continued its work on the property.

They drove on and found his truck at the plateau observation point. Sarah pulled up onto the shoulder and parked in front of his Ranger. She cut the engine and they both got out. They walked together to the guard rail and stared out over the town below. Clear Rock shone in the morning sun.

"Thank you for what you've done," Sarah said.

Frost nodded. "I'm glad the road led me where it did."

They stared out over the town in silence for a minute.

"I think we needed each other," Sarah said. "At this point in our lives, you know?"

"I think so."

She turned and faced Frost. "If you're ever able to stop running—if you're ever free—come back to me."

She kissed him and Frost pulled her in tight, returning her kiss as if it were giving him the last glimpse of daylight he would ever see. They parted after a minute and took one last look at the town below before walking back around to their vehicles. Frost stepped up to his

Ranger and Sarah to her car. She pulled her driver-side door open and looked back at Frost.

"I was thinking," she said. "Your name."

Frost looked over at her.

"Instead of Marion, why not just Ion? Sounds enough like Ian," Sarah said. "Ion Frost."

Frost smiled.

"You think it's silly," Sarah said.

"No. I don't think it's silly at all," Frost said. "That's actually what my mother used to call me."

"Really?"

Frost nodded.

"Well then," Sarah said. "Goodbye, Ion."

"Goodbye, Sarah."

And with that, they both stepped into their vehicles and turned their engines over. Sarah pulled out and Frost followed her down the mountainside. At the bottom of the road, Sarah turned and headed back into greater Clear Rock as Frost idled at the intersection, watching her go out his window. Soon her car disappeared down another road, out of sight. Frost turned and looked out his front windshield for a minute. He glanced over at the dashboard in front of the passenger seat. The Broncos cap sat upon it.

Frost grabbed the cap, set it firm on his head, and drove towards the highway that led out of Clear Rock.

FORTY-FOUR

The next morning, Frost emerged from the convenience store of a single-pump fuel station in Colorado Springs holding a protein bar, a large black coffee, and a new burner phone. He'd filled up, used the restroom, paid, and was ready to hit the road again. He felt possessed by a deep compulsion to put the entire state of Wyoming behind him as quickly as he could.

Yet before he started his truck, he thought for a minute about where he might actually want to go next, about what the road might have in store for him. It seemed impossible after the turmoil he'd endured in Clear Rock, but that draw was still there, and he thought he knew the source—Brakespeare's spark, that small but brilliant flame still calling for justice.

Frost gazed out across the state highway beyond the fuel station. The red rocks of the Garden of the Gods formation rose up in the distance, dwarfed by the great Pikes Peak mountain range behind it. Snow dusted the top of the surrounding Gambel oaks and pinyon. Hoarfrost veneered the blood-orange sandstone.

Somewhere warm might be nice, he thought.

He reached over to the passenger seat and picked up the box that held his new burner phone. He opened it, activated the phone and set it back down on the seat again. He took a sip of his coffee, threw his aviator sunglasses on, and started the truck.

Frost pulled out of the station and headed south. He glanced out at the horizon in front of him and the asphalt of the state highway disappearing beneath his hood. It was shaping up to be a nice day.

Then the phone rang.

Frost glanced over at it. He'd only turned it on a few seconds ago. *He* didn't even know the number yet. It rang again. And a third time.

Frost finally reached over and grabbed it and answered.

"Hello?"

"Mr. Frost," said the voice on the other line. "Glad to see that you received my letter. I think the time has come for us to talk."

Frost looked out at the horizon again. The open highway, the endless sky. It appeared the road wasn't done with him just yet.

END OF LETHAL JUSTICE
ION FROST BOOK ONE

PS: Do you like legal thrillers? Then keep reading for exclusive extracts from *Defending Innocence.*

ABOUT ETHAN REED

Loved this book? Share it with a friend!

To be notified of the next book release please sign up for Ethan's mailing list, at
www.relaypub.com/ethan-reed-email-sign-up.

———

Ethan Reed worked as a freelance journalist for the last twenty years. He has traveled to every state in America throughout his time as a journalist, investigating and writing articles for magazines and newspapers. He loved the simplicity of drifting from one state to the other, honing in on an electrifying story and then moving on.

In 2019, Ethan took the leap and started writing his first thriller under a pen name, pulling from his experiences on the road as a journalist and his extensive research of current events and military life. Ethan loves to delve into contemporary issues ripped from the headlines.

He has finally settled down and now lives in Lincoln, Nebraska with his wife and two kids, and his giant German shepherd, Cali.

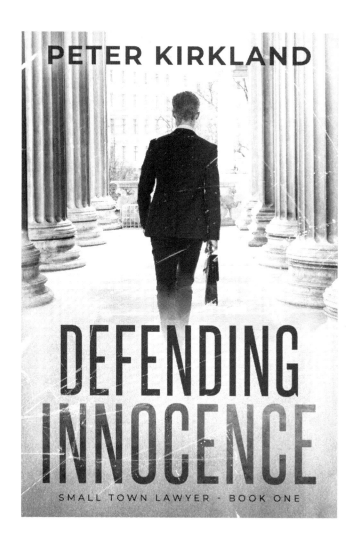

BLURB

An innocent client harbors dark secrets...

Defense attorney Leland Monroe lost it all: his big-city job, his reputation and, worst of all, his loving wife. Now he's back in his hometown to hit restart and repair the relationship with his troubled son. But the past is always present in a small town.

Leland returns to find his high school sweetheart hasn't had the easiest of lives—especially now that her son faces a death sentence for murdering his father. Yet what appears to be an open and shut case is anything but. As Leland digs deeper to uncover a truth even his client is determined to keep buried, a tangled web of corruption weaves its way throughout his once tranquil hometown.

Leland soon realizes it's not just his innocent young client's life that's at stake—powerful forces surface to threaten the precious few loved ones he has left.

Grab your copy of *Defending Innocence* (Small Town Lawyer Book One) from www.relaypub.com/blog/authors/peter-kirkland

———

EXCERPT

Chapter One

Monday, June 10, 2019

The Ocean View Diner, where I was waiting for my fried shrimp basket, was a dump with a view of nothing but the courthouse parking lot. It was already shabby when I was in high school, living on fries and coffee while I brainstormed the college application essays that were my ticket out. Much to the surprise of folks in my hometown, I'd made it to law school and beyond. I owned more than a dozen suits. I had tan for summers in the office, navy for opening statements to the jury, charcoal for talking to the media on the Charleston courthouse steps. My kid had admired me at an age when it was almost unnatural to think your dad was anything but a loser. I was a law-and-order guy trying to make the world safer. I'd thought I might run for office.

I nodded to the bailiff who walked through the door giving him a cordial "howdy", but he looked right through me, as he walked past. We'd certainly seen enough of each other in the courthouse, and I tried not to take offense at the slight but there's only so much a man can put up with when it comes to small town judgment.

They say pride goeth before a fall.

I'd seen enough, in my past life representing the great state of South Carolina, to know a man could have it a lot worse. The amount of depravity and human misery that had flowed across my desk made me know I ought to be grateful for what I still had left. My son, in other words, and my license to practice. I'd nearly lost both. The accident that took my wife had nearly killed him too, and even if he still hadn't entirely recovered from it, he'd come farther than anyone expected at the time, but Noah was incredibly angry all the time. Mostly at me but I tried not to let it get to me.

Like water off a duck's back, the little things ought not to have bothered me at all. It shouldn't have mattered that the locals at the next table had stopped talking when I walked in, apparently suspicious of anyone who wasn't a regular. Which I wasn't yet, since it'd been barely six months since I dragged my sorry ass back from the big city. Getting to be a regular took years.

A better man would not have been annoyed by the smell of rancid grease or the creak of ancient ceiling fans. It was even hotter in here than in the June glare outside, and a good man would've sympathized with my waitress, who was stuck here all day and probably never even got to sit down.

But I was not that man. I did say "Thank you kindly" when she dropped my order on the table and sloshed another dose of coffee in my cup, but I was irrationally annoyed that no one had ever fixed the menu sign on the wall between the cash register and the kitchen. The word "cheeseburger" was still missing its first R. When my friends and I were sixteen-year-old jackasses, we thought it was hilarious to order a "cheese booger." Now it was just pathetic that I was back. Especially since the reason I wasn't in the new '50s-style diner on the next corner—the popular lunch place for judges, local politicians, and successful attorneys—was that I couldn't afford it. Here, in exchange for tolerating the broken AC and worn-out furniture, I got decent shrimp at prices that were fifteen or twenty years behind the times.

The folks at the next table had gotten back to jawing, though at a lower volume on account of my being unfamiliar, I supposed. Between crunches of my dinner, I caught the gist: a body had washed ashore a little ways down the coast, where tourists rented beach houses. Maybe I shouldn't have eavesdropped. But although I wasn't a prosecutor anymore, I was probably never going to lose the habit of keeping a close eye on every local crime.

"Bunch of them Yankees was playing volleyball on the beach," the man said. "You know, girls in their bikinis, one of them thousand-dollar gas grills fired up on the deck." His voice held a mix of humor and scorn. "They were having themselves just a perfect vacation. And then this *corpse* washes up! This, I swear to you, decomposing *corpse* crashes the party!"

The table erupted with guffaws.

"So what'd they do?" a man said. "Hop in the Subarus and hightail it back to New York or wherever?"

"No, the thing is—and I heard this from my cousin, you know, the one working for the sheriff? The thing is, they thought a gator got him! Thought they had a gator in the water! And I'll be damned if they weren't pissing themselves like little girls, trying to get everybody back out of the water. Couple of them was so scared they started puking!"

They all lost it. One of them was so entertained he slammed a hand on the table, rattling the silverware. As the laughter started fading, one of them wondered aloud who the dead man might be.

"Aw, don't matter none," the storyteller said. "We ain't missing nobody."

I felt a sourness in my gut. I couldn't go a day here without being reminded why I'd left. In Basking Rock, compassion for your fellow man was strictly circumscribed. Tourists got none. The wrong kind of people, whatever that meant, got none. Your family and lifelong friends could do no wrong, and everybody else could go straight to hell.

I signaled the waitress and asked for a doggie bag. Might as well finish eating at home, away from present company. She scowled, probably thinking I was switching to takeout to avoid leaving a tip. I scrounged through my wallet, sure I'd had a few ones in there and grudgingly set down a five knowing I was leaving more than necessary. Making any kind of enemy was not my style. You never knew who might help you out one day, if you'd taken care not to get on their bad side. More to the point, I knew from friends who worked in health code enforcement that there were few things stupider than making enemies of the folks who make your food.

I'd parked my Chevy outside. It used to be the beater, until the nice car was totaled in the accident. When I fired it up, the engine light came on again. I kept right on ignoring it. I'd yet to find a local mechanic I could trust. The one I knew of had been a bully back in high school, and from what I'd heard, age had only refined his techniques. If he thought you'd gotten too big for your britches— which I certainly had, what with my law degree and my former big-city career—he took his rage out on your wallet.

The Chevy heroically made it home once again. I parked beside the clump of fan palms that were starting to block the driveway. I needed to get them pruned, and to fix the wobbly porch railing that would've been a lawsuit waiting to happen if we ever had visitors. I needed a haircut. My geriatric Yorkie, Squatter, who limped to the door to greet me, needed a trip to the vet. The to-do list never stopped growing, and checking anything off it required money I no longer had.

I tossed the mail on the table and scratched the dog on the head. He'd come with the house—the landlord said he'd been abandoned by the previous tenants, and I couldn't bring myself to dump him at the pound. As he wagged his tail, I called out to my son. "Noah?"

All I could hear was the breeze outside and Squatter's nails scrabbling on the tile. I was no scientist—my major, long ago when I thought I was smart, was US history—but I knew physics did not allow a house to be that quiet if it contained a teenage boy. It looked like I'd be eating another dinner alone. I'd texted Noah when I got to the diner, to see if he wanted anything, but he hadn't answered. I never knew where he was lately, unless he was at a doctor's appointment I'd driven him to myself.

After feeding Squatter I pulled up a chair, took a bite of now-cold shrimp, and flipped through the mail. The monthly health insurance bill—nearly thirteen hundred bucks just for the two of us—went into the small pile of things I couldn't get out of paying. Noah's physical therapy bills did too; as long as he still needed PT, I couldn't risk getting blacklisted there.

And he was going to need it for a good while yet, to have a shot at something like the life he'd been hoping for. We were both still hanging on to the thread of hope that he could get back into the shape that had earned him a baseball scholarship to USC in Columbia. The accident had cost him that, but he was determined to try again.

Or so he'd said at first. Lately he'd gotten depressed with how long it was taking, and how much fun he saw his high-school buddies having on Instagram. They'd gone to college and moved on with their lives. He'd started making new friends here, but to my dismay, they were not what you'd call college bound. College didn't seem to have occurred to them. One worked in a fast-food joint, and another didn't seem to work much at all.

I heard gravel crunching in the driveway. Even without the odd rhythm his limp gave him, I knew it had to be Noah; our little bungalow was an okay place to eat and sleep but too small to be much of a gathering place. I stuffed the bills into my battered briefcase. He didn't need to know we were struggling.

Squatter raced to the door to celebrate Noah's return and accompanied him back to the kitchen in a state of high canine excitement. Noah looked a little glum, or bored, as usual. Without bothering to say hi, he poured himself some tea from the fridge, sat down in the chair next to mine, and took one of my shrimp.

"I would've brought you some," I said. "I texted you from the diner."

He shrugged. "I didn't see it in time," he said, feeding the crispy tail to Squatter.

"That's a shame," I said. "What were you so busy doing?"

He glared at me. That look was a one-two punch every time. He had his mother's eyes, so it felt like the hostility was coming from both of them.

I knew I should back off, but I was never good at drawing the line in the right place. "Hanging out with Jackson again?"

He took another shrimp, got up, and went into the living room. At fourteen, Noah had perfected the art of sullen teenager. Now at nineteen, he'd turned it into a lost art as he immersed himself in the depression and apathy that comes with having your life turned completely upside down.

Grab your copy of *Defending Innocence* (Small Town Lawyer Book One) from
www.relaypub.com/blog/authors/peter-kirkland